Dedalus Original Fiction in Paperback

CONFESSIONS OF A FLESH-EATER

David Madsen is the pseudonym of a philosopher and theologian. Born in London, he studied for many years in Rome,
where he became fascinated by the teachings of the great
Gnostic heretics and their influence on the esoteric tradition
within Christianity. This inspired his first novel, the highly
acclaimed *Memoirs of a Gnostic Dwarf*.

He is currently editing *Orlando Crispe's The Flesh-Eater s Cook-
book*, which reveals some of the gastronomic secrets of the
notorious Thursday Club.

This book is dedicated to
Andrew Lyons
who prefers food to fashion

David Madsen

Confessions of a
Flesh-Eater

Dedalus

Published in the UK by Dedalus Ltd, Langford Lodge, St Judith's Lane, Sawtry, Cambs, PE17 5XE

ISBN 1 873982 47 X

Distributed in the USA by Subterranean, P.O. Box 160, 265 5th Street, Monroe, Oregon 97456

Distributed in Australia & New Zealand by Peribo Pty Ltd, 58 Beaumont Road, Mount Kuring-gai, N.S.W. 2080

Distributed in Canada by Marginal Distribution, Unit 102, 277 George Street North, Peterborough, Ontario, KJ9 3G9

First published by Dedalus in 1997
Copyright © 1997 David Madsen

Typeset by RefineCatch Limited, Bungay, Suffolk
Printed in Finland by Wsoy

Memoirs of a Gnostic Dwarf

'A pungent historical fiction on a par with Patrick Suskind's *Perfume*.'
The Independent on Sunday Summer Reading Selection

'David Madsen's first novel *Memoirs of a Gnostic Dwarf* opens with a stomach-turning description of the state of Pope Leo's backside. The narrator is a hunchbacked dwarf and it is his job to read aloud from St Augustine while salves and unguents are applied to the Papal posterior. Born of humble stock, and at one time the inmate of a freak show, the dwarf now moves in the highest circles of holy skulduggery and buggery. Madsen's book is essentially a romp, although an unusually erudite one, and his scatological and bloody look at the Renaissance is grotesque, fruity and filthy. The publisher has a special interest in decadence; they must be pleased with this glittering toad of a novel.'
Phil Baker in the Sunday Times

'. . . witty, decadent and immensely enjoyable.'
Gay Times Book of the Month

'Madsen's tale of how Peppe becomes the Pope's companion and is forced to choose between his master and his beliefs displays both erudition and a real storyteller's gift.'
Erika Wagner in The Times

'. . . its main attraction is the vivid tour it offers of Renaissance Italy. From the gutters of Trastevere, via a circus freak-show, all the way to the majestic halls of the Vatican, it always looks like the real thing. Every character, real or fictional, is pungently drawn, the crowds are as anarchic as a Bruegel painting and the author effortlessly cannons from heartbreaking tragedy to sharp wit, most of it of a bawdy or scatological nature. The whole thing mixes up its sex, violence, religion and art in a very pleasing, wholly credible manner.'
Eugene Byrne in Venue

I

The Incarceration of One Unjustly Accused

I did not kill Trogville. No matter what they say, I did not kill him. I introduced a mild narcotic into his glass of whisky; I subsequently stripped him naked, laid him face down on the parquet floor and inserted a courgette into his creamy, quivering anus; but when I quitted his apartment in the Via di Orsoline, he was still very much alive. That was at approximately nine o'clock. At a quarter to midnight he was discovered sprawled out like a stringless puppet, his chest yawning bloodily open, his heart torn out and placed neatly in the palm of his left hand. Now they are saying that I did it. I despised Trogville, I hated and feared him, but I did *not* kill him.

Allow me to introduce myself: I am Orlando Crispe, otherwise known as *Maestro* Orlando, and I am a great artist. Indeed, I am an artist of international repute. I am a creator, a demiurge, the image of an aeon, and the primordial material out of which I give birth to the children of my ideation is *food*. I am in fact a chef. A cook. I am one of the finest cooks in existence; actually, I consider my only rival to be Louis de Beaubois of the Hotel Voltaire in Cairo. I have no time for false modesty – if one is blessed with an extraordinary talent, one should not hesitate to declare it; if I say that I am probably *not* the best cook in the world I make a liar of myself, and if I say that I *am* – well, I fall into the immodesty of pride. That is such a short fall; hardly Luciferian.

My culinary studio is a *ristorante* called *Il Giardino di Piaceri,* which is situated in a small street just off the Piazza Farnese here in Rome; it possesses a secluded roof garden which I reserve for my very special guests, and it was at a table on this roof garden that I first served my now justly celebrated *farfalline di fegato crudo con salsa di rughetta, burro nero e zenzaro.* They told me that such a combination of flavours would never work, but they were all entirely wrong. It was served to Lady Teresa Fallows-Groyne, who married an American painter called Fleebakker, famous for mixing his colours with his own semen.

In my little cell here in Regina Caeli prison, they have provided me with writing materials, and I now pass the long hours of daylight composing these modest *excerpta* of the anfractuous history of my life; Helmut von Schneider – my dear friend Helmut, who shares my taste for flesh – has promised that he will arrange for private publication as soon as they are completed and edited.

I still blame that corpulent *poseur* Heinrich Hervé for precipitating the beginning of what was to be my downfall; he it was who tiresomely persisted in urging upon me the task of creating a unique culinary masterpiece, and it was because of him I eventually cooked my very special rissoles, *Heinrich Provençale, Andouillettes Hervé* and *Navarin of Heinrich*. Heinrich is (*was*, I should say) Danish by birth, but for many years lived in Germany, the country of his adoption, where he earned a modest living as a singer. He possessed a very powerful bass-baritone voice, yet one would not, I think, call it beautiful; Eiseneck of *Paris Match* once referred to him as an overgrown *fauvette*.

'These Jews!' Heinrich thundered, 'What do they know of art?' In Germany, force and power have always been preferred to subtlety and style.

Each night on the stroke of eight o'clock he would enter my restaurant, a grotesque *fantocchio*, and sing until the last diner had paid his bill and departed; he frequently begged, pleaded and commanded me (not necessarily in that order) to hire an accompanist, but this I refused to do – for one thing, my restaurant was not large enough to accommodate comfortably a grand piano. Then he would sit at his table near the kitchen doors – sometimes alone, sometimes with a companion, a young male prostitute picked up for the evening – and devour with gusto the meal I had prepared for him.

'Bah! I have had *Poussin à la Crème* at the Chateau Lavise-Bleiberger; in Florence I very nearly died and went to paradise on account of Maestro Louvier's exquisite sasaties; I have shared *Rosettes d'Agneau Parmentier* with le Duc d'Aujourdoi at *Maison Philippe le Roi*; where is your genius, Maestro Orlando? Where is the dish fit for angels that you keep promising me? Why have I not yet tasted the *raison d'être* of your culinary career?'

So I served him kangaroo steak, but – alas – this was not the ecstasy in flesh which he expected; next I tried grilled *côtelettes* of gerbil, then otter's liver, camel's heart, braised kidneys of polecat, even the testicles of an alsatian dog which – not knowing precisely what he was eating – he consumed with immense gusto but little appreciation; in the end, I became as nauseated by his passion for novelty as my customers were by his purgatorial nightly rendition of *Old Man River*.

However, I do not wish to anticipate my own story, and since the shadow of Heinrich did not darken the landscape of my life until some years after it had begun to blossom in the springtime of its own proper independence, I had better go back and begin – as they say – at the beginning.

II

The Object of My Desire

My first craving was for flesh. One morning I apparently attempted to bite off a chunk of my mother's breast as she was feeding me, and she ended up badly ulcerated; after that they put me on the bottle. A psychiatrist here in the prison – an absolute *blagueur* who sprays me with garlic-flavoured spittle whilst propounding his grotesque theories as to the origins of what he insultingly calls my 'mania' – told me that I am obsessed with flesh because I was thus precipitately torn from my mother's nipple, and that I am in some way trying to rediscover and connect myself to the 'ultimate source of nourishment'; this is complete and total nonsense, and I think it is Dottore Balletti who is obsessed – with breasts and nipples. His face sometimes assumes a very peculiar expression as he speaks to me of this *idée fixe* of his. Next time he pays me a visit I must try and see whether he also experiences an erection. Dottore Balletti misses the most significant point and confuses cause with effect: since my trying to bite into my mother's breast was the reason I was removed from it, it obviously *precedes* separation from the maternal nipple, and indicates that the craving for flesh is an *a priori* of my nature.

'*È una furia, quest' amore per la carne,*' he says.

'Like all respectable psychiatrists *dottore*,' I reply, 'your greatest talent is for pointing out the obvious. What is not obvious, you ignore, and when there is nothing obvious to point out, you invent it.'

'*Sì*, that is my job.'

'Meat' (in Italian *carne* means both flesh *and* meat) is too particular a term to properly describe the object of my craving; it is flesh which obsesses me, even though in my early years the only kind I ever tasted had once walked on four legs or had wings. Meat *is* flesh and vice-versa, yet the word 'flesh' captures the true flavour, the concentrated extract of the passion which rules me, and I infinitely prefer it. Flesh is my love; meat is what it becomes after I have lavished my creative culinary skill upon it. However, you will find that in the course of my narrative, I use 'flesh' and 'meat' interchangeably; this is purely for the sake of convenience and variety.

It is the raw material of my creative genius. I chose it (or rather, *it* chose *me*) as a painter might choose to work in watercolours or oils, as a composer might choose to specialize in opera; it is a subtle and enigmatic thing, this marriage of man and element, and the most one can say is that it does not occur by means of any purely mortal consideration – rather, there is the operation of what one might call a Higher Will (I borrow this phrase from Schœpenhauer) involved from the very beginning. And who knows when the beginning was? Why was Palestrina enraptured by the human voice? Why was Michelangelo in love with the cool smoothness of marble? Why did Albert Einstein surrender himself to a torrid intellectual affair with the structure of the physical universe? These are unanswerable questions, and they are therefore pointless. My *affaire du coeur* with flesh is to be located within the same dimension: it serves the high metaphysic of an inscrutable *dharma,* some inexorable purpose of fate – as I have said, the workings of a Higher Will – which weaves the textures of our existence together into a single fabric. In spite of Balletti's burblings about breasts and nipples.

My Father: A Harmless Idiot
As you shall soon hear, I was in my early teens when I discovered – in a rather dramatic way – that I did not want to be anything other than a chef, a true master in the culinary arts; indeed, their magic and mystery, their jealously-guarded secrets, their panoply of techniques and tools had intrigued and enchanted me even before I was tall enough to reach the handle on the pantry door. As a child – and without really knowing why – I used to spend hours pottering about in the kitchen: measuring, weighing, sniffing, tasting, concocting; my father, about whom the most charitable thing to be said is that he was a harmless idiot, expended a great deal of energy in trying to persuade me to adopt what he considered to be

more congruous interests, such as clockwork trains or football. Only once do I remember him executing an act of genteel violence upon me – for some minor domestic transgression the nature of which now escapes my memory. He beat me on the bare buttocks with a cricket bat; the bat itself he had bought for my eleventh birthday in the vain hope that it might encourage me to take an interest in the game. He made me take down my trousers and undershorts, and lean across the arm of his favourite chair, my face buried in the plump, yielding seat. I still recall the smell of warm, worn leather, enriched by the pungent tang of years of his anal sweat.

He administered three hard thwacks, but I was not hurt. My mother stood behind him, her hands at her throat; she uttered a strange, eldritch shriek each time the bat descended on my naked buttocks. I found this weird ritual mysteriously exhilarating; now, I suppose I would say that it was an *erotic* experience. After putting aside the bat (and breathing rather heavily) my father then did a strange thing: he reached down underneath my backside and grasped my little scrotum in his hand, exploring it shamelessly, tenderly kneading it with his fingertips.

'Oh yes, yes, that feels good,' he murmured. 'A beautiful pair! Never forget that God gave you balls, Orlando.'

The heat and softness of his hand was intensely pleasurable, as were the firm massaging motions he was making, and I was rather sorry when, after a moment or two, he stopped. That evening alone in my bedroom, I held myself between my legs just as he had held me, squeezing and rubbing gently. It occurs to me as I recall this delectable *scena* that my father must surely have found the whole experience as erotic as I did, even though neither of us would have been able (for different reasons) to classify it as such. In any case, it was never repeated.

'Love is a sacred thing,' he once remarked to me, coming unexpectedly into my room and delivering a preamble to what I supposed was to be a man-to-man chat about the so-called 'facts of life.' (Are they not, rather, merely possibilities?)

'Never be ashamed of what a woman makes you feel inside, Orlando.'

'Inside what?'

'That's how God meant it to be. Never be ashamed of it, and never abuse it; keep yourself clean and pure and manly, and you'll appreciate the act of love all the more, when the time comes for you to do it.'

Needless to say, I found this *bonne-bouche* of homespun sexual education excruciatingly embarrassing.

'I was a virgin on our wedding night,' he went on, 'so the joys of it came as a wonderful enlightenment to me. Oh, you'll be tempted, as we all are – but have the guts to resist, Orlando! Don't defile your body as some young men do; what could they ever know about the act of love? It's love that counts, Orlando, not biological urges.'

Then, abruptly switching gear, from mawkish ethical romanticism to clinical dispassion, he continued:

'The human penis is a marvel of power and precision, Orlando! When a man is fully erect –'

'I'm rather busy,' I said. 'Could we continue this fascinating conversation another time?'

He went out of the room with an expression of crestfallen surprise on his pasty face.

My father left no impression on the malleable texture of my young psyche; today, I can hardly remember the sound of his voice – it was somewhat high-pitched and querulous, I think. Whenever he comes to mind (which is seldom, now) he is but a nebulous figure enmeshed in the windswept nexus of a dark vacuum. I can discern nothing of significance. If Herr Doktor Jung's esoterically perspicacious observations on this condition are to be believed, the honour of having moulded and shaped me belongs entirely to my mother.

The Queen of My Highgate Childhood
I adored my mother. Psychologically-minded cynics will doubtless cluck and nod their theory-stuffed heads when I say that she was my one true companion and friend as well as my

mother, but it is so; there existed between us, from the very beginning it would seem, an osmotic bond which enabled her to intuit and assimilate my every mood, every subtlety of feeling, each summer cloud and autumn shadow that crossed the landscape of my soul, and to respond instantly. Sometimes I did not even have to voice my inner condition – merely to glance at her was knowledge and understanding enough for her capacious, empathetic psyche. Herr Doktor Jung also says that such a mother's son will turn out to be homosexual for her greater glory, but in my case the good physician's prognosis is not entirely accurate, for my tastes run to both sexes; the euphuistic carritch of modern sexologists would doubtlessly categorize me as bisexual, but since I have always regarded myself as a subject of celebration rather than an object of psychological inquiry, I prefer not to use this term. Let us just say that ripely-endowed ladies *and* callipygous young men hold equal appeal for me; this latter may be, I suppose, *ex consequenti* of the buttock-thwacking administered by my idiot of a father. He cherished the hope that one day I would meet a 'nice girl' and want to settle down with her.

'Don't you fret Orlando,' he would say with nauseating paternal confidentiality, 'Miss Right will come along soon enough.'

I found this prophecy utterly risible; after all, what girl – however 'nice' – could possibly live up to the nobility and goodness of my mother? She alone was the only woman in my life. I have made love to a great number of exquisite creatures of both sexes, but I have *loved* none save my Highgate queen.

My mother herself was extremely beautiful, and I often had cause to wonder what had attracted her to my father; he was certainly not handsome, neither was he graced in character or ability. Once I tried to satisfy my natural curiosity by asking my mother outright, but she did not seem inclined to intimate revelations.

'There must have been *something*,' I said, my hands resting on her knees.

'Oh yes, yes there was, Orlando.'

14

'What?'

'I hardly think, dear, that this is an appropriate occasion to engage in such a *personal* conversation. Neither your father nor I are the people we once were. We have changed, Orlando; everybody changes sooner or later, you know. I still love your father. I am not uncontent.'

'But *why* do you love him?' I persisted.

Mother smiled at me: a smile of infinite patience and compassion. She was *never* angry at me.

'Oh, Orlando dear, one day I will explain everything to you, and then you will understand.'

But she never did, and so neither did I.

Many years later, under the influence of an extremely fine bottle of *Chateau Neuf du Pâpe,* I was indiscreet and foolish enough to speak of this to Heinrich Hervé.

'Maybe he had a twelve-inch cock?' he said, sneering lasciviously.

And there, dear unknown reader of these confessions, is the measure of the man. As a matter of fact I do not know what the size of his cock was, but if the rest of him was anything to go by, it must surely have been a pallid, uninspiring, wrinkled, nondescript little thing.

In her earlier years my mother had been a successful actress with a repertory company, touring the country with light romantic comedies such as *Heartbreak Avenue* and Quincey Cavanagh's *Fickle Passions,* both of which were highly regarded in their time; however, after she had met my father and he – by some fantastic means the nature of which I could not even begin to guess at – had persuaded her that he was worthy of her love, she relinquished (*sacrificed,* I would say) her career and settled with him in the house in Highgate where I was conceived, born and grew up. Sometimes, in a nostalgic mood, she would sit me on her knee and speak to me of her golden years on the stage.

'I was a queen Orlando, a queen! Men would come night after night to the same play, just to see me again. Oh, I was beautiful then.'

'You still *are* beautiful!'

'Alas, I am not as I once was; you must understand that. Then – well – I had my share of admirers, I can tell you. They were heady days. Even the Duke of Manchester . . . have I ever told you what the Duke said to me after the first night of *Love Requited?*'

'Tell me!'

'He came to the stage door after the performance, and when Marie (my retarded but faithful French dresser) showed him into my dressing-room, I was helpless, completely overcome. I could hardly utter a word! I was inexperienced and nervous, Orlando – what was I to think? The Duke of Manchester! I can still recall how wildly my heart beat in my breast. "Madame," he said to me, "Madame, tonight I have had the privilege and the pleasure to witness one of the finest performances on the northern stage – indeed, of any stage in this country! You will be a great star, Madame. I count myself blessed that I have witnessed your first waxing." Then he asked me whether I would do him the honour of dining with him at the *Maison du Parc* – (it was the most fashionable restaurant in the city at that time, and Sybil Thorndike had once received a proposal of marriage from the Comte de Beauchaise there) – but I had to refuse, for I knew that there was also a Duchess of Manchester, and the possibility of scandal was very real. Besides, I had my career to consider. Oh, Orlando, I refused him! Yes, I refused him, even though he pressed me, and every evening for a month thereafter I received a dozen red roses together with a little card which said: *'From one who pines beneath the light of a new-born star.'* Oh, Orlando, can you imagine how giddy with pleasure that made me? I, a young and probably foolish girl –'

'You, foolish?' I would cry. 'Oh, mother, I swear that you were *born* wise!'

Then she would pat me fondly on the head and laugh softly, and when my father came into the room – all five feet four inches of him, with the ridiculous little moustache that overhung his top lip – I would burst into uncontrolled sobbing.

Yes, my mother was a queen, and I have remained her most

loyal subject. I must also make it clear, in order that her memory may remain pure and untainted, that there was never anything improper about the intensely intimate bond which bound us together; we understood each other perfectly, she and I – she by empathy and I by devotion – and I do not think that there could possibly have been two more precisely aligned souls than ours. Our love ran exceptionally deep, our relationship was remarkably complex and profound, yet I assure you (*pace* that sex-obsessed old Hebrew Freud) that it was ever chaste. You can well imagine therefore how unendurable it was for me to hear Heinrich Hervé impute grossness of sexual appetite to that noble, dignified, sensitive woman. Those *afficionados* of the Œdipus theory who wallow in their disgusting spermy daydreams of little boys murdering their fathers and having intercourse with their mothers could never begin to understand the beauty of the relationship which existed between my mother and me; their minds are too poisoned for that. It is certainly true that I frequently felt like murdering my father out of sheer pique, but neither an iota nor a jot of carnal intention ever shadowed the bright sunshine of love that shone in my heart for *her*. I find the very thought of such a thing utterly repellent.

The Incident in the Garden: A Mystical Marriage is Announced

At the back of our Highgate house we had a large garden which grew more-or-less wild, since my father only ever made desultory attempts to induce it to submit to some kind of suburban order, and heavy work with a spade or hoe was quite beyond the constitution of my mother, who was governed by that sensitivity and subtlety of temperament she had cultivated, *de rigueur*, as an actress; she who had once enchanted the Duke of Manchester with her exquisite portrayal of a woman torn apart by the conflict between love and duty, could hardly be expected to go wading about the convolvulus in wellington boots. On occasions I would wander among the cherry trees that grew close to the wall; beyond the wall was the garden of a funeral director called Jolly – an absurd

17

name, which must surely have accounted for the final demise of his business, hinting incongruously as it does of flippancy and horseplay. No-one could be expected to entrust the final dispatch of their loved ones to a man called Jolly, and in the end no-one did.

On this particular afternoon – I still recall the shimmering heat, the vast expanse of blue sky, and the sound of quavering, grief-stricken voices raised in plangent lament coming from Jolly's chapel-of-rest – I had gone into the garden to escape yet another paternal homily, when quite suddenly, there in the long grass, I saw the trembling, fluttering body of a small bird (perhaps it was a sparrow, but I can't be certain), clearly in its death-throes. It had been badly mauled by a cat, as far as I could discern. Its globular black eyes (they were rather like the jet buttons on my mother's best winter coat) were glazed and vacant; the torn wings flapped agitatedly but uselessly, and I could see the tiny thump-thump of its little heart still beating within its bloodied breast.

I was overcome with horror. I wished to put an end to its sufferings at once, but did not know how to do so; I could hardly just stamp on it, nor did there seem to be any implement to hand with which to carry out the task. There is no such thing as a special item of equipment designed for practising euthanasia on mortally wounded or terminally ill small animals and birds, and there never has been; bearing in mind the range of services we have developed for the benefit of the sick and suffering of our own species, I consider this a lamentable state of affairs. As it happened however, the poor creature itself relieved me of my distress by simply expiring. I picked up the mutilated body and cradled it tenderly in my hands. I brought it up to my lips to kiss it.

Then something very extrordinary happened: quite without warning, I was overwhelmed by the urge to suck its flesh. I could smell its still-warm body – a kind of tangy, sour-sweet, meaty odour rather like that of a wet dog. I was simultaneously comforted and excited by this. I didn't want merely to smell it, I wanted to *taste* it too. Oh, how hard I had to fight against the desire to sink my teeth into its breast and insert my tongue into the rich, moist antrum, all darkly slick with blood! Strange images popped into my mind: small, blind creatures, new-born pups squashed tightly together in a deep, dank burrow beneath the surface of the ground ... the pungent ripeness of animal haunches sweating after a swift run ... the carious breath of a mother on the quivering snout of her whelp as fresh meat passes from the salivating jaws of one to the other ... oh!

Shocked by this strange internal flux, yet certain that I had alighted upon some immensely significant and hitherto concealed item of self-knowledge, I threw the dead bird back in the long grass and ran into the house. In the privacy of my bedroom I stripped off all my clothes, lay on the bed, cradled my genitals between my cupped hands, and crooned softly to myself until I fell asleep.

That was the beginning of a recognition of what Dr Balletti calls my 'mania.' I myself do not accept it as anything of the kind, however; on the contrary, I believe it to be a true love affair – as true and as durable and as divinely preordained as Chopin's infatuation with the pianoforte. That hot afternoon in our Highgate garden I encountered for the first time the workings of the Higher Will which was to govern the course of my life; moreover, without being able to identify or name the process, I knew deep in my heart that I had submitted to this Will without reservation. I had been introduced to the amniotic fluid in which I was hitherto to live and breathe.

I kept the secret of that recognition to myself; after all, I was not certain how sympathetically any self-revelation on my part would be received. Neither was I quite sure (indeed, how *could* I be, at that young age?) about the moral texture of it – I mean, was it laudable, or was it not? Did other people possess it? Now of course I know that they did – albeit that the elemental partner in their mystical marriage was other than mine: Michelangelo and his marble, Shakespeare and the English language, Herr Doktor Jung and the deep-sea waters of the human psyche. What are these if not perfect examples of his *Mysterium Coniunctionis*, the consummated nuptials of genius and medium? And to this list must surely be added the name of Orlando Crispe and his moist, yielding, blood-fragrant, tractable *flesh*.

My First Great Dish of the World

It was on my thirteenth birthday that I finally realized what my endless potterings in the kitchen and concocting of various little dishes had been leading to; I suddenly saw them – distinctly, aglow with the patina of retrojective significance and meaning – for what they were: a preparation, a training, an extended novitiate in the culinary arts. I knew then beyond any uncertainty that I was at last ready to be fully initiated into the beguiling secrets of the kitchen and to make my final vows to that Higher Will which had assembled the disparate fragments of my destiny into a coherent whole, before even my ridiculous father – panting and gasping and crooning glutinous inanities, no doubt – had first plunged his florid tool into the milky-white body of the woman it was my honour to call *mother*. In short, I was ready to dedicate my life to the vocation which divine grace had bestowed upon me. *I would become a chef.*

The manner of thus discerning my future path in life was in itself quite simple. My mother (with all her customary perspicacity) had brought me a little book called *Great Dishes of the World Made Easy*; my father's birthday gift to me was an advanced chemistry set – his perspective was clearly that of the analyst whose essential task is that of decomposition, whose curiosity impells him to break things down into their disparate parts without having the slightest idea how to put them together again. My mother however, could not fail to understand that I had entered this world with the soul of an artist, born to create, to recompose, inspired by an intuitive visionary grasp of the whole – a vision as essentially divine as the analyst's is demonic. As it happened, the first recipe upon which my eyes alighted as I riffled excitedly through the pages was for *Boeuf Stroganoff*; in that moment of magic and grace, I *knew*, beyond any doubt or uncertainty, oh! I knew that I had fallen irredeemably and irretrievably in love.

20

Boeuf Stroganoff

2 ounces (50g) of butter
2 large onions, coarsely chopped
4 ounces (100g) mushrooms, sliced
½ ounce (15g) plain flour
1½lb (750g) fillet steak, cut into thick strips
1 tsp (5ml) mixed herbs
1 tbsp (15ml) tomato purée
2 tsp (10ml) French mustard
¼ pint (150ml) soured cream
½ pint (300ml) beef stock
salt and black pepper to season
chopped parsley to serve

Melt half the quantity of butter in a pan on a low heat and brown the onions. Turn up the heat, add the mushrooms, and fry for several minutes. Then remove from the pan and keep warm in a dish. Season the flour with salt and black pepper and toss the strips of steak in the flour so that they are well covered. Melt the remaining butter in the pan and quickly fry the steak until browned. Add to the dish with the mushrooms and onions. Stir in the beef stock, herbs, tomato purée and mustard, return to the pan and bring to the boil, stirring thoroughly. Pour in the soured cream. Heat without boiling, stirring all the time. Serve sprinkled with parsley.

This was of course only a beginning, but it was a great success; my dear mother was generous enough to compliment me on the meal I served to the three of us – it was my father's evening for his motor maintenance class, but out of sheer curiosity he had stayed at home, no doubt anticipating that my first attempt at one of the great dishes of the world would be a humiliating failure.

'Well,' he said, chewing on a sliver of beef, like a ruminating cow, 'it's all very well messing about in the kitchen for a hobby, if that's what you like doing Orlando, but soon enough you'll have to start thinking about the future.'

'This *is* my future,' I replied manfully.

My father shook his head slowly, a patient little smile appearing beneath his absurd, juice-smeared moustache.

'You can't make a living out of stew,' he said.

'It was *Boeuf Stroganoff*.'

'It tasted like stew to me.'

'I am going to be a great chef,' I said.

To be perfectly fair, I have to say that he did not actually laugh in my face, but the expression of contempt and pity commingled that came over him was far worse than laughter. I never hated him more than at that moment. My mother, immutably self-possessed as always, sat in front of her empty plate without saying another word; however, as I got up to leave the table, she looked at me with perfect understanding shining in her lovely eyes.

I myself was utterly enraptured: the thought of how I had transmuted the flesh of a living beast – by some wondrous alchemical process, like lead into gold! – transported me into a higher, brighter dimension of reality; sweetened, spiced, enriched, the bouquet of its precious ichor lingered in my mouth like the aftertaste of a classic wine, the luxurious grace of a sacrament bestowed orally. More than this: it was flesh absorbed by my flesh, the two becoming one, a passionate act of giving, receiving and uniting far sweeter and more durable than the slippery jiggling of buttocks and groins in which I confess I have so often indulged. For me, it was a true *exstasis*.

The Light of My Life Untimely Expended

The dear, sweet, beloved queen of my heart passed from this earthly life shortly before the end of my schooling. Her constitution had never been robust; personally, I am inclined to believe that her early career on the stage had drained her of all vital energy. After all, the life of a successful actress is physically, emotionally and mentally demanding, requiring as it does total dedication of body and soul (all true art makes this demand upon the one who worships at its altar), and it is to be expected therefore, that suffering will inevitably accompany creative genius. I myself have been plagued by hæmorrhoids for years.

And yet, I was completely unprepared for her going. It was

my father who first informed me that there was something seriously wrong with her.

'You'd better sit down, Orlando old chap,' he said, his face grave.

'Why? What's wrong? Is there something the matter?'

'Yes. With your mother.'

I began to tingle all over with an electric current of apprehension.

'Mother is ill? Where is she? If she's ill, she will need me –'

'No, Orlando, no. She's upstairs, but Doctor Silvermann says she musn't be disturbed.'

'Why didn't you tell me before?' I cried, shaking an ineffectual little fist at my father. I couldn't bear the thought that he had shared such a secret with my mother, excluding me from knowledge of her condition; indeed, I did not wish to contemplate the possibility that he knew *anything* about her that I didn't.

'We just didn't realize,' he replied, shrugging his shoulders helplessly. 'You know what your mother's like, never one to complain. She – well, she just left it too late, that's all. The poor woman.'

'My mother is not a woman,' I screamed, 'she is a *lady!*'

'Don't upset yourself, old chap. We'll see what Doctor Silvermann has to say.'

It transpired that what Doctor Silvermann had to say was this: my mother was dying. I was never told what exactly she was dying *of*, but instead had to be satisfied with callously vague statements such as 'completely exhausted,' or 'no resistance left,' and 'just wants to sleep.' But who has ever died of *sleep* in the name of God, except (so I once read) undernourished natives in remote, swampy parts of the African hinterland, where all kinds of noxious vapours and horrible crawling things thrive? One did not die of sleep in Highgate, of that I was sure. My efforts to discover the truth were thwarted relentlessly and cruelly by my father, and every question I put to him was met by unsubtle evasion.

'Why won't you *tell* me?'

'There's nothing to tell old chap, believe me.'

'How can there be nothing to tell? What's *wrong* with her?'

'She's dying, Orlando.'

'I know that already. What I want to know is *why* she's dying.'

'The poor woman. She's no resistance left.'

Hearing that phrase yet again, I turned and fled from the room, my cheeks hot with unstoppable tears.

A week later, my mother was dead.

The Great Lie

It was the explanation my father finally gave me, barely a month after the funeral, that finally pushed me into the first major (and, in retrospect, one would have to say the most important) decision of my life. Even now, I have to make an effort to prevent myself from trembling with rage when I recall the magnitude of his wickedness! How he could for one moment have expected me to believe him, I simply do not know. I have since considered the possibility that grief had unhinged him, but it is more likely that being jealous of the deep bond between mother and me, he was attempting (vainly, I need not say) to slander and befoul the pure memory of that sweetest of women, which he knew I cherished as a sacred trust. This was precisely what I thought at the time, and I still think it now. I was of course surprised (not to say shocked) at the manner in which this attempt was made, but not that he was capable of it. Poor mother was blind as far as my father was concerned, for wifely duty and loyalty to her husband had always been an inviolate principle of her life; the irony is that if she had been a person of less exacting ethical standards, she might not have been obliged to spend the greater part of her cruelly short life saddled with such a nonentity as my father. Our sojourn in this world is chock-a-block with 'ifs,' so they say.

I was in the bath when he made his vile announcement; I do not know why he chose this particular moment, but I imagine that he thought my nakedness would render me more vulnerable, less capable of expressing outrage and disgust than I otherwise might have been. He was quite wrong. At the time, I was even prepared to get out of the bath and face him squarely, even though this would mean exposing my puckered genitals; in fact I actually did so, as you shall shortly learn.

'I suppose it's time you were told,' he murmured, in a tone of voice which made it very clear that some dreadful information was about to be imparted.

'Told what?' I asked, making sure that there was plenty of foam between my legs; I still retained a disturbing (but far from unreservedly unpleasant) memory of the time he had lasciviously explored my scrotum.

'About your mother.'

'She died of sleep, didn't she? That's what you and Doctor Silvermann said.'

I did not attempt to hold back my bitterness.

'I know how you must feel,' replied my father, and to my horror he placed one hand on my back. Then it moved down a fraction.

'You can't possibly know,' I said with great dignity.

'Yes I can, and I *do*. Of course I do. Don't you think I still grieve for her, Orlando? I've lost her too, haven't I?'

Ominously, the hand slithered, a capriolated alien thing, round to my chest. I shuddered.

'I'm trying to take a bath.'

'And I'm trying to tell you about your mother, Orlando.'

'It's too late for that,' I said.

He looked down at me and smiled. It was nauseating.

'It's never too late,' he answered, like someone encouraging an octogenarian to take up driving lessons or evening classes in pottery.

'Then what is it you have to say?'

'Something that should have been said a long time ago, if she had allowed it.'

'Allowed it? What do you mean?'

My father uttered a small, apologetic cough.

'You and I – well – we never really had any man-to-man chats, did we? Never sat down together and really talked about things?'

'No.'

'Like father and sons *ought* to do, Orlando.'

'Ought they?'

'You were never interested in that, I dare say.'

'You're right – I wasn't.'

He sighed, and the hand on my chest began to move in a slow, circular motion.

'Don't make it harder on me than it already is, Orlando, *please*. It's just that – well – just that you wanted to know, and now I think you're prepared for it. As God is my witness, I never wanted to keep it from you! But what could I do? We discussed it often, your mother and I, although she was always adamant that you were never to be told anything while she was alive. "He's just a child," she said. "How can you expect a child to understand?" So I let her have her way, and we said nothing. Besides, we often wondered whether or not you had a *right* to know. Even a mother is entitled to her own secrets, Orlando –'

'There were no secrets between her and me!' I cried, and the soap slipped out of my hands, plopping into the water through the foam I had piled up between my legs; I peered down into the hole and saw my wrinkled penis bobbing languorously below the surface.

'Ah, but there *were*,' replied my father. 'Well, at least one, anyway. The *big* secret, the shame of your poor mother's life, and – and in the end – the death of her. Oh, Orlando, don't hate me for what I'm about to tell you! Don't despise me for giving you the truth you've asked for so often.'

I despise you already, I thought.

'It's hard for me, believe me! I loved that woman to distraction, but what can I do? How can I alter the facts to make them more palatable than they are? I can't. If you must know, then you *will* know, but you must never think I wouldn't have had things otherwise; I'd give the world to be able to tell you a different story, but that's not possible.'

I was by this time thoroughly frightened, and quite unable to interrupt my father any further – I knew he would go on, I knew it would be ghastly, but I could not stop him; neither, in fact, did I wish to. I sat in the tepid water shivering; he perched on the side of the bath, and all the while his hand inched lower and lower, creeping towards the folds of my stomach like a loathsome, many-legged giant insect.

'Your mother,' he said in a hushed, quavering voice, 'had been ill for years, Orlando.'

You're lying! I wanted to scream, but I could not even open my mouth.

'Yes, for years. She was ill when I married her. That's why she – well – why she was devoted to me, you see, because I married her anyway, in spite of everything. Oh, she told me; I mean, there wasn't any point in her trying to hide it, was there? I would have found out sooner or later – considering the *nature* of the illness, that is. But I loved her – oh, I truly did! – and she was terribly grateful for the offer, and over the years, if you really work at it, gratitude turns into love. That's something you should always remember, Orlando. In spite of what all those sex-doctors with letters after their name say, you don't have to start with fire or passion or uncontrollable desire – why, that burns itself out sooner or later, be sure of it. What your mother and I had was so much finer, more lasting: a real respect for each other, deep feeling, and a long, exquisite voyage together into the discovery of love. Who could ask for more than that? Years ago I told you that I was a virgin when I married her, and it's true – she was the first woman I did it with.'

Still shivering, I screwed my eyes shut tightly.

'Of course, your mother had done it with dozens of men.'

Then I screamed – or at least I *thought* I had, but when the agonizing, attenuated muscle-spasm had expended itself, I realized that no sound had actually come out of my mouth.

'Not surprising really, not when you consider the profession she was in. Actresses are notorious for their easy virtue, for being available. And by God, your mother was well and truly available. Of course, it helped her career; she wasn't exactly what you call talented, but she got by in the smaller roles. The only thing is, she had to do a lot of jumping in and out of bed to get those roles: directors, producers, stage-hands, leading men (even a leading *lady* in one particular case), electricians – she had it off with the lot.

'It's a lonely life up there behind the footlights, she told me that herself. A girl gets to thinking of men a bit more than she otherwise might, out on the boards night after night, walking back to her digs in the cold and the dark after the evening performance. Moving around from place to place doesn't help either – no stability, no sense of permanence, no – well, no *home*. Your mother told me that she was always thinking about a home and a husband, a family; but the show must go on as they say, and there just wasn't any time for anything like that. I suppose the one-night stands were a sort of compensation.

'It was some aristocrat who infected her with the syphilis – she was fairly certain of that, although she'd had so many partners she couldn't be absolutely sure. The Duke of Manchester, she told me –'

I think I must have exploded and *imploded* simultaneously. I leapt out of the bath, sending water and foam cascading everywhere, and threw myself at my father with all the savagery of a wild beast, clawing and kicking and lunging. Although I had clearly taken him by surprise he fought back with ferocity and we fell together, crashing against the tiled wall (turquoise dolphins in a pale viridian sea-spray); I heard his head crack.

'Orlando!' he yelled, 'stop this! You must believe me, it's the truth!'

'*Liar!*'

'Please, Orlando, *please* - I loved her, I really did – I haven't lied to you! It wasn't always easy, knowing the kind of life she led –'

'I hate you!' I shouted. 'I hate you! I've always hated you, and I always will. You're *nothing* compared to her – nothing! She was a goddess, she was pure and gentle and sweet, and she would never have done all those horrible things. Never! I don't know why she ever married you, she was far too good for you, she was way above you; mother was clever and talented, but you – what did you ever amount to? I've been

28

ashamed of you for as long as I can remember. You – you're the *worst* father anybody could have had. Oh, I know what you're trying to do! – you're trying to make me think vile things about her just so that you can feel better – but it won't work! Look at you: what are you? Nothing. Now I shall *always* hate you. I shall never, ever forgive you for the cruel lies you've told.'

'Orlando, please –'

'You *disgust* me.'

Then the *cauchemar* began anew, and slipping on the sopping floor, I fell; I managed to haul myself up again by grasping my father's belt – his trousers came slithering down to reveal pallid legs. I aimed a somewhat feeble blow at his testicles, then I began pummelling him on the chest with my clenched fists.

'Stop this, you young fool – oh, for Christ's sake!'

He was panting and wheezing, but he disabled me by suddenly and quite unexpectedly grasping my penis in one hand and yanking on it hard. The sensation was at once both intensely pleasurable and dreadfully painful. To my embarrassment, I felt the quiverings of a nascent erection.

'You sicken me,' I managed to say. 'Utterly and totally.'

His hands fell from my shoulders. When I saw that there were tears trickling down his flushed cheeks, I was momentarily disconcerted.

'Oh, Orlando,' he murmured, 'have you *never* loved me?'

'Loved you?' I snarled, regaining my sense of outrage. 'Loved you? I've never even *liked* you.'

'I had hoped,' he said in a suddenly weary, infinitely sad voice, 'that you and I could be friends.'

I was lost for words; after all this, he dared to say such a thing? He must surely be mentally deranged.

'Friends?' I managed to echo.

'Yes,' he mumbled. 'Friends.'

I drew myself up to my full height and looked into his eyes.

'I promise you this,' I said with a child's bravado, 'not only am I going to be one of the greatest chefs in the entire world, I shall also *never* speak to you again as long as you live.'

And that was a promise which, as you will see for yourself, I eventually broke in the most spectacular manner.

***

Report of Doctor Enrico Balletti to the Chief Medical Officer of Regina Caeli Prison
7th July 19—
(Translated from the Italian)

I first saw prisoner 022654, the Englishman Crispe, at the evening session of general examinations in the Santa Caterina block, last Thursday, July 2nd. I was at once impressed by his general air of self-confidence, his control, the apparently reasoned and reasonable content of his conversation with me. That is to say, I was impressed by the absolute certainty with which he conducted himself in a perfectly sane manner, because absolute certainty belongs only to the insane.

022654 believes that he is a victim of a miscarriage of justice; he stated to me at least half a dozen times in the same fifteen minute session that he did not kill Arturo Trogville, the celebrated food writer and critic – indeed, in my opinion, he is obsessed with this man Trogville. 022654 is apparently entirely unconcerned that he stands condemned for a second murder – one with even more horrifying implications. When he insists that he did not kill Trogville, maybe he is stating the simple truth or maybe not, I do not know; what I do know however, is that he demonstrates no remorse of any kind. It is my belief that 022654 assumes that we regard his deeds in the same light as himself – that is, as works of art.

He has expressed his intention of keeping a diary, or a journal, or perhaps of writing an account of his life – I am not quite sure which; I approve of this unreservedly, since it is bound to make access to his psyche easier for me. Catharsis of some sort is certainly required; in any case, I suspect that progress will be slow. I have promised 022654 that I will obtain a supply of writing materials for him.

The mother is at the root of his psychosis – of this, I am convinced. He speaks of her to me in tones of hushed reverence, as one might speak of

God or a lover, or of some ineffable secret. He does not take kindly to any cross-questioning, however discreet or gentle, as far as the woman he calls his 'Highgate queen' is concerned; he merely states facts, which I am expected to accept at face value: that his mother was a paragon of womanly virtue, that she was gifted to the point of genius, his one and only companion in life who understood him perfectly, a victim of his father's shameless duplicity . . . and so on. On the two occasions I attempted to have him enlarge on these 'facts', 022654 became agitated, then aggressive, clearly suspecting that I was challenging their accuracy.

I would like to know more about the father, but any information must be drawn out of 022654 with the greatest circumspection; in my opinion all the elements of a textbook Œdipus complex are present – the markedly sexual character of his relationship with the mother and his undisguised contempt for his father, for example – but I am not yet in a position to make an unambiguous diagnosis. The precise fate of the father, of course, is as unfortunate as the fact that he is no longer available for questioning. I intend to work on the asumption that the father in some way – either deliberately or unwittingly as the case may be – attacked the child's image of the mother, and in so doing, undermined his sense of connectedness with the most basic stratum of life; this stratum seems for 022654 to have been totally identified with 'mother,' who was sustenance, nourishment, food, life. Furthermore, I have no doubt that this sense of connectedness was destroyed altogether when 022654 was removed from the mother's breast; the records I received from the clinic of the late Dr Stephen McCrae indicate that the breast became ulcerated after being bitten during a feeding session.

Much as I despise the old fraud, I shall have to re-read von Schielberg's The Incestuous Meal: Mother-Love and Meat-Eating.

On a purely personal level I do not think that 022654 likes me – twice during our interview he accusd me of spitting at him. However, I do not think this will interfere with our work together; I recommend that for the time being we continue the medication prescribed for 022654 at the time of his arrival here.

Enrico Balletti.
Report registered by Luciano Casti, Chief Medical Officer.

III

Learning the Hard Way

I began my apprenticeship in the art of the gods at Fuller's Hotel in Trowbridge, under the magisterial Egbert Swayne. Egbert Swayne was a man of immense proportions: he was in fact hugely fat. He also had an extravagant personality to match. When I first saw him – totally bald, pop-eyed, full-lipped, slightly swarthy of complexion, thundering through the kitchens and bellowing with the exaggerated rage (his voice was resonantly fruity) of an *opera buffa* villain – I was overwhelmed; not, you understand, with fear and trembling, but with an irresistible sense of the ridiculous. Egbert Swayne was in fact totally absurd – his only *gravitas* was his culinary creativity – and he ruled over his private kingdom with all the self-indulgent theatrical absurdity of a manic despot, for the kitchen of a true master is alien to democracy. His dedication to his art, however, was complete and total, and to watch him at work was to worship at the altar of his genius. He would brook no shoddiness, no half-heartedness, and he could not tolerate to have about him those whom he considered unworthy of their high calling. We were, in his sight, acolytes who served in the temple of which he was the supreme archpriest.

'Is there no-one among you buggers whose head is not stuffed with pigshit instead of brains?' he would bellow (his very words, I assure you).

Utensils would fly through the air like thunderbolts from the hand of an irate Zeus.

'Live or die with me, boy!' he screamed at me in particular. 'Live or die by my side, and at my caprice. Surrender your freedom of will completely to me, and I will give you godhood. Do you understand me?'

'Yes, Mr Swayne.'

'You may call me Master.'

'Thank you, Master.'

'All that there is to learn, I will teach you. I will lead you from ignorance to understanding, from darkness to light. In return, I ask for your body and soul. Are you willing, you loose-limbed young lackey?'

I nodded my head vigorously.

'Yes, Master,' I said. 'I am willing.'

And he pecked me on my right cheek.

It became obvious as my apprenticeship proceeded, however, that my body interested him rather more than my soul, for one evening as I was about to leave the kitchen and make my lonely way up the back stairs to the room that I had been assigned high in the attics of the hotel, I found him barring the doors – a great mountain of sweat-bedewed blubber, an ambiguous smile puckering his empurpled face.

'Where do you think you are going?' he said.

'To bed, Master.'

'With whom, may I ask?'

'With no-one at all, Master.'

'Wrong. You are going to bed with me.'

'What?'

'Lead on, boy! Lead on, that is, if you wish to *get* on in this place. You catch my drift?'

'Yes, I think so.'

And as we climbed the caliginous, dust-webbed stairway, he pinched my right buttock between a ceratoid thumb and forefinger.

Servicing Master Egbert was not quite as bad as I had imagined it might be; indeed, he was fairly conventional in his requirements. He was incredibly hirsute; what impressed me most was his vast belly – an infinite landscape clouded over with the cumulo-cirrus of fuliginous hair, a rugose immensity criss-crossed with myriad little folds and creases in which his body moisture had collected like oleaginous puddles after a shower of rain.

'Ah, the joys of dispassionate lust.'

I dipped the tip of my tongue into the salty shadows of his fonticulus, and he crooned in sheer delight.

'Gobble me up!'

Then he commanded me to perform a routine series of sexual acts upon him, which I will not bore you with by describing here. As soon as he had effected his pre-dawn departure, trailing his voluminous, stained underpants behind him like a bag of excess skin, I went to the sink and rinsed out my mouth with *Mint-o-Fresh*.

From that time onward, Master Egbert displayed a marked personal interest in the progress of my career; occasionally a little promise of advancement, together with an accompanying kiss on the lips, was delivered clandestinely in the subfusc uterus of the cold-store:

'I'll put you on bread next week, my dear.'

'Thank you, Master.'

'And tonight you shall have the privilege of fellating me into a state of unconsciousness.'

'Thank you, Master.'

The cold-store was (inevitably, I suppose) the tabernacle before which I made my own private devotions, for there the great carcasses hung – alluring and suaveolent, raw and richly sweaty; sometimes I stood for five or ten minutes at a time, perfectly motionless, my face pressed against the smooth marble-veined flesh, my nostrils caressed by the perfume of coagulated blood, rapt in ecstatic dulia. And I contemplated the phantasms that projected themselves upon the silkscreen of my ravished imagination. My penis trembled. On these occasions I was in a state of intense aching, of bitter-sweet longing for my apprenticeship in the art and science of self-expression in flesh to commence; running the tip of my tongue slowly and salaciously across the fibrous plane of a wine-dark flank, I craved the sweetness of that communion between creator and primal matter which only those who burn with the flame of genius can truly know or comprehend.

Meanwhile, I had to be content with bread.

The Stuff of Life
As a baker of bread I was a mere sub-deacon in Master Egbert's sacerdotal hierarchy, and the day when I would stand,

fully ordained at the altar of flesh to work my own miracles of transubstantiation, seemed as far off as ever; even so, there was a great deal to be learned, and it was not a lowliness entirely without its compensations – the fragrance of new-baked bread is quite unique and intensely pleasant, for one thing. I was allowed to use only fresh yeast. Referring to the dried variety, Master Egbert once screamed:

'I will not have that dehydrated camel-sperm in my kitchen!'

I was taught by Flavio Fulvio, the chief baker, how to discern that precise moment in the kneading process when the texture of the dough becomes pliable and elastic – an essential condition for producing fine bread; that it happened quite suddenly continued to take me by surprise for a considerable time (much dough was wasted as a result) but Signor Fulvio was infinitely patient.

'You weel learrn. *Coraggio, amico mio,* such skeels are not – well, well.'

Signor Fulvio suffered from a peculiar inability to finish his sentences.

'Acquired overnight?' I suggested.

'Esattly, esattly! I weel teessh you, you see. *Piano piano, si impara.*'

And indeed, little by little, I did learn.

The incredible variety of the different kinds of bread impressed me greatly, for I had been reared on the humble seedy bloomer (the only sort my father would eat): the *pecorino* breads, the herb, olive and capsicum Mediterranean breads constituted an entire species by themselves, to say nothing of their fruity relatives – bread with nuts, sultanas, honey and cream, bread with nougatine or chocolate chips, bread with sweet rice. Then there were milk rolls, brioches, raisin loaves, spiced buns and almond *stollens*; there were malted banana batches, a huge range of rye breads, mango curls, Panastan bread, Seville bread, Kentucky sweet corns, Toledo bread, pitta bread, and (my own favourite) Viennese fig-and-chicory plaits.

Each of these delectable creations demanded their own

special care and attention, and I discovered that it was necessary for me to put myself into the correct frame of mind before beginning work – to assume, so to speak, the *weltanschauung* of the culture to which the kind of bread I wished to bake properly belonged. Does this sound *de trop*? I assure you that it is not. It would be entirely incongruous for example, to begin a batch of Bavarian ryes in what, *faute de mieux*, one might call a 'Mediterranean mood,' for the primal stuff beneath your fingers will sense the alien vibrations, and react accordingly. One cannot successfully bake the bread of a people who dwell in some cold northern fastness when one's mind dances with images of azure seas or a broiling southern sun. I might tell you that listening to a little Mozart the night before I was due to work on Viennese fig-and-chicory plaits invariably ensured perfect results.

No-one should be surprised at this; after all, here we are talking about the passionate osmosis between a master and his material, which requires total dedication to each and every detail – no matter how apparently nugatory – of the creative act. It is quite simply a matter of seriousness of purpose. Andrei Rublev is said to have prayed and fasted for three days before beginning his icon of the Trinity – which, moreover, he painted in the open air in order to acquire the proper degree of translucency; D'Annunzio attired himself in a shot-silk dressing-gown and strewed his room with rose petals before setting pen to paper; what difference is there then, between perfect religious art, perfect poetry, and perfectly-baked bread? Absolutely none of course; only a buffoon would rate the genius of the master baker below that of the master poet, for genius is without degree.

A painful and humiliating realization of my own inexperience soon dispelled the heresy (to which I confess I was initially addicted) that all the initiations preceding that into the great *gnosis* of the transmutation of flesh, are of lesser significance; I had to learn that every sacrament of the kitchen bestowed its own unique grace, and like any tyro, arrogance caused me to make a great many mistakes.

For example, the amount of time it takes for dough to

properly rise constituted a serious problem for me in the beginning; again and again I succumbed to the temptation to lift the dampened cloth covering the great glazed bowls and snatch a quick peek, not realizing that the resulting disruption of temperature would hinder the very process I was so impatient to see completed.

'Donna try too ard, *caro amico*. Let eet be. Eet does okay by eetself. Donna assle eet. I tink you gotta ave – yeah.'

'More patience?'

'*Preciso.*'

Rising times do of course vary with room temperature; in a warm place for example it will usually take about an hour, but put the dough in a refrigerator, and you may have to wait a whole day for results. Furthermore, it must always return to room temperature before baking.

Brioche

1½oz (40g) fresh yeast
5 tbsp (75ml) milk
5 tbsp (75ml) water
8oz (225g) extraction flour
1½lb (750g) wholemeal flour
1½oz (40g) heather honey
8 eggs, beaten
½ tsp (2.5ml) salt
14oz (400g) melted butter

First mix the yeast with the milk and water, then stir into the extraction flour and make a dough. Put into an earthenware bowl, cover with a damp cloth, and leave at room temperature for 30 minutes to ferment. Add the wholemeal flour, honey, eggs and salt, and knead until the dough is pliable. Then pour on the melted butter. Continue to knead the dough until it is properly clear. Once again put it in the bowl, cover it, and leave to rise. It is ready when the dough has approximately doubled in size and is springy to the touch. Knead it lightly and divide into four pieces. Put in lightly greased brioche tins, cover, and leave to prove in a warm place. Then back in a preheated oven at 220°C/425°F (gas mark 7) for 30 minutes.

A Kiss is Just a Kiss

The day I drew my first successful batch of brioches from the oven I received a continental-style kiss on both cheeks from Signor Fulvio.

'You remember wad I say? You tink I'ma right enough now? You tink – oh, yep.'

'Yes, I remember, Signor Fulvio. You said you would teach me, and you have.'

Smouldering with ridiculous theatrical jealousy, Master Egbert also kissed me – on the lips – and squeezed my crotch for good measure.

'Know wad,' Signor Fulvio whispered in my ear as the Master waddled off, 'if *il Maestro* wasn't *un Maestro vero,* I'da say he was some kinda *finocchio.* Know wadda mean? You look after your *bel culo, amico mio.* Watch your ass.'

Alas, it was a little too late for such homely counsel as that.

In bed that night, interrupting a little post-coital ditty that he was humming to himself, I asked Master Egbert:

'Do you love me?'

He made a small, unnecessary adjustment to the black calotte he sometimes wore, and which presently reposed on his patinated crown.

'Of course not,' he replied, surprise temporarily afflicting him with a slight breathlessness. 'Why should I *love* you, my adorable boy? It's purely and simply a matter of lust. I crave intimate communion with all that corporeal excellence I lack in myself; to wit – your seductive Dionysian glance, your perpetually moist cherry lips, flawless skin, inviting muscularity, your ripe young cock. I desire you all over, but I don't love you.'

'Good.'

'What?'

'That makes it all the easier to ask,' I said.

'Ask what?'

'A favour.'

'Ah. What favour, precisely?'

'I want to move on to sauces.'

'You are weary of Viennese fig-and-chicory plaits so soon?'

'Not entirely, Master. I simply want to move on.'

'Signor Fulvio was right then,' he said, and I detected a slight fremescence in his voice.

'Signor Fulvio?'

'The very same. He told me that you lack patience.'

'He's always saying that,' I objected. 'It doesn't mean anything.'

'Perhaps not. We shall see.'

'You agree, then?'

Master Egbert sighed a massive internal sigh, and the blubbery vastness of his great bulk shivered like a fractured terrain settling down after a mild earthquake.

'Did I say I agree?' he murmured.

I reached down between his legs.

'How about if I do *that?*' I said.

'Ah – oh no, don't stop –'

I took his hand and placed it between my own legs, and at once my father's pale, fratchety-looking face rose up unbidden before my mind's eye.

'Or *that?*' I said, bending forward to kiss an exquisitely tender spot.

'Oh, oh, oh! Did I ever tell you that I suffered from a constriction of the prepuce, as a young man?'

'I don't believe you were *ever* young,' I said. 'I think you were born as you are now: a fat, hairy, middle-aged whale full of piss and wind.'

'Oh, you blue-eyed bastard.'

'And if I do *this?*'

I sucked hard.

'Yes, yes, for God's sake! Oh, *wonderful!* Yes, I'll put you on sauces – oh –'

And the very next day he did.

Mirror, Mirror on the Wall

I had now discovered something very important about myself: *I was physically attractive to others.* Oh, set down baldly like that it doesn't sound terribly significant, but you must remember that I had hitherto never contemplated myself in this way; I

39

was too busy with my dreams of professional advancement, too concerned with the great and singular *obsession* of my life to have any time or energy left over for other kinds of self-knowledge. Even my regular bouts of sexual horseplay with Master Egbert had never led me to envisage the possibility that I had something which other people might desire. In short, I had no occasion to stand naked in front of a mirror and realize that (to use Master Egbert's own description) my 'seductive Dionysian glance, perpetually moist cherry lips, flawless skin, inviting muscularity and ripe young cock' constituted a delicious temptation. *Jeunesse doré!* This is hardly surprising, really – physically hideous as he was, I merely supposed that the Master was happy to take anything he could get. However, since being translated from bread to sauces – clearly the result of an attraction that entirely transcended Master Egbert's limited opportunities to satisfy his carnal urges – a whole new horizon had opened up for me, and I determined to take every advantage of its radiant promise.

Late one evening I *did* stand naked in front of the mirror, and I saw that indeed I *was* beautiful; I had my sweet mother to thank for that, of course. The calumny which my father had heaped upon her sacred memory faded in my mind when I began to consider the possibilities newly made available to me, and the pain which until now had been an inevitable corollary to every recollection of her dear face and her gentle voice, suddenly became a paean of exultant gratitude. Even after her death then, she continued to bestow her grace. If the favours I might be obliged to dispense in order to advance and strengthen my vocation had to be sexual, so be it. This prospect, in any case, did not seem entirely unpleasurable to me. Perhaps at last I would find myself embracing at least one counsel of my father's: never to forget that I had balls; well, I apparently had rather luscious balls, and I made up my mind to put them to good use.

A Potted History of Fuller's Hotel
Fuller's Hotel was the grandest establishment in Trowbridge. To those of you who might conceivably imagine that

Trowbridge is not conducive to grandiosity, let me tell you that in 1897 the Earl of Bridgeford gave a sumptuous dinner party in the Prince of Wales Banqueting Hall (now a ball-room) for two hundred titled or otherwise egregious persons, during the course of which Miss Maude Alleyn danced on the Earl's table dressed as a Hottentot. Neither does Fuller's pedigree depend merely on the lustre of nostalgia, because some years after my departure, the Society of Distinguished Britons held its Annual General Meeting (with a champagne supper to follow) in the Peacock Suite, and although it is true that he did not dance on the table dressed as a Hottentot, Sir Oswald Fucques delivered one of the finest and most penetrating critiques of the brand of consumerist philosophy that later came to be known as 'Thatcherism'; there can be little doubt that its success was in no small measure due to the excellent *Bollinger Special Cuvée* selected and served by Georges-Claude Marais, our *Maître d'Hôtel*.

Fuller's Hotel had been constructed in the early years of the nineteenth century to satisfy the pretensions of the head of an old wool merchanting family, who regarded it (for want of the genuine article) as his country seat; however, less than five years after the death of Sir Frederick Fuller ('Firebrand Freddy') it had been renovated and refurbished as an hotel by an exceedingly wealthy French entrepreneur. It was Monsieur Charles Cluzac who installed Maître Chavasse-Laclos in the kitchens of Fuller's Hotel, thus ensuring it a reputation second-to-none among the best country hostelries; *Framboises Marie Lloyd* were created by Jean Chavasse-Laclos, as you may well know.

In 1924 a particularly gruesome murder took place at Fuller's Hotel – a psychotic lawyer called Hawkes hacked his mistress to death with an axe as she slept, and was later hanged for doing so; oddly enough (human nature being what it is, I suppose) this did not have any deleterious effect whatsoever on custom, but rather actually increased and enhanced it, and for a good many years after the murder it was considered highly fashionable for professional men to take their mistresses to Fuller's to enjoy a weekend of illicit passion. Alvin Alton's sensation-mongering account of the crime, *An Axe Among the Axminsters,* put an end to this boom by making it perfectly clear that Fuller's Hotel was used by solicitors, bankers and clerks-of-the-works for precisely this purpose; indeed, the author seemed to imply that they did so with the full connivance of the staff, who constituted nothing less than a depraved *camarilla* whose sole object was to corrupt the morality of the middle-classes. Quieter times inevitably followed, and the hotel was eventually acquired by Lawrence Denning-Smith – presumably as a sop to his conscience, for it was Lawrence Denning-Smith who started the *Sizzlin' Sausage* fast-food chain. I will speak no more of him.

Fuller's had been all but forgotten until Egbert Swayne brought it out of the doldrums, artfully seducing (quite literally in one case, I gather) the Michelin assessors, and lifting it to the glittering heights of culinary professionalism with a succession of utterly astonishing gastronomic offerings which were not only solidly based upon classical tradition, but also looked forward towards adaptation and innovation, demonstrating all the skill and inspiration which only a true master possesses; a slightly inebriated Egon Ronay was once moved to declare:

'Tonight I have dined in the house of the Lord.'

Master Egbert had enough courage to discover his own personal style, trust it, and – *fortiter et recte* – stick to it; fashions in food are notoriously volatile in any case, and when *nouvelle cuisine* arrived, he screamed:

'More fucking tomfoolery! Half a hamster's tit and two peas floating on a raspberry haemorrhage for thirty quid? God in heaven, do they take us all for dizzards?'

He saw what many others saw, but he had the guts to say it. He also knew, despite all the trimmings and trappings of *haute cuisine*, despite the effete posturings of the new generation of sophisticates, that what people want more than anything else is first-rate food, perfectly cooked, unobtrusively served in pleasant surroundings, for a reasonable price. And this is exactly what he gave them. The *Good Food Guide* referred to Egbert Swayne's style as a *via media,* which did not displease the Master, for it was essentially accurate; he always avoided extremes, but was more than happy to take the best of diverse cultures and traditions, bringing them together to create something surprisingly new. He contrived a harmony between the thrill of novelty and the patina of tradition. He was, I suppose, a true eclectic.

Allow me to give you two typical examples of his style:

MENU FOR THE ANNUAL DINNER OF
THE BISHOP BERKELEY SOCIETY

Jambon Persillé

Pissaladière

Rosettes d'Agneau Parmentier
Spiced Cabbage Salad
New Potatoes Roasted in their Skins

Millefeuillé de Chocolat Arlequin

Comtesse de Saillon-Felée, Vin de Table Blanc
Hautes Côtes de Beaune, Danton Frères
Billecarte-Selvaux NV

Augustus Pratt, President of the Bishop Berkeley Society, commented:

'Consuming a meal like *that* really brings home the old boy's dictum that *esse est percipi*. Wouldn't you say?'

MENU FOR A PRIVATE DINNER PARTY
SIR REGINALD AND LADY DARTINGTON

Salade de Poivrons Rouges aux Anchois

Roast Quails with Bacon and Sweet Vinegar

Paupiettes de Boeuf

Braised Celery Hearts
New Potatoes in a Honey and Thyme Dressing

Lemon Tart à la Crème Chantilly

Mâcon-Villages Blanc, Danton Frères
Rioja Criana, Caste Palacio y Palmaios
Muscatel de Valencia

Although the French *jambon Bayenne* was imported, Master Egbert obtained his hams from a dedicated, incontinent elderly widow named Mrs Pikemain, who specialized in breeding the old varieties of pig such as Gloucester Old Spots and Landrace. Both her smoked and unsmoked hams possessed an utterly unique delicacy of flavour; whether her incontinence had anything to do with this, it is difficult to say. Mrs Pikemain soaked her hams for at least ten days in a brine solution, then hung them up to dry; after this they were either simmered slowly or smoked over a mixture of oak and beech, the result of which was a translucent golden glow. Master Egbert's professional relationship with old Mrs Pikeman lasted until she died at the age of ninety-one; thereafter, he continued to do business with her burly, tousle-haired grandson, with whom he also began a torrid affair.

'He's crazy,' the Master once observed to me, 'but I adore him, not least of all because he's got the cock of a rhino. You know what he said to me after we'd done it for the first time? He looked at me with those liquid chocolate eyes of his and he said, "Well it's better than shafting the pigs, anyway."'

'Obviously an incurable romantic.'

Master Egbert imported his Parma ham from Casa Casta-Minerva, a small family concern whose London agents were Graziano Viletti, and it was in my opinion the very best: silky in texture, deep pink in colour, moderately salty, creamy, wonderfully fragrant, with the merest nuance of the Italian farmyard, and an angel's kiss of herby moistness – oh, yes! – it was the best! It is the fat of course, which gives Parma ham its unique, richly sumptuous flavour, and Master Egbert used almost to weep when plates were returned to the kitchen bearing shreds of fat torn from the meat and abandoned. The ham itself comes from huge, mature pigs, and it is dry-salted and air-dried for anything up to two years, which bestows a gloriously sweet ripeness. Served translucently thin, the best Parma ham needs no accompaniment whatsoever, and certainly no condiments, although I once saw an obese, florid-faced diner cover his with tomato ketchup (I did not inform Master Egbert of what I had witnessed, for fear of provoking an attack of hysteria); together, fat and meat – pink fringed with creamy white! – constitute a taste – and foretaste, so to speak – of paradise. To one eating Parma ham for the first time, the sensation can be positively erotic.

The Things That Money Can Buy

It was my Béchamel sauce that did it. It was my Béchamel sauce that led me to Ariadne Butely-Butters, and it was Mrs Butely-Butters (or rather, her money) which brought my dream of culinary independence and supremacy significantly nearer to becoming a reality.

'You're wanted in the Grill Room,' Master Egbert said to me in a snappish tone.

'Who wants me?'

'Hadn't you better go and find out for yourself?'

'Is there a complaint?'

'Quite the reverse. Oh for Christ's sake, get out there and see.'

Mrs Ariadne Butely-Butters was an ancient, powdered *habitué* of the Grill Room, who in her time had been (so I was later told) a high-society flapper, a Windmill girl, briefly notorious for throwing an egg at Archbishop William Temple, a modestly successful *chanteuse,* the author of a scurrilous *roman à clef,* and the wife of a Hungarian aristocrat, tragically widowed after only six months of a tempestuous marriage; she was now an incredibly wealthy woman, having inherited the fortune of her second husband, a Nottinghamshire sanitary-ware manufacturer. She was also bored, lonely, and suffering from an obsession with the imminence of final disintegration.

45

'Young man, come here and sit by me.'

The fragrance of *Chanel* did not quite mask the odour of irreversible decay.

'I have called you here in order to compliment you.'

'Thank you, Madame.'

'No – thank *you*. I have been coming to Fuller's Hotel for a great many years, but tonight, for the first time, I have tasted perfection. I mean your Béchamel sauce.'

'I'm glad you liked it.'

'*Liked* it? It was heaven! I was ravished. As you know, a good sauce is not merely an accompaniment; the role of a good sauce is equivalent to that of the pianoforte in the art of *lieder* – I have been a singer myself, you understand – it constitutes an inseparable element of the whole composition, contributing to that wholeness and enhancing its clarity, its accessibility. It encourages, it expounds, demonstrates and synthesizes. Wouldn't you agree?'

'I agree absolutely,' I said, slightly disconcerted by what sounded like a lecture, but fascinated by the gorgeous pearl choker that surrounded the fibrous, desiccated threads of skin that were her neck.

'What is your secret, young man?'

'Dedication.'

'You needn't be coy with me. Tell me your secret.'

I shrugged.

'Don't allow the milk to reach boiling-point before adding the onion, parsley, peppercorns and bayleaf – don't allow it to boil, not even for the fraction of a second.'

'Ah!'

'So many people do, you know – it's fatal. They should go in just *before* boiling-point, then the saucepan should be removed from the heat at once, and at least twelve minutes allowed for infusion.'

'Twelve minutes . . . you are that precise?'

'Of course – precision is an essential ingredient of dedication. Then one has to take into account so many other factors, naturally.'

'Such as?'

'Room temperature, the weather, even one's own mood. The medium always responds to the mood of the artist. The longest I have ever allowed for infusion is fifteen minutes and thirty-five seconds.'

Mrs Butely-Butters laid a spotted, skeletal claw on my forearm, and as she gazed into my eyes, I had the uncanny sensation of being propositioned by a corpse – an experience, albeit fleeting, that was an unpleasant commingling of fascination and horror. But then – oh, then – the horrid nearly always *is* fascinating.

'Yes, you *are* dedicated,' she whispered.

'Thank you, Madame.'

'I do so hope we shall be able to meet again. And now I must return to my Calvados, and you to your duties.'

She had been right about the nature and function of sauces, of course. In the grand classical tradition the rule used to be sauces, sauces, and the more sauces the better (French patrimony actually boasts of nearly four hundred different varieties), but now the emphasis is decidedly on integration, complementarity, lightness but sureness of touch; the bad old days of poor storage, inadequate refrigeration and questionable freshness which gave rise to the axiom 'C'est la sauce qui fait passer le poisson' have long since gone, and no serious *gourmet* or *gourmand* relishes a cloying buttery blanket whose chief purpose is to distract or mask. Every sauce should declare itself clearly and precisely but with modesty, and what it has to say should be entirely in accord with the statement uttered by the final dish; the two personalities must be harmoniously distinct, true twins in both nature and spirit, combining to make an integrated whole. It is not so much a matter of thesis, antithesis and synthesis, but rather of definition, synonym and fullness of revelation.

The *grandes dames* of the classical sauces – Hollandaise, Mousseline, Bordelaise, Béchamel, Béarnaise, Soubise and Mornay – demand nothing less than complete perfection, otherwise their essential simplicity will fail to astonish and delight, and such perfection comes only as the result of faithful dedication to tradition; for example, one would no more consider innovation in the case of Béchamel than a Grand Master would think of changing the rules of chess or ignoring the classic openings created by the great exponents of the past. However, with regional specialities such as Raïto, Meurette de Sorges and Aillade, one can be a little more subjective and introduce an element of creativity, since experimentation and adaptation is the nexus from which these *jeunes filles* emerged.

Sauce Aillade

3 cloves of garlic, crushed
Handful of peeled walnuts
¼ teaspoon of salt
Freshly ground black pepper
5 fl oz (150 mls) walnut oil
2 tbsps red wine vinegar
1 soft-boiled egg yolk
1 tbsp chopped fresh parsley

Pound the garlic and walnuts to a paste in a mortar. Blend in the salt, pepper, oil and wine vinegar. Add the egg yolk and, when it is well-blended, add the parsley.

This sauce is a speciality of the Languedoc region, frequently served with *magrets de canard;* the proportions of the ingredients do vary considerably, and experimentation according to personal taste is therefore permissible.

Later that evening (and, I confess, not entirely to my surprise) I was summoned to Mrs Butely-Butters' suite. I arrived to find her in bed, wearing a ridiculously feathered, friand nightgown; she was propped up by many pillows, drinking champagne, and it was obvious to me that she was also slightly drunk.

'Dear boy! Orlando – (yes, I asked them your name – and so much else about you!) – indulge a foolish old woman, and sit here on the bed.'

She patted the quilt coyly.

'You are young,' she said. Then she sighed. 'So young. I adore youth! Here, have some champagne.'

I was astonished that such a brittle hand, attached to such an emaciated wrist, had the strength to hold the bottle steady. She filled my glass and I sipped.

'*Laurent Perrier*,' I murmured appreciatively.

'Yes. Did you take a sneak peep at the label?'

'I didn't have to, Madame.'

'For heaven's sake Orlando, call me Ariadne!'

'Ariadne, then.'

'Do you know dearest boy, I have drunk champagne every day of my life; or at least, every day for the past – well, God alone knows how many years – and I still can't tell one from the other. Does that surprise you? Shock you, even?'

'Not at all. You clearly know what you like.'

One hand was now on my thigh.

'Yes my dear, I do. And I like *you*. I like you very much indeed. You're very good-looking, did you know that?'

'I inherited my mother's looks,' I answered. 'She was an extremely beautiful woman.'

'I dare say she was. And you are an extremely beautiful young man.'

'My mother was a talented actress. She was a true *artiste*.'

I drank some more champagne, then I said:

'What am I doing here, Ariadne?'

'I want you to make me happy; I told you, I adore youth. And – and *I* want to make *you* happy, Orlando. What would make you truly happy? Tell me.'

'Truly happy?'

'Truly happy.'

'Independence,' I said.

'Independence?'

'Fuller's Hotel is just a stepping-stone for me, just a stop on the route; I want my own restaurant eventually, my own kitchen where I can create my own masterpieces. I want – I *intend* – to be a great chef. One of the greatest ever. That has been my dream since the beginning. True happiness for me is making the dream a reality.'

'Oh, Orlando!'

She leaned forward and kissed me on one cheek; it was a

strange sensation, like being tickled with a strip of warm, wet chamois.

'Perhaps, my dear, we can make each other happy?'

'Perhaps, Ariadne.'

'At least for a short while. I meant what I said about your Béchamel sauce.'

'Yes, thank you.'

'It wasn't *just* an unsubtle ploy, you know. I really meant it.'

'But it was a ploy all the same?'

She giggled, and it put me in mind of the meaningless chuckle of the irreversibly senile.

'Of course. All that pretentious rubbish about sauce being like the piano, I read in a fashionable cookery magazine; it was an article by Arturo Trogville. I looked it up especially for the occasion. The whole thing was *planned,* you see! I noticed you one evening crossing the hotel foyer and I made up my mind there and then to find out who you were, and to meet you. You remind me just a little of Stan, when he was young.'

'Stan?'

'Yes. Was that terribly naughty of me? Are you very angry?'

'I am charmed, Ariadne.'

'I *can* be naughty, you know. Oh, indeed I can.'

The vagabond hand was now fumbling at the zip of my trousers, the keloidal knuckles crunching audibly.

'Ariadne, you really musn't . . .'

'I bet you've got a beautiful willie-wonkie,' she said in a revoltingly glutinous tone of voice, and with surprising frankness.

'As a matter of fact, I think I have. But this isn't right.'

'Just like Stan had.'

Who the hell was Stan?

'Ariadne, who was —'

She eventually managed to pull down the zip, and her fingers slipped in.

'Look,' I said, 'this sort of thing will get me into serious trouble with the management —'

'Who's to know?'

'The staff are strictly forbidden —'

'Oh, Orlando, I've lived too long to be forbidden anything!'

'All the same, Ariadne . . .'

She giggled again.

'Besides, I mustn't take advantage of you,' I said.

'Why on earth not? Anyway, I'm the one who's taking advantage of *you*. Darling thing, can't you see I'm trying to *seduce* you?'

I felt my cotton briefs snag on one of her corrugated fingernails.

'Don't you want me to help make your dream come true?' she said.

'Of course – but this is all so – well – so unexpected –'

'Don't you find the prospect of seduction rather thrilling?'

I certainly found the prospect of even a fraction of her wealth thrilling, and so despite my revulsion, I was careful with my words.

'That's a foolish question,' I said.

'Of course it is. Youth cannot but succumb to sweet seduction . . .'

In the course of subsequent reflection upon this grotesque incident, I was quite astonished at the high degree of proficiency in the art of mercenarism that I seemed to have acquired with such ease and rapidity; having once glimpsed the roseate promise of self-advancement which this malodorous old hag's financial resources offered, I went all out to grasp it. Neither was I in any way ashamed to do so, for had I not vowed that I would put my physical charms to good use? They were, after all, a legacy from the dearest of all mothers – my Highgate queen! – and to profit by them was surely to glorify her beloved memory. My only real problem was how to get as much as I could out of Mrs Butely-Butters for the minimum return, for even my willie-wonkie had its pride, and I would have preferred not to have it invaginated; nevertheless – when I contemplated what she could do for me – it was a case of being *in utrumque paratus*.

'Oh, Orlando, Orlando,' she whispered, a trail of champagne fizz snaking out of the corner of her mouth and trickling down over her wrinkled chin.

Then she said:

'I think I'm tight.'

'Actually Ariadne, you're completely pissed.'

'I'm going to throw up.'

She slumped towards me, her head banging against my shoulder, and I was disconcerted and confused to observe what appeared to be an erratic slithering movement of her entire scalp, until I realized that she was wearing a wig. To my relief, the furtive encounter of her crablike hand with my shrivelled manhood suddenly ceased.

'Am I dreaming?' she murmured through the rattle of spittle.

'No,' I said, 'but you *are* tired. Perhaps you ought to sleep.'

'Sweet Orlando . . .'

'Sweet Ariadne.'

I left her as she was, sprawled across the pillows, and tiptoed out of the room. The following afternoon I received a gift-wrapped Raymond Weil watch, accompanied by a little card in the shape of a heart, on which were scrawled the words: *Perhaps we can make each other's dreams come true.*

I saw Master Egbert eyeing me up and down as I slipped the watch onto my wrist.

Feelings are Forever

The Raymond Weil watch was followed by a Mont Blanc fountain-pen, a pair of solid gold cuff-links engraved with my initials, a pigskin wallet, and a second invitation to her room for champagne.

Master Egbert hissed at me:

'If you're humping that calcified old cow, you disgust me.'

'Jealous, are we?'

'As a matter of fact, *yes*. But there's also something object-ively foul about dipping your lovely wick with a woman her age. She ought to be ashamed.'

'I am not a gerontophile, and I am *not* dipping my wick, as it happens.'

'But you're leading her on, you pitiless gigolo.'

'That's quite a different matter.'

'If your Hollandaise sauce suffers on account of this, you'll be sorry for it. I'll spank your buttocks until they bleed.'

'Promises, promises.'

On this second occasion I found my prediluvian *geldmutter* recumbent upon the satinate bed, wearing a casually unfastened *chinoise* blouse and green knickers; she looked absurd, but was unfortunately quite sober, which seemed to indicate that she meant business. Her naked thighs were like strips of bleached, rotting rubber. Oh, is there anything quite so hideous as really *old* flesh? Her rheumy eyes, coal-black in their rouged and ravaged hollows, glittered with frank expectation.

'Orlando, dearest boy,' she trilled, 'Come, come!'

This was precisely what I was hoping *not* to be required to do.

'I've been waiting for you.'

'Hello Ariadne,' I said.

'"Hello"? So formal, so aloof? Ah, Orlando, so *cold* towards your adoring girl?'

'Thank you very much for the watch. And the pen. And the cufflinks – look, I'm wearing them.'

She waved one thin arm in the air, creating a sudden cloud-burst of talcum powder.

'Trifles!' she said, 'bagatelles! You know what I want to do, don't you?'

'What?'

'I want to make your dream come true.'

I shook my head slowly.

'That would take quite a lot of money,' I said.

'I've got oodles of money. How *much* would it take, exactly?'

'I couldn't say, offhand . . . I'd have to find the right kind of place, first. I'd have to be sure. It would be a matter of starting out with sufficient capital. I couldn't even begin to look at the possibilities without proper resources –'

'I can have Lawrence Digby draw up suitable arrangements in the morning.'

'Who's Lawrence Digby?'

'My solicitor, silly boy. He'll take care of everything, you wait and see. Your darling girl will show you how grateful she can be.'

'Tomorrow is Sunday.'

'Lawrence will make arrangements for me to buy Buckingham Palace on Christmas Day, if I tell him to,' she said, a steel-hard note of resolution suddenly in her voice. Then she began to purr again. 'Come here to me, Orlando. I want you near me. I want to bask in your youth.'

My heart was beating and my mouth was dry; could it really be quite so easy? Was that how it was done, just by snapping the fingers? The sheer power of it excited me, and together with the realization that Mrs Butely-Butters was to all intents and purposes offering me my own restaurant, caused my willie-wonkie to stir inside my underpants.

'Oh!' she cried delightedly, immediately deflating it again, 'are you eager for embraces? Naughty boy!'

I climbed up onto the bed and stretched out beside her.

'Don't touch me Orlando, not yet . . . I'm frightened.'

'Frightened of me?'

'No. Yes. Of everything. Oh, Christ! Is this what I've dreamed of for so long?'

'It's certainly what *I* have dreamed of,' I said with complete honesty, but doubtlessly a very different frame of reference.

'Oh, Orlando . . .'

Mrs Butely-Butters emitted an odour that was, it seemed to me, a blend of three distinct and uncomplimentary smells: *Chanel*, White Horse linament and the sick lassitude of excessive wealth.

'Be good to me, Orlando,' she crooned, her voice varnished with the rich *craquelure* of desperation that one so often comes across in the reluctantly senescent.

'And you be good to *me*, won't you?' I said.

I opened her blouse and uncovered one breast. It was hideous, collapsed in on itself like an old suede bag; the maculate nipple, stippled with feeble silvery hair, hung down from a tangle of wrinkled fibres. It could have been the air-sack of an obsolete Celtic wind instrument.

'I am still beautiful?' she asked.

'That is a totally absurd and unnecessary question,' I said.

She smiled gratefully.

'You say the kindest things, Orlando! You know how to make an old woman feel young again, young and desirable.'

I closed my eyes and kissed her on those desiccated, papery lips. Her breath was, I should imagine, somewhat similar in odour to the first farting flutter of air to escape an Egyptian tomb opened after three thousand years.

'Do I excite you, Orlando?'

'Need you ask?'

'It's just that – well – you're going about things so formally, so objectively, if you know what I mean. You seem *detached*.'

'Oh, my dear lady, I *must* be so! I am restraining myself, quite deliberately controlling my passion. If I did not do this, it would all be over and done with too quickly. It is not easy for me – you inflame me – '

'Orlando, I want you to *do* things to me – you *know* – where's your lovely young willie-wonkie?'

There was no doubt about it of course, not after such disheartening precision of terms: I knew I would have to penetrate the decrepit old sow. This was not a pleasant prospect, but the corollary possibilities of advancing my career certainly were.

Gently, gingerly, I drew down her green silk knickers. Silvery scales of dead skin rose up in a puffball and floated down again like a slow-motion fall of snowflakes. What I saw was the fluff of a goat's beard set in a sunken mound of grey, corrugated flaky pastry.

'Oh, oh, oh!' she moaned. 'Will I get the *feeling*, Orlando? The one Stan used to give me in Kew Gardens?'

'Look, who exactly *is* this Stan?'

'Stanley,' she gasped, twisting her bewigged death's head on the pillow. 'Stanley Baldwin.'

'You mean – ?'

'It's been so long since I had the feeling. I want it. I want the feeling, Orlando. Oh please, give me the feeling . . .'

I presumed that she was referring to an orgasm. Had this

repulsive ossification once been Stanley Baldwin's mistress? Or had the incident in Kew Gardens been merely the casual diversion of a single summer's afternoon, heady with the fragrance of exotic hothouse blooms?

'You *knew* Stanley Baldwin?' I said, as much astonished as curious.

'Well, only in the biblical sense,' she answered.

'Stanley Baldwin?'

'We used to meet every Saturday afternoon in Kew Gardens, outside the rare orchids house; he always loved orchids, always sent me an orchid on my birthday. We'd sit on the bench with a rug over us, me on his lap, him with his arms around my shoulders, and nobody ever knew, ever guessed, what was going on underneath that rug.'

'But this is quite incredible,' I said. 'You and *Stanley Baldwin?*'

'Yes. We used to give each other the *feeling*,' Mrs Butely-Butters went on, her upper set of dentures slipping out and being sucked noisily but expertly back in again, as her speech became more excited in the heat of recollection. 'Stan had the most gorgeous willie-wonkie I've ever seen..'

'Oh? And how many have you seen, Ariadne?'

You will appreciate that curiosity, not jealousy, prompted this question.

'Oh, hundreds. He used to caress my womanly parts with his fingertips; it was like a butterfly fluttering down there between my legs, so delicate and so unbearably arousing – oh, oh, then the *feeling* would overwhelm me – the lovely feeling –'

Indeed, it appeared that Mrs Butely-Butter's lovely feeling was beginning to overwhelm her once again at this very moment, without any aid or assistance from my otiose willie-wonkie: her scrawny limbs were executing a graceless little fandango all of their own as she made strange clutching gestures with her fists – one could almost *hear* the joints gravelling in the agonizing novelty of exertion; her withered dugs flapped uselessly on either side of her visible ribcage; the vellum-yellow eyelids were screwed tightly shut. Traces of a translucent ozaena glittered on her hair-frilled upper lip.

'Oh, Stan – Orlando – oh –'

Amazingly, she was bringing herself off, the recollection of Stanley Baldwin having been resurrected from some labyrinthine nidus of her memory, and it was clear that breaching the *ne plus ultra* of her passion would be a purely private accomplishment. I had acted merely as a catalyst. Was this all she had ever required of me, or had Stanley Baldwin and I merged together, our separate identities reconstituted to form a single archetype of lost love recaptured?

'Enjoy your feeling,' I urged in a soft, discreet voice. 'Let it take you, let it cradle you in its caress. It's been such a long, long time, hasn't it?'

'Yes, oh yes, the feeling . . . it's been such a long time . . .'

She twisted and turned for some moments, then settled into a foetal position; her claws moved feebly between her thighs. A slow, sibilant, attenuated thread of graveolent breath issued from a pinprick-point between her papery lips, like a prelude to the hushed cadence of approaching expiry.

'Aaahhh . . .'

Without looking down, I tickled the unlovely bearded *mons* with a fingertip.

'Like a butterfly,' I whispered.

'Like a butterfly,' she said in a voice which was barely audible.

Before I had finished stuffing myself back into my underpants, she was fast asleep and snoring gently.

Two days later I received notification from Lawrence Digby of Digby, Digby & Peacock, that a deposit of twenty thousand pounds had been lodged with Coutts in my name, and that further instructions from me were awaited.

And So to Bed

The remaining hours of that night, a night pregnant with the intoxicating realisation of opportunity, I reserved for myself and my beloved alone. I selected a juicy, pungent flank from the cold-store – one that seemed to have been waiting for my coming, aching for my embrace, soundlessly crying out for the worship I alone could give! – and carrying it on my shoulders like a bride across the threshold, I bore it aloft to my little attic room.

I stood for some moments absorbed in contemplation of the huge crimson-deep, fat-speckled expanse of flesh; it lay on the bed like an expectant lover, its silence a high eloquence, its motionless passivity an initiation of seduction rather than a response to it – both paradoxes of passion. Its entire presence was a metaphysical contradiction: it was dead yet shockingly alive, moving perpetually in its own stillness; it was dumb, but the nexus of emotions it aroused in me constituted a lyrical epiphany in honour of stupendous obsession. Oh Christ, what wonders were to unfold? I trembled all over, as with a fine fremitus.

I undressed myself slowly and clumsily, with all the shy *gaucherie* of a virgin lover: I hopped from one foot to the other as I pulled off my trousers, catching my sock on the buckle of my belt; a shirt-button snapped and split; my keys slipped out of my pocket. When at last I had finished, standing there erect beneath my underpants, sweating and shaking, I understood with poignant clarity how patient and how courteous my beloved had been; it gleamed richly in the amber-gold light of the shaded lamp, waiting only to satisfy my hunger, to satiate, to plunge me into ecstasy.

I placed my body carefully across it, tucking my arms underneath it, so that we were locked in an embrace; I lay my cheek against its lightly corrugated surface and, inhaling deeply, was at once inebriated with the sour-sweet odour of chill clotted blood, of heady amino-acids, of a hundred other numinous ichors exposed, expelled and inspissated – this, surely, was the intoxicating perfume that quickened the nostrils of Yahweh as he stirred his forefinger into the chaotic primal slime which was to become Adam!

With much deliberation I drew my underpants down over my buttocks, so that the revelation of my final nakedness came gently to my beloved, with subtlety and finesse – a last love-offering, a final token of foreplay before the great consummation; they slipped to my ankles and I kicked them to the floor. The impress of damp, ripe flesh, the solid interstratification of flesh and fat against my exposed genitals, was sensational. Then I spread my thighs as widely as I could, curling my legs around each side, pulling myself up and over the great meaty bulk. I kissed its fibres lingeringly, I licked it, gnawed at it with exquisite tenderness, as a young husband might lick and gnaw the stiffening nipples of his new bride. Under the heat of my body it was becoming warmer and slightly greasy, so that when I began the first slow, tentative thrusts, I found myself slipping and sliding in an exquisitely arousing manner, and I knew for certain that at this moment, my beloved was answering the urgent call of my increasing passion.

I could no longer see the room or its contents, nor do I think I was actually aware of them; I swam, like a foetus in amniotic fluid, in an infinite ocean of blood-red flesh. I was conscious of my movements but not their immediate intention; hence, I knew precisely what I was doing when I rolled onto my back, opened my legs, and pulled the great carcass on top of me, but not quite *why*. I was reduced to a pure and simple empiricism: everything was sensation, nothing was reason. We moved together like a horse and rider, my beloved and I; when I arched and bucked, so too did the carcass; when I lifted myself and sank back again, it did likewise; when I parted my arms and thighs to embrace, the contours of the resulting concavities were instantly sealed by dead-weight, wine-rich, blood-red flesh.

Moaning, moaning and shuddering, I clung to my beloved in a sexual systalsis as I released my seed – helplessly, copiously, repeatedly – naked flesh to naked flesh, meat to meat, perfectly and completely made one in a true and mysterious conjunction.

I heard a voice, which was my own and yet entirely unfamiliar, whisper:

'Oh, I love . . . love you!'

Then:

'What the hell are you *doing,* for Christ's sake?'

Master Egbert stood in the rectangle of harsh yellow light that was the doorway: huge, shocking, like an unpredicted eclipse.

'*Fucking a side of beef?*'

It was then that I lost consciousness.

Mrs Butely-Butters died two days before I left Fuller's Hotel; ironically enough she did not finally expire of decrepitude, but slipped off a bar-stool and cracked her skull open. I was unable to attend the funeral, but I did send a small spray of orchids, bearing the inscription: *Feelings Are Forever.*

Master Egbert was briefly inconsolable.

'You've been with me eight years,' he said. 'How am I going to fill the lonely nights without you?' he cried, pulling me to himself and squeezing my backside with a meaty, hairy hand.

'Oh, you'll find someone. Actually, that new kichen-boy looks quite nice.'

'George? I hardly think so. His room is full of grubby photographs of women in their corsets.'

'How do you know that?' I asked.

'I make it my business to know *everything* about my hirelings and minions,' Egbert replied, winking naughtily. 'Only one thing I never found out about you, until it was too late.'

'And that is, pray?'

'That you like shafting sides of beef.'

Later, in bed, while Master Egbert was running his car-uncular nose through my pubic hair, I said:

'Preparing and cooking, eating, having sex — it's all the same to me, you know. It's the *act of communion* that matters — becoming one. All true artists of genius are one with their chosen medium of self-expression.'

'Am I a genius, then?'

'You know you are. Of course you are.'

'And do I find myself impelled to poke my dick into a cow's carcass?'

'You are deliberately misunderstanding me,' I said. 'The method is neither here nor there — it's the consummation, the union. *That's* what it's all about. Listen: preparing and consuming a *Navarin* is, for me, just the same as – well – as what you saw me doing with that carcass. I worship flesh! I want to be *one* with it, whichever means I choose to accomplish, express and manifest that oneness. It's the stuff of my life, the *prima materia* of my creative urge. Don't you think God felt exactly the same when he looked down upon the universal primal slime and the idea came to him to beget his own image?'

'God knows what God felt, my boy. I think, perhaps, you are ever so slightly crazy.'

'That's what my father thought too.'

'You have a father? I had always imagined that you slipped down to this earth entire and whole from the apex of Olympus. And, by the gods on Olympus, I shall miss you!'

'What a kind thing to say.'

'This will be our final night together. I'd better make the most of it.'

Master Egbert turned over onto his vast belly like a helpless beached whale, shuddering and gasping for breath; he grasped his sweating, hair-dark buttocks and prised them open.

'There,' he said in the manner of a nanny offering her fractious charge a tempting *douceur,* 'all yours.'

And for the last time, I lost myself in those miasmally tenebrous depths.

***

Report of Doctor Enrico Balletti to the Chief Medical Officer of Regina Caeli Prison
14th September 19—
(Translated from the Italian)

This is the third time I have seen prisoner 022654, the Englishman Crispe; the previous occasions were general examinations in the Santa Caterina and San Marco blocks, prisoner 022654 having been transferred from Santa Caterina to San Marco after attempting to gnaw off the right leg of a fellow inmate as he slept.

I am making a conscious effort to be objective in this case, if only for the sake of my professional integrity, but I am finding objectivity an increasingly difficult virtue to attain; to my shame, I am forced to admit that I dislike prisoner 022654 intensely, and I regret having come to the day when personal feelings have interfered with – or at least, seriously hindered – the progress of my work. Crispe despises me, I know, but this is not why I feel such revulsion in his presence – far from it! Indeed, I am proud to say that I have always been perfectly indifferent to my patients' feelings towards me. No – I loath him precisely and simply because he is loathsome. There is something about the man, some inner thing which I cannot as yet quite grasp – an impression, a radiation, a self-revelation, call it what you will – that I find totally abhorrent. The beliefs he espouses, it seems to me, are simply a revolting outer manifestation of this inner, spiritual corruption – that he is corrupt, I have no doubt whatsoever, for only this morning he described to me in lascivious detail how he made a very particular Fricassée de Rognons de Veau au Vin Blanc with juices extracted from – scraped from – the private parts of a prostitute, which he then proceeded to serve to a restaurant full of unsuspecting and innocent diners. Even worse, he tries to convince me that this was in fact an act of profound creativity. Even though it humiliates me as a member of my profession to be obliged to say it, say it I must: Orlando Crispe is a monster.

I had originally thought that Crispe's mother, his 'Highgate queen', was the single dominating influence in his life, but now I discover – somewhat to my surprise, I admit – that this is not so; he begins to talk of two people, twins I believe, whom he calls Jacques and Jeanne. It would seem that these individuals – whether they be figments of Crispe's depraved imagination or not – have played a significant part in his descent into murder and madness, and I therefore need to persuade him to talk much more about them than he has done so far. The man is so impossibly arrogant! Every question I ask, every suggestion I make, every possibility I pose, he dismisses with contempt. Only when he speaks of his mother does he become in the least pliable or responsive, and if therefore I can bring him to the point where he will talk to me about these twins, Jacques and Jeanne, as he does about his Highgate queen, I shall have made a great advance.

I have discovered that Highgate is a suburb of north London – Karl Marx is apparently buried in the cemetery there; however, I do not think this fact has any bearing on the case. I recommend continuation of the present medication for prisoner 022654.

Enrico Balletti.
Report registered by Luciano Casti, Chief Medical Officer.

IV

Il Bistro

It was called quite simply *Il Bistro*. Situated in a narrow street very near Cambridge Circus (and therefore ideal for theatre-goers), it was nothing outwardly impressive, but it did have a certain *chic*, the location was enviable, and it was all mine. There was, moreover, a two-bedroomed flat above the premises on a ninety-five-year lease, with seventy years still to run. I finally made up my mind to acquire it after learning, genuinely to my surprise, that Mrs Butely-Butters had left me another twenty thousand pounds in her will. God bless the repulsive old sow.

The previous proprietor, Jean-Claude Fallon, had bought himself a luxurious country hotel in Devon (I shall not name it, since he is still there and prospering in his old age) and was anxious to move out of London as soon as possible.

'What will you do about Jacques and Jeanne?' he asked, two days before I was due to move in.

'Who?'

'Did I not explain about Jacques and Jeanne?'

'No Jean-Claude, you did not.'

'They come with *Il Bistro*.'

'Not if I don't want them to,' I answered guardedly.

'Ah, but *mon ami, mon cher* Orlando, you *will* want them to, once you meet them. You can't throw them out; where would they go, what would they do?'

'Well, what exactly do they do?'

'Jacques helps in the kitchen and Jeanne waits at the tables. But that is inadequate – they do everything you need them to do. They are superb, *mon ami*. Jacques is a very talented young man, and Jeanne has every customer completely in love with her. Come to that, so does Jacques. They are both excellent for business.'

'There isn't much time for me to get to know them, Jean-Claude.'

'Believe me Orlando, that will not take long. Jacques and Jeanne have been my right and my left hand – is that what you say in English?'

'Very nearly.'

'Good. Then that is what they are. Oh, Orlando, wait and see for yourself!'

And for the time being I had to be content with that.

The Terrible Twins

The surprise was entirely mine when I finally met Jacques and Jeanne. Unsurprisingly, they were twins, each pale, grey-eyed, ovular face a perfect replica of the other; they both had blond hair and there was a small mole at the corner of each perfect little mouth, a subtle but irresistible invitation for discreet kisses, I thought. Jean-Claude had not prepared me for two such peculiar creatures; there was something distinctly fey about them, but I also detected a steel-like hardness beneath the surface, an indefinable blend of inflexibility and determination, almost a kind of ferocity. I suspected that they would share a single will when this ferocity had occasion to be exercised. I was suspicious of them, but frankly attracted. They were also just a little too self-confident for my liking – cocky, even.

'We shall be happy to serve you as we served Jean-Claude,' Jacques stated, with just the trace of an accent.

'I'm obviously faced with a *fait accompli*,' I said.

Jeanne's eyes widened slightly.

'You would not think of dismissing us?' she asked.

'Well not that, exactly.'

'Then what?'

'It's just that – I think I would have liked to decide for myself.'

'But Jean-Claude told us –'

'It isn't his bistro anymore. It's mine, now.'

'And so are we,' Jacques said.

'You will never regret it, you will see,' added Jeanne.

She smiled, but there was something odd about it, and it did not have the effect of reassuring me, which was obviously the intention.

65

My new sense of freedom and independence induced euphoria in me. I was, even though by all the standards and principles of my training still a tyro, my own master. I was monarch of my own kingdom. Above all, I was now at liberty to immerse myself in the esoteric delights of my beloved flesh: to love, honour and obey flesh; to lavish all my culinary skill upon it; to work my alchemical magic and transmute the base matter of flesh into the pure gold of the great classic dishes; to experiment, devise, adapt, and create lavish masterpieces of my own. I was possessed by the fiery flux of commingled apprehension and joy – what a responsibility I would carry! I felt as Michelangelo must surely have felt when faced by the great naked mass of new-quarried marble from which the youthful *David* was soon to emerge, entire and whole, a perfect and breathtaking clarity of form born from the chaos of formlessness. I was a midwife of flesh, a mage and a master. And yet, my initiation had barely begun.

Cynics will doubtless sneer when, in speaking of – say – an *Entrecôte Bordelaise*, I employ terms such as these – communion, surrender, mystery, ultimate giving and receiving love – but I have never worried about the cluckings of cynicism. The most exquisitely spine-shuddering of sexual climaxes, believe me, cannot be compared in any degree to the *exstasis* of communion by consumption; moreover, the sweetness of the latter derives not from the spasm of lubricated orifices, but solely from *knowledge*. It is knowing precisely what process one is setting into motion – it is in *gnosis* – that the true joy resides.

Entrecôte Bordelaise

4 steaks, trimmed, approximately 8oz (225g) each
3 tblsp groundnut oil
Salt and black pepper
Sprig of fresh thyme
2 tblsp red wine vinegar
5 fl oz (150 ml) beef stock
2 tsp coarsely ground black pepper

Pinch of cayenne pepper
1 tablespoon butter
3 oz (75g) shallots, finely chopped
4 garlic cloves, chopped
1 pint (600 mls) red wine
1 bay leaf
2–3 beef marrow bones
5 tablespoons red wine vinegar

Rub the steaks with a little oil, season with salt and pepper, then cover and refrigerate for at least two hours. Remove them from the refrigerator about an hour before cooking.

Mix shallots, wine, garlic cloves, bay leaf and thyme in a saucepan; boil for approximately 15 minutes, reducing by just over half. Strain. Discard the bay leaf and sprig of thyme. Wrap the marrow bones in cloth and bring to the boil, then simmer for ten minutes. Drain, and remove the marrow jelly.

Heat a tablespoon of groundnut oil in a pan then when it is very hot, add the steaks. Cook for precisely two minutes on one side; season with salt and pepper, then cook for five minutes on the other side. The steaks must be pink within. Remove the steaks from the pan, cover with half of the shallot, wine and garlic mixture, and cover. Set aside.

Into the still-hot pan put the wine vinegar, boil for two minutes, making sure to blend in all the juices; add the beef stock, the remaining half of the shallot, wine and garlic mixture, then the black pepper and cayenne pepper, and boil until reduced to about 10 fl oz (300 mls). Add the butter and stir well.

Heat what is left of the oil in a different pan and cook the steaks for approximately two minutes on each side. Spread the marrow jelly on top of the steaks and grill for a minute or so. Serve the steaks on hot plates, and spoon over the sauce.

'When are we to re-open?' asked Jacques, and I was irritated to find myself annoyed by his importunity.

'I thought next month.'

'People have been inquiring.'

'What people? Who has been inquiring?'

'Friends of *Il Bistro* . . . '

'Have we friends?'

'*Mais oui*, of course we have. Regular customers and clients.'

'Anyway, I've decided. We shall re-open next month.'

Jacques nodded thoughtfully, smiled at me, and glided away. Both he and Jeanne had a habit of gliding; I can think of no other word to describe it, since they appeared and disappeared silently, unobtrusively, sometimes rather disturbingly. They were a little like cats.

'Our friends and our clients will expect a grand affair,' Jacques remarked to me some time later that day. The twins had quite obviously gone away and thought about what I had said.

'Yes,' Jeanne added. 'We must not disappoint them.'

'Therefore there must be a proper re-opening.'

'Look –' I began, but was interrupted by Jacques.

'We shall have someone of great importance present,' he said.

'A well-known and respected figure,' Jeanne declared.

Then they both said, speaking more-or-less at the same time:

'It will be good for business.'

'But I'm afraid I don't know anyone of great importance,' I told them. It was perfectly true and, I immediately thought, rather sad.

'We do,' announced Jacques.

'Who, for example?'

Jacques shrugged his shoulders.

'It is a matter of indifference who,' he said. 'We know so many. Most of the clients of *Il Bistro* are respected figures of importance.'

'I can't believe this. Jean-Claude said nothing to me.'

'Your business with Jean-Claude was precisely that – business. Did he never tell you about us?'

'No, I can't say that he did.'

'We shall serve you as we served him.'

'Yes, you said that already. I just don't know anything about you. And as *I* have said already, this is *my* bistro.'

Jeanne nodded.

'Of course it is,' she agreed. 'Have we ever denied it?'

'No, but –'

'But nothing,' Jacques said. 'Believe me, we know that you are an artist; we understand the workings of your creative genius, we sympathise with the needs of your soul. Neither I nor my sister would ever trespass upon them. We would never set foot in the realm which properly belongs to you.'

I was mollified, and they saw it.

'We are here to ensure that you are left free to pursue your high calling,' he went on, his voice softly, discreetly seductive. 'We look after the business, we see to the smooth running of daily affairs, we attend to the comfort of our customers and clients.'

Then Jeanne said a rather strange thing:

'Not all of the customers are clients, of course.'

Immediately, Jacques shot her a furious glance, and she withered before its intensity.

'You will see,' he said. 'Everything will be wonderful, just like before.'

'I'm still not sure about this personage of great importance,' I said.

'Leave that to us. We will do what is necessary.'

I was not happy. I was beginning to like them, but I was still deeply suspicious of them. Despite their obvious loyalty to *Il Bistro* and to me personally, I could not help but feel, deep down (which is where feelings really matter), that they would turn against both of us, instantly and without a qualm, should they find it expedient to do so.

Opening Night Success

I could hardly bring myself to believe it when they told me that Jean Cocteau would be the 'someone of great importance' to re-open *Il Bistro*.

'You mean *the* Jean Cocteau?' I asked the twins.

'I was not aware that there is more than one Monsieur Cocteau,' Jacques answered smoothly.

'Monsieur Cocteau is unique,' Jeanne added.

'He certainly is. I thought he was dead. I can't begin to imagine how you managed to persuade him – I mean, are you actually *friends* of his?'

Jeanne allowed a slight smile to flicker across her face.

'Jacques knows him better than I do,' she said.

Being well aware of Jean Cocteau's appetite for beautiful young men, I did not doubt this statement in the least.

'I don't know what to say,' I murmured. 'It's quite fantastic. In fact, it's quite – well – quite incredible.'

'You are pleased?'

'Pleased? Why, I'm delighted. But when will he arrive? I must make arrangements – a special menu, of course –'

'You may leave all the necessary arrangements to us,' Jacques said, and I knew that 'may' actually meant '*will*.' 'Apart from the menus, of course. Monsieur Cocteau is safe in our hands.'

Jean Cocteau had the most enormous nose I have ever seen on a human face. From photographs in books it was of course evident that the nose was prominent, but I suppose this fact must have registered only subliminally in the stagnant pond-water of my mind, as secondary facts and philosophical accidents do; besides, however obvious a distinguishing physical feature may be at one remove, nothing quite prepares one for the sight of it in the flesh. (Flesh!) It was truly huge. In fact, I experienced considerable difficulty in keeping my eyes off it – you know how the embarrassing, the shameful and the simply horrid exerts an almost irresistible fascination; furthermore, human nature being what it is, the first thing one does when one is told to take no notice of something, is to give it one's undivided attention. The more I exhorted myself to ignore the Cocteau hooter, the more I became both obsessed and repelled by it. I also found myself wondering whether what they say about men with big noses was actually true. In point of fact, Jacques was later able to assure me that it was decidedly *not* true – not in the case of Monsieur Cocteau, anyway.

The opening (rather, I should say *re*-opening) of *Il Bistro* took place on Wednesday 22nd March 19— at 7.30pm precisely. Monsieur Cocteau cut a pink ribbon ('Pink in Monsieur's honour,' Jacques said quite seriously) that had been tacked up across the door, and made a flamboyant little speech in French, waving his arms about a great deal and gesticulating. I, of course, was completely preoccupied with his titanic proboscis. Jacques and Jeanne had invited several restaurant critics and food writers from some of the classier Sunday newspapers (including the man who was to become my implacable enemy, Arturo Trogville), and the obese author of *Dishes To Die For,* Reginald Crane. If the truth be told, I was rather impressed.

Cocteau sat at a table of honour, laden with such fresh flowers as were available at that time of year, looking for all the world like a mischievous, wild-haired elf, picking at the food which (with the help of Jacques and Jeanne) I had laboured so hard in the heat of the kitchen to produce. With consummate tact, he chose dishes which were not inspired by the great French classical tradition. The critics and writers had come with their companions who, of course, ended up with a complimentary dinner for doing nothing; this, I was later to learn, was a manoeuvre completely typical of their breed. The remaining tables I am happy to say were all occupied by *bona fide* customers.

Late that night, after the last diner had departed and the door had been locked, I came to learn the precise difference between a 'customer' and a 'client.' This had in fact puzzled me ever since Jacques had rebuked Jeanne with a furious glance for implying that there actually *was* a difference.

It happened because I thought I had mislaid Jean Cocteau; yet could you actually mislay a man with a nose so enormous it can be seen quivering and twitching across a crowded restaurant? Was it possible to misplace a person whose outstanding physical characteristic so occupies your attention that you can concentrate on little else? Apparently it was, for at the evening's end, after the final shrieks and guffaws and surreptitious farts had returned to the primal silence from which they came, *Il Bistro* was suddenly and disconcertingly devoid of human beings apart from myself; there were stained, crumpled napkins littering the floor, innumerable cigarette-ends overflowing the ashtrays, empty and half-empty bottles cluttering the tables, dessert plates piled high – but there was no Monsieur Cocteau. And then of course an even worse possibility presented itself: had I let this justly celebrated *homme de belles lettres* and flamboyant creative genius simply slip away in the crowd without even thanking him? I broke out in a sweat merely thinking of this. Where, moreover, was Jacques? And Jeanne? Oh, why had they failed me? Was this all their promises of efficiency amounted to? God damn them both.

'Jacques!' I screamed at the top of my voice. 'Where the devil are you?'

He was not in the kitchen, which glittered and steamed with the chaotic afterbirth of my culinary labours. Certainly, I thought, he could not possibly be upstairs in *my* quarters, for he would never dare perpetrate such an impertinence. Just to be sure however, I checked – but he wasn't up there either.

'Jacques! Jacques, you intolerable bastard! Where are you? Where is that old queen Cocteau? I have lost Monsieur Cocteau!'

In a fury now, I made my way down to the basement, where the storerooms were; as a matter of fact (and strange as it may seem) I had never ventured there before, since Jacques and Jeanne took charge of them as they had done for my predecessor, and they guarded every inch of their kingdom with ferocious jealousy. It was, so to speak, their own private domain – a realm of sweet-smelling, fruity, fusty darkness where most of the best wine was kept, where sacks and wooden crates lined the cold stone walls. Somehow, it did not accord with their light, almost translucent beauty or their cat-like natures; like cats, I had imagined that in their leisure hours they curled up somewhere in the sun.

Then I saw the door. It was a plain, unpainted wooden door set in the wall of the second storeroom; odd, I reflected, that it should be there. *Why* was it there? It was, I thought, a very *personal* door; it was *somebody's* door, not just any old door. It was a door which led – undoubtedly – to some*one* and not some*thing*.

This speculation about a door was madness.

But was it? I thought I heard noises coming from behind this son-of-a-bitch of a door; weird, staccato noises, a kind of intermittent rasping or gasping, like Morse code made by someone suffering from tonsillitis. I cocked my head and listened as intently as I could. Then, quite without warning, I distinctly heard a voice say:

'Jacques, mon petit oiseau – mais non! – petit? No, comme tu es vraiment magnifique! Oh Jacques, je t'adore!'

I recognized those shrill, histrionic tones immediately.

Trembling all over, I turned the handle of the door and pushed it open.

'Maître Orlando –'

The cosy little scene which greeted me quite took my breath away: in the middle of the room (an extremely well-appointed room, I managed to observe) was a huge double bed, and on the double bed lay Jacques, stark naked, his legs spread wide, his arms tucked behind his head, an expression of smiling unconcern on his face. And on top of Jacques was an equally naked Monsieur Cocteau; *his* face however, was a mask of pure horror.

'Don't worry Maestro,' Jacques remarked with a casualness which infuriated me, 'Monsieur Cocteau is a client.'

At that moment a voice behind the door spoke; I turned and saw Jeanne.

'He is now, anyway,' she said.

Customers and Clients

The story that I subsequently had from Jacques and Jeanne was a grotesque one, and you shall hear it for yourselves.

After the departure of Jean Cocteau (a limousine from the Carbourne Hotel called for him shortly after one o'clock), I summoned the twins to my office, sat them down, and demanded a full explanation.

'What the hell do you think you are playing at?' I said.

'We are not playing. It is not a game.'

'You're right about that, at least. Well? What have you to say for yourselves? Are you going to tell me that this was one unplanned and stolen night of love, and that you regret it with all your heart, and that it will never happen again? Because if you are, I shall not believe you.'

'No, I am not going to tell you that,' Jacques said cockily. I felt like striking him.

'Then what the devil *are* you going to tell me? I demand a satisfactory account of yourselves!'

'You will have to start at the beginning,' Jeanne said sadly, shaking her head.

'Yes,' I went on, 'the *beginning*. You can tell me what that room is doing down there. That room, that door – '

'The room is ours, Maestro,' said Jeanne. 'We live there.'

'Who lives there?'

'I do. And Jacques. *We* live there.'

'You live in the basement of my restaurant?' I cried, outraged.

'No,' Jacques said, 'we live in *our* room.'

'Since when, pray? And why have you never told me?'

'Since the time of Monsieur Fallon. And we never told you because you never asked.'

'Did you ever think to ask us *anything* about ourselves?' Jeanne said, and I detected a chiding note in her voice.

'Don't lie to me,' I said, ignoring her.

'It is true. *Maître* Fallon constructed the room for us, and he put in the door. The second storeroom used to be bigger.'

'Jean-Claude did not tell me that you lived in my basement,' I said.

Jeanne put in:

'We live in our room.'

'Whatever you like to call it. Furthermore, it strikes me that there are a number of things which Jean-Claude did not tell me. Too many, for my liking. How can it be that you have been living in my basement – *your room* – without my knowledge?'

'As I said, you never asked us,' Jeanne answered, and that same sad, reproving tone was there in her voice again.

'Why should I have asked?' I cried, feeling helpless now. 'I didn't realise – how could I? – I didn't know, for God's sake! You come in every evening –'

'Come *up,* Maestro.'

'And you go out – alright, alright, go *down* – in the early hours of the morning – what the hell was I *supposed* to think, to know, to ask?'

'We never disturb you,' Jacques said. 'You must agree to that.'

'I don't have to agree to a damn thing!' I shouted, helplessness having given way to anger. 'How *dare* you live in my restaurant without my permission?'

'No, we never disturb you,' Jeanne insisted.

'You are satisfied with our work?' Jacques asked.

I could not speak for a moment or two. I thought of the success of our opening night, of Jean Cocteau, of the critcs and writers, of the menus we had produced – I thought of all that and I knew that in all probability none of it would have been possible without the twins.

'That is an unfair question,' I said at last. 'You know that I am more than satisfied with your work – '

'Then, *cher Maître,* where is the problem?'

I slumped a little in my chair.

'It isn't so much a problem,' I said, 'as a principle.'

'Monsieur?'

'Look, damn it, I ought to *know* what goes on in my restaurant –'

Jeanne said:

'And now you *do.*'

'Yes, *now* I do, and that is precisely my point – I ought to have known before.'

'You are angry about Monsieur Cocteau,' Jacques said.

'That came as a shock, I'll admit. I thought I had – had lost – him.'

'*Lost* him?'

'Put like that of course, it sounds absurd – but that's what I thought – I mean, yes, I thought he'd just *gone* – and I didn't know –'

'Monsieur Cocteau became a client this evening,' Jeanne said, helping me out of my confusion.

'And what precisely does a 'client' mean?'

'It is a customer who sleeps with Jacques.'

'I see. So customers are people who just eat here, and clients are people who eat here, then sleep with Jacques. Correct?'

'Absolutely correct.'

'Or with *you*, if that is their wish, I take it?'

Jeanne nodded.

'Or with me. But most of them prefer Jacques. The women cannot resist him of course –'

'Oh, of course –'

'And the men surprise themselves with their own feelings. We are much alike, my brother and I, are we not? Sometimes they think he is me; when they find out he isn't, it's too late, and they are enjoying themselves too much to stop. Usually, I take the photographs.'

'The photographs?'

'Of course. Without the photographs, they do not pay so well.'

Everything suddenly became shockingly, nauseatingly clear.

'I don't believe this,' I managed to whisper. 'I *won't* believe it –'

'But I assure you it is true.'

'It has helped Monsieur Fallon to buy his hotel in the country,' said Jacques, 'and it will help you also, Maestro. *Il Bistro* will flourish thanks to its clients. Also, as you saw for yourself, Jeanne and I have some nice things.'

Some 'nice things'? I recalled that moment of pushing open the door, and now suddenly details which were then seen blurrily, out of the corner of my eye, hardly registering in my awareness, became blindingly obvious, bathed in a sumptuously garish clarity: pictures in antique frames, gilded mirrors (also probably antique), porcelain, tapestries; it had been like opening Tutenkamun's tomb – gold, everywhere the glint of gold.

'We try to make ourselves comfortable,' Jeanne said, in the manner of an incongruously prim madam explaining to a prospective client: *'We always try to keep our girls clean . . .'*

'Jacques has sex with them, Jeanne takes the pictures, and

76

then comes the blackmail,' I murmured, but it was a statement, not a question.

'Oh, no!' cried Jeanne, horrified at what she clearly considered the gross impropriety of this suggestion.

'No?'

'No! Our clients *like* us to take the photographs. They *ask* us to take them. That is how it began – one day a gentleman said, "Jeanne, please will you take pictures of me with Jacques?" and – pouff, like that! – we have been doing it ever since.'

'I see. And the negatives?'

'We still have them, Maestro. In our room. They are well looked after.'

'I don't doubt that for one moment,' I said. 'You seem to be a very thorough pair altogether.'

'Thank you.'

'I didn't mean that as a compliment, Jeanne –'

'No, Monsieur.'

It was clear, nevertheless, that she intended to take it as one.

'And how long has this – this *activity* – been going on?' I asked. Then I said: 'No, no, don't tell me, I don't want to know.'

I was overcome at that moment by a vague, imprecise intuition, a kind of sixth-sense grasp of something other than sex-sessions and photographs – something, perhaps, a little closer to an unambiguous violation of the law – but I managed to fight it off.

'It has to stop of course,' I said. 'And those negatives must be destroyed.'

'But surely not! Why, why?'

'If I need to tell you that, then you do not have the intelligence I have hitherto credited you with,' I answered.

'Monsieur – please –'

'No, Jeanne. No. What you have been doing is terribly wrong. Worse still, it is probably illegal. It must cease from this moment on. Do you understand me?'

They did not respond.

'Do you understand me?'

Sullenly, Jacques said:

'Perfectly.'

'Good. You may continue to live in the base – in *your room* – for the time being. As you have pointed out, I am satisfied with your work and you do not disturb me.'

'Thank you,' Jeanne said gracelessly.

'Do you both live in that room?' I asked.

'We *sleep* there.'

'Both of you? In that bed?'

'Yes. But there is no intercourse.'

'I should hope not.'

I rose in a dignified manner from my chair.

'I think that will be all for now,' I said. 'You may go. There is a great deal of work to be done before tomorrow evening. The restaurant is a mess. Those food writers are pigs.'

'We shall come up at five o'clock precisely, Maestro.'

'Thank you. I bid you goodnight.'

'It is now morning.'

'I bid you good morning, then.'

Then he looked up at me and said:

'I am sorry we have offended you, Maestro. Whatever Jeanne and I have done was for the benefit of *Il Bistro*. It has been that way for a long time. Neither my sister nor I can see any harm in it, and we are – I frankly confess to you – surprised that you do. The people who pay us for the photographs are not poor; more than this, they have had their hour of pleasure with me – and I can tell you that it is very rarely a pleasure for *me*. Some of them are old or fat or both, some of them like me to do strange things to them, things which I would rather not do. But it is for *Il Bistro*, as I have explained to you. I do not think Jeanne cares very much to stand there watching until the moment is right, then – click-click! – take her photographs. But we are people of business, of profit, of interest in the well-being of *Il Bistro* – and of you. We wish only to serve you. That is why we are here. We love to serve. Again I say to you, we regret that we have given offence.'

He executed a strange little bow, and I was overcome with an appalling sense of guilt.

'Your apology is accepted,' I said, putting one hand on his

shoulder. The flesh beneath his cotton shirt was warm and supple.

Then Jeanne said in a whisper:

'Monsieur is kind to us.'

Suddenly she leaned forward and kissed me gently on the mouth. Her lips were sweet and soft, apple-scented.

'It would please me very much,' she murmured in my ear, 'if you would permit me to have intercourse with you when you feel in need of pleasure. When you want someone, let it be me.'

'And there shall be no photographs,' Jacques added – a little unnecessarily, I thought.

'Good. We will talk again tomorrow.'

And with the taste of her mouth still lingering on mine, I watched them go. Back down to *their* room.

The Sweet Smell of Success

Il Bistro did indeed flourish. Actually, it did a great deal more than that; between us, Jacques, Jeanne and I managed to transform it from a well-regarded but essentially (I honestly admit it) *average* London eatery into a top-class establishment with a discriminating and monied clientele that included a goodly clutch of well-known names from theatrical and literary circles. We figured regularly in the food and eating-out pages of the better Sunday supplements, and the critics (all except one, of whom you shall shortly hear) were invariably generous. We were booked solid, every night, for weeks in advance. I took on a young student called Axel who came in the evenings to wash up, and I also hired two waiters for weekend work, when we were at our busiest. Indeed, as time went on, I began to think of installing a manager so that I could be left undisturbed in the kitchen, but both Jacques and Jeanne were against this idea.

I knew why, of course: it was true that the twins served me well, but it was also true that they served themselves equally well; I once put this to Jacques, and in a rather indifferent manner he more-or-less admitted it.

'Yes, it is true,' he said. 'Is it not an arrangement that suits the three of us? My sister and I – we make money for ourselves as well as for you. And why not? We are always at your disposal, you know this.'

A manager would be an intrusion into this cosy set-up, I could see that; the twins clearly intended to guard their prerogatives jealously. *My* prerogatives, naturally, pertained first and foremost to the kitchen.

Oh, the kitchen was my paradise, and I was the god who presided over it! There among the gleaming pots and pans, the sweat and swink and the gurgling of water, there in my fragrant, boiling, bubbling, meat-rich kingdom, I was sole monarch. Yet so much of my creative labour was still study, study and learning and initiation; the rubrics I knew by heart, the rituals I performed to perfection, but the sacred art of transubstantiation – this was still the sweet mystery whose innermost secrets I was as yet only just beginning to penetrate. I was pontiff and prelate, arch-priest of the liturgies I had created for the worship of flesh, and yet my education continued. There were black days when I felt like a mere novice, hopelessly inadequate, totally unworthy of my high calling, for I was easily discouraged by failure or poor results; yet never once did I doubt that I *was* called – called and chosen to serve my blood-rich deity. And at all times I was keenly – painfully – aware of his presence, of his crimson-rimmed and critical eyes upon me, watching my every move, judging my efforts with merciless objectivity, assessing and evaluating and passing sentence. The shades of the great masters of my art were with me too, bending low from their niches in the starry heavens, urging me on, exhorting me never to be satisfied, whispering words of encouragement or reproof; they were my companions in dreaming and in waking, and the knowledge of the triumphs they had won inspired me, ceaselessly, to greater dedication. To fail them, to leave their expectations unfulfilled, I vowed must be an impossibility; for they had kindled the fire of their spirit in me, and it was my life's task to keep that fire burning.

★

The only serpent in this demi-Eden was Arturo Trogville whom, as you know, I now stand accused of murdering; however, I told you at the beginning of these confessions that I did not kill Trogville, and I tell it to you again now: *I did not kill Trogville*. On the other hand, you will shortly learn for yourselves why I hated him so, and how without any reasonable motive (as far as I can see) he conducted a cruel and vicious campaign against me and my art; the insufferable brute even followed me to Rome, never once giving me respite. I think he must have been mentally unstable.

His first attack – a subtle one compared to what he was to write about me in later years – came shortly after *Il Bistro* had opened; it was in the restaurant guide of *The Out-of-Towner*. Jacques showed it to me.

'Do you know this Trogville?' I asked him.

'Not personally, Maestro.'

'He was never a client of yours, then?'

'I thank heaven that he was not,' Jacques said, making a little grimace. 'If he had been, he would not be daring to write this.'

'Is it bad, then?'

'Read it for yourself. It is what the English call "damning with faint praise."'

I did read it for myself, and I was not pleased.

An Egg is an Egg is an Egg
Arturo Trogville

Who does Orlando Crispe think he is? He is in fact the proprietor of Il Bistro in London's West End; he is indeed the *chef* at Il Bistro, and clearly a talented one; but who does he *think* he is? A poet, perhaps? Or a philosopher of romanticism? A writer of lyrical libretti? At any rate, certainly someone with pretensions to an artistic or literary vocation, for *pretension* was the dominant characteristic of the meal that I and a companion shared on the opening night of Il Bistro last week. Monsieur Jean-Claude Fallon, as we all know, was a middle-of-the-road, no-nonsense and no-frills cook, whose customers knew what to expect and were never disappointed: classic French cuisine creatively handled, well-prepared and charmingly served. Jean-Claude Fallon was thoroughly *reliable*. We might have to wait some time before the same can be said of Orlando Crispe.

Do not mistake me: my companion and I very much enjoyed

our meal, and I have no complaints about the service; nevertheless, I am old-fashioned enough to dislike culinary flippancy: like the doughty Miss Prism's ward Cecily, when I see a spade I call it a spade, and therefore when I am eating mushrooms, I do not care to be told that they are '*enfants du forêt*'. I point out this eccentricity not through critical peevishness but rather because it was symptomatic of the evening: pretension frequently disguising mediocrity. Many of Mr Crispe's offerings (advertised as 'creations' which my companion and I prudently avoided) were based on a combination of flavours and textures that bordered on the bizarre – novelty for novelty's sake, it seemed to me. Or if you prefer, *pretension*.

However, I have said that we enjoyed our meal, and this is true enough. Both my companion and I chose the *petite bourse froide d'oeuf mollet* as a starter: pancakes quaintly tied up like purses and filled with cold soft-boiled egg in a surprisingly piquant mayonnaise. These could not be faulted, and I would dearly love to know precisely which spices went into the mayonnaise – my companion was convinced it possessed aphrodisiac properties.

As a main course I chose the *côte de boeuf poêlée au confit d'echalotes*; my one complaint about this otherwise adequate pan-fried rib of beef is that the shallots were over-caramelised, tasting slightly bitter, and having an unpleasantly mushy texture. My companion, not a meat-eater, decided to try the cheese souffle with macaroni and mushrooms (Mr Crispe's '*enfants du forêt*') and pronounced it good; the essence of a souffle is of course its *lightness,* and I was duly advised that this *soufflé au fromage aux macaronis* was meltingly, hauntingly light, the marriage of gruyère and macaroni delightful. The '*enfants du forêt*' added that touch of earthiness – subtle enough not to dominate but unmistakably a presence – required to anchor the *buoyancy* of the *soufflé.*

The walnut tartlet I chose for my pudding was disappointingly heavy, and it was not accompanied by a dessert sauce, which I would have preferred. My companion had *oreillon d'abricot meringués au coulis de framboises,* and informed me that she could have eaten them twice over – not so much because of their irresistible deliciousness, but because of the dainty size of the portion.

Truly, I wish Mr Crispe luck with his venture; he seems, on the whole, to have struck the right balance as far as choice and variety goes, and prices are reasonable. The wine list is unambitious, but again, good value for money. But, oh dear! – *please* let us have no more of this 'children of the forest' nonsense. As far as I am concerned, whatever fancy name Mr Crispe might care to give it, to paraphrase Gertrude Stein: *an egg is an egg is an egg.*

'It is beneath contempt,' I said.

'Do not distress yourself unduly,' Jacques murmured. 'Trogville is only one critic among so many.'

'But an important one, Jacques. And to think I also had to feed that fat, bejewelled cow who was with him. His 'companion.' Who was she?'

Jacques shrugged.

'A lady of aristocratic birth. I understand that Monsieur Trogville has a *penchant* for such creatures.'

'He's also got a *penchant* for bile,' I said.

'This is not like you. Do not yield to bitterness. Think: tonight we introduce *magrets de canard* on to the *à la carte* menu; your mind and heart must be free of all such petty rancours –'

'Of course you are right, Jacques. Ah, *magrets de canard.*'

I began, even then, to tremble with both apprehension and expectation. Jacques slipped noiselessly from my side.

Pride Before a Fall

It is entirely amazing that the leanest part of the duck – indeed, the *only* lean part really, for *'magret'* means 'lean' – was, until three or four decades ago, the part which no-one really bothered to use. The thighs for example (and also the drumsticks) are cooked and then preserved in fat to be used in the winter months for a whole variety of different dishes; the gibblets and the bones are used to enhance and enrich soup, and I hardly need to mention the heavenly *foie gras.* But the breast? Ah, now we really *know* what to do with the breast! Grilled or sautéed, served blood-rich, sumptuously pinky-rare, it compares to the finest entrecôte, in my opinion. They may also be steeped in marinade or glazed, cooked with citrus fruits or fruits of the forest, served with *pommes frites* or potato *purée,* with cherries, peaches, white grapes or chunks of apple – oh, these tender slices of flesh lend themselves to an almost infinite spectrum of possibilities!

That evening my *magrets de canard* were prepared and served to fifteen customers, and they were a triumph, a homage to the glory of classical simplicity. I was exultant. As a matter of fact, I made up my mind that such success deserved to be celebrated, and that I was in just the frame of mind to celebrate it with Jeanne down in *the room;* I would therefore take advantage of her touching offer of photograph-free inter-course. The thought of that fragrant mouth pressed against mine, of those vulnerable, yielding limbs, stirred me to a heady degree of anticipation perfectly congruous with the general mood of triumph inspired by my *magrets*. I would, I thought, do as much as I could to bring form and order to the chaos in the kitchen, then repair to my own apartment for a shower, before descending to Jeanne. I decided to say nothing to Jeanne herself, for I wanted my little visit to come as a surprise.

As it happened however, I never made it into that subfusc *nidus* behind the enigmatic door, let alone Jeanne's bed.

I allowed myself the luxury of a long, hot shower; I stepped in, goosefleshed, and turned the control to maximum heat. I used a musky-fragrant shower soap that Master Egbert, who obtained his supply from a 'friend' in Tunisia, had given me as a parting gift; I worked up a delicious lather, covering my whole body with it before washing it off under the steamy spray. I towelled myself dry and splashed on liberal quantities of *Maison Le Comte Laliques*. I dressed myself in dark grey slacks and pale cream silk shirt. Then, standing in front of the full-length mirror attached to the inside of my wardrobe door, I passed judgement on myself: *I was ready for love,* as romantic novelists like to say.

It was almost one o'clock by the time I descended to the amethyst twilight of the basement, made my way gingerly through the chill of the second storeroom, and stood in front of *that* door. I knocked gently. Then again. There was no response. I leaned forward a little and listened, but could detect no noise within. I knocked for the third time, rapping on the wood with my knuckles. Where the devil were they?

'Jeanne?' I whispered, feeling more than a little foolish; certainly, I had no intention of turning myself into a love-sick Romeo crooning inanities in the night to an unseen Juliet. I had my dignity to consider. Any more of this, and I would return to my apartment and the cool chastity of my own bed.

'Jeanne? Are you in there?'

At that moment I stepped back with the shameful but practical intention of peering through the keyhole, when I trod on what must have been a piece of rotten fruit – it was extremely slippery, at any rate – and I fell; I tried to grab at something in order to lessen the shock of making precipitate contact with the floor, but succeeded only in pulling a large wooden crate down onto my head. I seemed to hear the crack of bone. I was suspended, momentarily, between a state of shock and a state of unconsciousness, awaiting the inevitable moment of impact and wondering why it had not yet come. Then, legs turned to jelly, I quickly sank.

V

Illumination

Almost two hours later I regained consciousness, waking cold, stiff, sore, and with a throbbing head; the air was still heavy with the cloying fragrance of *Maison Le Comte Laliques*. At once, I became aware that something extraordinary had happened to me – something caused by my fall and with a very precise neurological explanation I have no doubt, yet something which seemed to me to have come from a higher, more esoteric realm, where explanations, neurological or otherwise, have no meaning.

In the first place, I knew – *I knew!* – that there was a definite philosophy at the heart and centre of my art: a philosophy with its own structure, principles, logic and syllogistic self-validation, no less intelligible than Decartes' rationalism or Heidegger's pseudo-mystical existentialism – and certainly more practicable than the latter. This sure and certain knowledge thrilled me more than I can say, no less for its implications than for its apparently gratuitous and totally unexpected bestowal! Even with all the confidence I had always had in my technical skill, with my unshakable sense of vocation and dedication to its demands, it almost seemed as if I had been pressing on in the dark, a practitioner without a sustaining theory, a ritualist lacking a theology, a magician with a rabbit but no top hat; now, because of a fall and a bang on the head, it would appear, I suddenly found myself with all three – a theory, a theology, a top hat.

Oh, how pompous, how slick this all sounds, and how utterly inadequate! Yet the gift I had received was in itself essentially simple: before my fall, I knew the *how* of my art – after the fall, I knew the *why*.

At the heart of the flesh-eater's philosophy is a movement of love: it is intense and immediate, and the flesh-eater aches for flesh as an erect boy aches for a moist girl; it is patient and long-suffering, and the flesh-eater yearns for flesh as a mystic yearns for the kiss of God; it is obsessive and all-possessing, and the flesh-eater longs for flesh as a barren woman longs for a child.

Think about it, I beg you: is it not obvious beyond any reasonable doubt that this world entirely depends for its continued existence upon the movements of surrender and absorption? Do these principles not constitute the essence of corporeal extension? For where I am – or at any rate, where my body is – you, your body, cannot be; simply by existing physically, I take up space, and the space that I take up is unavailable to you. Therefore, unless violent competition is to destroy us utterly, the rule of natural law which governs the survival of every species – from the human being to the amoeba! – is that of surrender and absorption. Some are born to surrender, and others to absorb; the impala springing nervously through the dusty scrub belongs to the former species, and the lion which brings it down in a sudden red rainburst of blood and tissue belongs to the latter. As do my kind, the flesh-eaters.

The work in hand is always to become *conscious* of this dual movement. There is no valid comparison to be made between a true flesh-eater and – say – a man who slurps down stew on a tray in front of the television, as my father frequently did: the first, being above all supremely aware of his high calling and exquisitely sensitive to the demands of his art, is a carrier of the light of knowledge; the second, being entirely ignorant of the process in which he is involved, remains bogged down in a deep intellectual darkness. The first is a lover, the second a brute beast. Then there are some – a unique and precious breed! – whose special genius enables them to transform conscious participation in the soul-workings of nature into a rare and lovely art; I, Orlando Crispe, am one of that breed.

Yes, I knew, at that moment of astonishing intellectual enlightenment that I had discovered a *philosophy* behind my alchemical art – a metaphysic which was its matrix and ground. I immediately christened it *Absorptionism,* and I tell you now that it eventually came to constitute the entire perspective of my life. It remains to me what the world of Forms was to Plato – both subject and method, the lodestone of his thinking, feeling and doing. Do I call this art *mine?* But no – surely it belongs to the world!

Let me say it again: it is most akin to the labours of the alchemist, for I transmute the base into the rare, the lower into the higher, I turn dead flesh into *rôti de porc aux pommes*, and I have absolutely no doubt that in so doing, I am manifesting on the physical plane a transmutation of spiritual significance, a soul-change high and noble, of which hot fat in the cast-iron pan and the savour of baked meat is but an outward significa-tion, as words are symbols, and indicate a reality beyond themselves.

They struggled against impossible odds, those singular clowns of mystical chemistry – oh, how they dreamed of what they could never achieve, and, despairing of the dream, pressed on with the achievement, men obsessed with an indirigible labour, inspired by the radiance of a light so pro-foundly inward, they could not even detect its heat, and took its existence on trust. From *nigredo* to *rubedo;* from the black-ened formlessness of the *prima materia* to the *lapis philosopho-rum;* from two kilos of boned shoulder of lamb to *Navarin d'Agneau Printanier* – can you see the progression? They tried to turn base metal into gold, and in doing so they described the evolution of the soul towards divinity; I turn dead pig into *Colombo de porc frais,* and do precisely the same. Through the double movement of surrender and absorption, the flesh of the lesser creature is changed into that of the greater: dead pig becomes Orlando Crispe. Can there be a more astonishing transformation than this?

In the second place, I discovered that my fall and bang on the head had left me with a very strange ability which, I admit, I still occasionally find disconcerting, and which I now know is called *synaesthesia*. Quite simply, it is the ability to perceive existents with senses other than the one designed to perceive them. A roast chicken, for example, might evoke curved shapes in the eye of the mind, or the smell of roses produce the sound of violins in the inner ear. I came to learn that this extraordinary ability occurs naturally in only ten people in every million; moreover, in them it is an involuntary phenomenon and not subject to conscious control. I, however, could switch mine on and off at will, which made me something of an oddity.

Since I am writing this here in my little cell in the Regina Caeli prison on a Wednesday, I might as well tell you that Wednesdays are the loveliest shade of deep blue; Fridays, which is the day I have my interview with Doctor Balletti, are aggresively red. Roses, as I have implied, always make me hear violins playing a sweet, high melody that is at once both melancholy and uplifting; flowers which have been cut and put into vases however, *weep* - that is the only word to properly describe the slow, falling cadences of cello-sound accompanied by a shrill, grating tinkling of percussion that I invariably hear in my head if I tune in to my synaesthesia in the presence of cut flowers. The number three has the soul of a triangle, while four is two parallel lines, and seven, the sum of three and four, is a perfect circle; one might say that three is the goal, four the way, and seven the attaining of the goal. Seven, you must know, has always been regarded by esotericists both ancient and modern as a number of high mystical importance, and I for one am not surprised – it reveals such a beautiful circle, frequently tinted a pale, almost translucent amethyst. The higher the number, the smaller the shape produced.

Red causes the sound of bright, clear trumpets, and yet strangely enough, trumpets make me see huge, tree-like extensions of the purest gold; the viola has become my favourite instrument however, because it reveals that deep and lovely blue I now associate with Wednesdays. I think if I were to hear someone playing the viola on a Wednesday I should succumb to a surfeit of blue – gently, peacefully, sweetly drifting into a blue eternity. I loath any kind of drum, which at once overwhelms my inner vision with a vast, bone-dry expanse of irregular black shapes, like alien things, sloughed-off reptilian skins, mutated insect life forms. I consider the drum to be a malign instrument.

For the record, unknown reader of these confessions, I may tell you that an orgasm (one's own or another's) is a starburst of brilliant white light whose centre and heart is a little circle of water-colour; to pass through that circle is to cross over into no-time and no-place – an infinite suspension, if you like – and to be there forever, because there is no way back. Fortunately, the human orgasm is of insufficient intensity for this to happen – only in certain tantric techniques does the peril become real; I once read of an Indian monk who practised tantric intercourse with a cow – he lost consciousness moments before climax and never regained it again. I do not know what happened to the cow.

The Colour of Flesh

And – oh! – what a new and undreamed of horizon opened up onto the landscape of my creative vision! To properly describe the dazzling world of multiple sensations into which I was suddenly plunged, would be altogether beyond the utility of words. Now, I didn't just see the flesh I used for my masterworks, I *perceived* it, I *heard* it. It became breathtakingly alive in my hands, singing to me, bathing me in its own glorious colour. I moved among shapes and images and I was transported to undiscovered terrains.

Each kind of meat – of flesh – carries its own unique evocations. Beef, for example, bears me away to the world of primary colours – simple, strong, immediately intelligible; it is in some way therefore, the foundation and first principle of my culinary alchemy, corresponding to the *nigredo* of the ancient alchemical process.

Picture, if you will, a vast virgin landscape: every form in it is simplicity itself, uncluttered and without complication, a world of clean black lines, smooth contours, configurations that lead to other configurations with clarity and precision. This is creation as it first emerged from the Creator's mind, as it first took shape in his mighty hand, and it is immediately comprehensible. No-one has to ask: 'What is this?' because everything is perfectly and completely itself, requiring no mediation. Red, white and black predominate, with splashes of secondary colour in between the spaces – like a painting by Fernand Léger, who happens to be an artist I greatly admire.

Beef is the calling and singing of bold brass – the horn,

the tuba, trombone, saxophone, cornet, trumpet – never overpowering yet always firm, courageous; the more complex and subtle a beef dish is, the more other timbres are added to this basic sound – usually lower strings, but sharp sauces or condiments produce an overtone of shrill percussion. Beef Bourguignon, with a juice so rich it is almost black, is for me invariably associated with the tremendous passages for brass in the *Dies Irae* of Berlioz's *Grand Messe des Morts*.

Beef is the sexual potency of young men before it has been squandered; it is the pliant strength of newly developed muscles and the power of the erect male member; it is the intensity and passion of fire, the warrior's prowess, the king's authority. It is, I am obliged to say – *pace* our contemporary social sensibilities – a *masculine* meat.

To my mind, the dish which most perfectly allows the Légeresque simplicity of the soul of beef to shine through, which least interferes with its uncluttered formal purity, is a classical *Steak Tartare*.

Steak Tartare

For each person
¾ lb (220g) of fresh fillet of beef or sirloin, finely minced
1 egg yolk
½ tsp Worcester sauce
1 small onion, finely chopped
1 tbsp tomato ketchup
1 tbsp parsley, finely chopped
1 tbsp capers
1 tbsp extra virgin olive oil
Black pepper to season

Mix all the ingredients together in a deep bowl except the meat and the oil; use a wooden spoon for this. Add the olive oil, and when the mixture is thoroughly blended, add the meat. Take a handful of the blended mixture and shape it into a thin but firm round disk. Serve garnished with tomato and watercress.

The following day, just to be on the safe side, I went to the local general practitioner to have a thorough check-up, and to my relief the result was entirely satisfactory.

'Well Mr Crispe, it seems that your little tumble didn't do you any real harm, apart from giving you a headache.'

'Thank you, Dr Levi.'

'If you do have any trouble in the weeks to come, just pop back and see me.'

I hesitated at the door for a brief moment, then I said:

'Doctor, what would you say if I told you I could – well – could *see* sounds and *hear* colours? That whenever – just for example, you understand – whenever I hear a trumpet, I see gold and red?'

Dr Levi frowned. Then he shrugged his shoulders.

'I'd say you had synaesthesia,' he said. 'It's an extremely rare condition, but it exists.'

'And what would you say if I told you that I could switch this 'condition' on and off at will? Use it only when I wanted to, I mean?'

He smiled.

'I'd say you were mad. Good morning, Mr Crispe.'

You know my opinion of doctors already, of course.

An Unpleasant Surprise

It would be very difficult for me to adequately convey my feelings the moment I saw my father standing just inside the door of *Il Bistro* with a tarty-looking woman beside him; shock, disgust, anger, horror – none of these by themselves would suffice to fully describe the *thump-thump* that rattled my heart in its encaging musculature. I suppose, above all, I was *transfixed*. For several minutes I could not move. I stood there, dumb, staring at the pair of them.

Then Jeanne was at my side.

'I allowed them to come in. He said – he told me – he said he is your father.'

By a supreme effort of sheer psychic exertion I managed to reply.

'Yes,' I muttered in a hoarse, strained voice. 'This man is my father.'

I had not forgotten my youthful promise never to speak to him again.

'Hello, son.'

Perceiving my distress, Jeanne tried to help.

'Maestro Crispe cannot see you now,' she said.

'Of course he can see me. I'm his father. Orlando – *son* – I've come to put things right between you and me.'

Put things right?

'I know it hasn't always been easy. It's been very lonely for me without your mother. I missed her terribly, you know. This – this is Lydia, Miss Lydia Malone. She has done me the honour of consenting to be my wife.'

'Oh, for God's sake!' I screamed, unable to restrain myself any longer. 'Come in and shut that door! Or do you want the whole world to know our business?'

'I don't care if the whole world *does* know, old chap. Lydia and I love each other. Is there anything wrong in that?'

I took her in – and I mean the whole of her, inside and out – in a single, contemptuous glance: cheap, tawdry, avaricious.

'I know your mother wouldn't want me to be alone for the rest of my life, Orlando.'

'Don't befoul her name by speaking it,' I said.

'I didn't speak it. I just said –'

'I heard what you said. And how would *you* know what my mother wants? You've never known. You disgust me! If you think you can simply walk in here – oh, for God's sake close the door. Jeanne – leave us. I'll deal with – with – these people.'

'As you wish.'

She tiptoed stealthily away.

'I vowed never to speak to you again,' I said after Jeanne had gone.

'I knew you didn't mean it. It was just –'

'Just what?'

'Look, I've always meant to make it up to you Orlando,' my father said.

He had not changed, not one iota: still small and pasty and ineffectual, still speaking about the impossible as though it were the probable.

'You cannot know what you are saying.'

'What happened before – I mean – that's all over and done with. It's in the past, and best forgotten. Your mother would be the first to say so.'

'Please stop telling me what my mother would or would not want to say.'

'I only mean –'

'I know what you mean!' I cried. 'What you mean is that it's all "water under the bridge" or "live and let live" or "can't we start again," and a dozen other mawkish clichés lurking inside that ridiculous bald head of yours. Isn't that right?'

'Can't we be friends, Orlando?'

'I told you once before, and I'll tell you again: I don't love you. I never have. I don't even like you.'

'There's no need to be rude to your father, I'm sure,' said Miss Lydia Malone, speaking for the first time.

My father sighed patiently.

'It's all right, Lydia, he can't help it. He's been rude to me for most of his life. I'm used to it.'

'You fucking *saint*,' I said.

'Language, Orlando.'

'Look – I don't think we have anything to say to each other. Why don't you two just leave quietly?'

They glanced at each other. Miss Lydia Malone nodded almost imperceptibly at my father.

'Actually, we've come here for a purpose,' my father said in a quiet, rather sly tone of voice.

'Oh?'

'Not just to put things right between us, I mean; although God knows that's reason enough for me to be here.'

'Well?'

'You're making it very hard for Lydia and me, taking this high-handed attitude –'

'That is precisely my intention.'

'We've heard of your success, of course. Lydia showed me

something in the food page in one of the Sunday supplements, so I cut it out and kept it. You're doing quite well for yourself, Orlando. Quite well indeed.'

'Get to the point.'

'As I say, you're making it very hard for us –'

'The point is,' Miss Lydia Malone interrupted, 'we want to get married in the Spring and set up house. There are too many memories of – of *her* – in that Highgate dump. We've seen a lovely little cottage up in Suffolk, and I – *we* – have set our hearts on it, haven't we baby?'

Baby?

My father nodded.

'Only it's a bit beyond our means, at present. I'm not working, and your father only gets a small pension – and we thought – seeing as how you were so successful in your business and everything – we thought –'

'You thought I might lend you some money, yes?'

'Not exactly,' she said, with incalculable nerve. 'We thought you might *give* us some. Just enough to buy the cottage.'

'Excuse me,' I said, just able to get the words out. 'Would you mind if my father and I had a private talk in the next room?'

Miss Lydia Malone sniffed.

'If it'll help,' she said.

'Oh, it will, believe me.'

She pulled a little brush out of her handbag and began to buff her nails.

I dragged my father by the collar of his polyester shirt into the kitchen – now cold and still and silently gleaming.

'How *dare* you!' I cried, anger pouring out of me unstoppably, deliriously, deliciously, like semen out of a throbbing penis.

'What?'

'How dare you walk back into my life as though nothing had happened between us, dragging that cheap tart behind you, besmirching the memory of my mother and demanding

95

that I give you money? Have you entirely taken leave of your senses?'

'I don't understand, Orlando –'

'No, you never did, did you? That's what killed my poor mother.'

'She killed herself with that awful disease, I told you that before, only you wouldn't believe me.'

'And I still don't.'

'You think she was a saint, is that it?'

'I *know* she was.'

'Even after what I told you that night?'

'Lies, all of it. The whole dirty story. Products of your filthy imagination. Lies, lies, lies. You'd like nothing better than to sully her saintliness and purity in my eyes, wouldn't you? My mother – she – she was a *queen*. I've always said so.'

My father looked at me and suddenly seemed to make up his mind about something; his eyes narrowed and grew hard, his scrawny chest made a pathetic attempt to puff itself out as he drew in a long, apparently meaningful breath.

'Alright,' he said. 'It's about time you heard the whole truth.'

'From you? That's about as likely as hearing blood drip from a stone.'

'You call her a saint,' he said, his voice quavering, 'but I call her a whore. You call her "mother", and so she was – but Christ knows who your father was.'

'My father?'

'It could have been any man out of hundreds. She would never tell me. For her sake I brought you up as my own. You *owe* me, Orlando. When that so-called saint was out night after night shagging everything in trousers, I was looking after you and bringing you up as if you were my own.'

At that moment a great, pure, radiant light descended from some ethereal heaven, rich as a benediction, inexhaustible as the ocean, beneficent as the sun, wise as the sum of all earthly knowledge – oh, my salvation and my joy! That light covered me with its infinite mantle and the voice of an angel breathed sweetly into my ear: *This man is not your father.* Suddenly, I was a captive granted liberty.

Then I, too, made my mind up about something; my eyes, too, narrowed and hardened.

In a carefully controlled, even-toned voice, I said slowly:

'Do you remember that day you hit me with the cricket bat for some trivial misdemeanour or other?'

He was momentarily disconcerted.

'Please, don't let's go over the past like this, old chap – not after what I've just told you –'

'Just answer my question. Do you remember?'

'Yes, yes I do.'

'And do you further remember what you did to me after you had hit me?'

He looked down at the tiled kitchen floor, not daring to raise his eyes to mine.

'I squeezed your balls,' he murmured.

'Yes, you squeezed my balls.'

'I was wishing you *had* been my son, you see. I'd always wanted a son, someone to carry on the family line, someone – well –'

'Someone to perpetuate your own image?' I suggested.

'That too – yes – I suppose so. Is there anything wrong in that? Doesn't every father yearn to know that he's brought another *man* into the world? The bond between a father and son – it's a miracle old chap. Yes, I wanted a son – yes, I wanted another man in the family – I *wanted* to be your father, Orlando. Can't you see that, don't you understand?'

'I've really no idea what every father yearns for,' I interrupted, 'but I do know this: you have made me the happiest man in the world.'

He looked up at me and I saw his flabby, pasty face alight with unexpected hope.

'What? *Happy*, Orlando old chap?'

'More than you will ever realise.'

I unbuckled my trousers and let them fall to the floor. Then I pulled down the front of my briefs.

'You may not actually be my father, but I suppose that's hardly your fault. Let's pretend, shall we? They're somewhat larger now, of course. Why not feel for yourself?'

'Oh God – Orlando – do you mean it?'

'Go ahead – *father*.'

He reached out and held my balls in the palm of one pale, trembling hand. He began to knead and squeeze them in that unutterably delicious manner I remembered so well, rolling the thick, hair-dappled skin between his fingertips, tugging and rubbing gently.

I was tempted – only momentarily, I admit – to surrender to that lascivious hand and succumb to the exquisite sensations it was producing, but I knew that if I did, I would be deflected from the purpose upon which my mind had only minutes ago resolved.

'Stand up, I commanded.'

'Just a few moments more, Orlando – please – let me feel them just a few moments more –'

'Stand up!'

He did so, clearly unnerved by the severity of my tone.

'What is it, son? Are we reconciled, is that it? Is there forgiveness between us? Oh, Orlando, you don't know how I long for you and me to put things right!'

'And for the money to buy your little cottage, I assume.'

'Now don't be like that –'

'Listen to me. When I said you had made me the happiest man in the world, I meant it; I have hated you from the very beginning, and I hate you now. You were *nothing* compared to the woman I adored – all you ever amounted to was a vulgar, ineffectual little nobody, and I have never been able to fathom why that queen ever soiled her life by entwining it with yours. To learn that you are not my father is a liberation and joy of a magnitude you can hardly begin to imagine – I never *wanted* you to be my father, I always wished you *weren't* my father, and now I know that truly you are *not*. It may well be – and indeed I suspect this is the case – that my mother found someone who was able to give her the respect and devotion you never could; if this means that – fleetingly, perhaps even painfully, since she was unfailing in a loyalty you never once merited and therefore knew that it must end – she discovered joy with a man who was worthy of her, then I do not cherish her memory any the less for that. I don't care *who* my real father was if he adored her as I adored her. I'm simply deliri-ously happy it wasn't *you*.'

My father screamed – a single, attenuated howl of fury. I did not think such a small man could produce so great a sound. My synaesthesia showed me, in my mind's eye, a great slash of zig-zag black lines, like the contours of an anfractuous mountain range.

'You bastard!' he cried. 'You ungrateful bastard! Is that all I am to you – someone you never wanted to be your father? After all I've done, putting up with her whoring, giving you every care and attention a child could have, even though you weren't my own flesh and blood? You could have been any-body's – *anybody's*, do you hear me? And all you can do is go on pretending to yourself that your mother was a bloody saint – *a saint?* For God's sake, listen to what I'm telling you –'

But I wasn't listening, not any more.

'– it makes me sick, the way you idolise that whore –'

I reached out to the nearest oven and picked up a large cast-iron frying-pan, grasping it firmly by the wooden handle. It was very heavy. I lifted it as high as I could without losing my balance.

'You once struck me with a cricket bat,' I said. 'Well, I don't happen to have a cricket bat handy, but allow me to return the compliment with this.'

And I brought it down with tremendous force upon the top of my father's bald head. It sounded like an egg cracking.

He looked up at me, whimpered once, then fell to the floor in a spray of bright blood.

***

Report of Doctor Enrico Balletti to the Chief Medical Officer of Regina Caeli Prison
1st October 19—
(Translated from the Italian)

I have seen him again. I had to see him, it is my job. It is my vocation. Ever since I was a child – and you, Luciano, you know only too well how deprived that childhood was – I have wanted to be a great doctor of the soul, a healer of the psyche, a psychiatrist; indeed, I neither thought nor dreamed of being anything else but this. And now Orlando Crispe enters my life like a great chunk of cosmic debris entering the earth's atmosphere, crashing downwards in a cascade of fire and heat – oh, worse than this! – he has smashed into the globe of my professional faith and certainty, and I'm not on terra firma *anymore. In fact, so much of my world has been turned upside down by this monster that I don't know quite where I am.*

Forgive me, Luciano, for that totally unwarranted outburst. I wrote it, regretted it, but left it as it is, even though I feel somewhat calmer and more rational now, in order that you may at least understand how this Crispe creature sometimes affects me.

He has inexplicably changed his mind, and now states that he will not let me read the account of his life that he is presently writing. I cannot understand this; despite the revulsion I feel in his presence, I am unfailingly polite. Occasionally, and particularly when I attempt to bring him round to the subject of breast-feeding – or in his case, the lack of it – I catch him peering in a peculiar manner at my crotch; naturally, this is most disturbing for me. My first thought was that he is a pervert – but then I immediately had to remind myself that he is far worse than that: he is a vicious murderer – and, as he frequently reminds me, a master chef as well.

It would seem that he has endowed this beastly obsession of his with a rationale – a 'metaphysic' he calls it, a philosophy, if you please. I once read the Englishman de Quincey on the 'art' of murder, and I laughed gently to myself; when I am obliged to listen to the insane ramblings of the monster Crispe, I am almost physically sick. Indeed, I was constrained to order Nurse Petti to bring a vessel into the interview room, so certain was I of being unable to control myself. Thank God I have not (yet) had to make use of it. He likens himself to Plato – to Plato, Socrates, Aristotle – and is convinced that what he terms 'Absorptionism' belongs to the high and noble philosophies of the world. Disgust is a most unprofessional emotion for a psychiatrist to succumb to, but I freely confess I have been quite over-powered by it.

*Do you believe in evil, Luciano? Oh, I don't mean the sordid medi-
ocrity of our collective moral failings − I don't mean our sweaty
adulterous couplings, our unsophisticated acts of greed, our loathsome
abrogations of integrity and the stifled voice of midnight conscience −
but, rather, an absolute principle or − dare I say it? −* power *of evil. If
you and I, Luciano, still practised the Catholic faith of our childhood,
I might well be asking you: 'Do you believe in the Devil?' Because
with every day that passes, I am finding myself obliged to struggle
against the temptation to believe that Orlando Crispe is possessed.
Centuries ago our Church burned schizophrenics at the stake,
imagining them to be infected by demons, and exorcism was the
Church's cure for the manic-depressive; God knows, I, of all people
tremble at the thought that the science of the psyche should ever take
one step back towards that age of abysmal ignorance, and yet − yet I,
Enrico Balletti, I who swept all contenders aside to win the coveted
Prix d'Italia Alberto-Prout with my 'An Investigation into Aspects
of Narcissism in the Celibate Life' − that I should have my sleepless
nights tormented with the unworthy suspicion that my patient is
possesed by the Devil! It is humiliating.*

*Crispe now refuses to tell me anything more about these so-called
'twins' Jeanne and Jacques, and I am coming to believe that they are
wholly figments of his imagination. I have therefore changed my mind
again, and I am now sure − all talk of possession aside − that this
Highgate queen of his lurks deep at the bottom of his psyche, wreak-
ing terrifying havoc there. Crispe makes it clear that he idolised his
mother in life, and worships her − as a devotee worships his* numen −
*in death; yet he was denied the maternal nipple in his earliest months,
and I cannot but think that this has marked him − perhaps indelibly
so. At least, this is the speculation upon which I am proceeding. For −
think, Luciano! − if consciously he nourishes himself on an inviolate
memory, could it not be that* unconsciously *he is driven by the need
to nourish himself on the flesh he was denied? He imagines that his
Highgate queen was a saint, but deep, deep within him is the buried
knowledge that her breast rejected him − these conflicting predicates
torture him. Now, firstly, he must avenge himself on the flesh that was
taken from him and, secondly, consume as much of it as possible in
case it is taken away from him again. It is the inner child, Luciano,*

who is possesed by the passion for meat – oh, there! I have said it! – it is the inner child who is possessed! *Perhaps my tormenting and humiliating suspicions were not so far from the truth after all; I remind myself that I speak as a psychiatrist, not a theologian, and from this I shall draw my consolation.*

Cavaradossi from the Department of Prison Welfare asked me to dinner yesterday evening with his wife Arabella – you know how I have always admired that delightful creature from afar! – but he has a great liking for tripe, and since I could not bear the thought of sitting opposite him while he forked in great mouthfuls of entrails in tomato sauce, I was reluctantly obliged to refuse. Oh God.

Enrico Balletti
Report registered by Luciano Casti, Chief Medical Officer.

VI

Surrender to Love

Yes, I killed my father! I was a parricide – the crime most difficult to live with, they say, after murder of one's own mother; well, I for one knew that I would have no difficulty whatsoever in living with my crime (if one can call it that, with such a victim as my father) – my only difficulty, such as it might be, was making sure I didn't get caught.

I knew that Miss Lydia Malone would have to suffer a similar fate, since I could not afford to have her on the loose, telling all and sundry that she had left my father alive and well at *Il Bistro*. Accordingly, I telephoned to tell her that my father had decided to stay with me for a few days in order to settle things between us, and that she was invited to a 'peace conference' the following evening.

It enraged me to think that she had established herself in the Highgate house where I had grown up in the radiance of my mother's presence – in the very rooms through which my goddess had walked, her cheap tawdriness fouling the air that she had breathed – oh, it was intolerable! This rage made the task I had to perform so much easier. Well, Miss Lydia Malone would go to join my father – most immediately in the cold-store, where I had hidden his naked corpse, and ultimately, I fervently hoped, in the eternal fires of hell.

Believe me, it was such a simple matter! Allegiances and loyalties were changed as easily as one changes a pair of socks. I was amazed that even my so-called father was enough of an idiot to have fallen for this brazen opportunist.

'I kept telling him that I needed a younger man,' she crooned. 'He wouldn't listen. He's so in love with me, you see.'

'Love is blind, Lydia.'

'What if he catches us? I mean – suppose he comes back? Oh, God.'

'I told you, he's out for the evening.'

'What about this – what did you call it? –'

'A peace conference,' I said. 'To settle things between us. The three of us, all friends again. That's tomorrow, my darling – didn't I say? Tomorrow we'll put everything right, you'll see.'

'Oh, baby. Do you think he'll be terribly angry?'

'Not in the least.'

'You seem so sure . . .'

'I am, believe me.'

'He can still come and live in the cottage, can't he? He'll like that. You wouldn't mind, would you, Orlando? I don't want to see him hurt, honestly I don't. Oh, am I shameless?'

'Completely.'

'Do you think he'll understand, in time?'

'Of course.'

'Do you think he'll forgive us?'

'Absolutely.'

'I feel such a tramp.'

'Is that so bad?'

'Oh, Orlando, how *can* you!'

I had fed her sumptuously and had slipped a fairly strong sedative powder (easily obtained on prescription from Dr Levi) into her third glass of wine. Her deepest motive for returning to *Il Bistro* was, I knew, the inability to resist taking on the challenge of having both father *and* son, nor could she quite disguise the thrill of victory with an affectation of reluctance and remorse. In the end she simply gave it up as a bad job and fell upon me with the manic hunger of an old soak for booze.

We lay entwined together on the sofa in front of the fire; flesh and firelight – a perfect combination! The gaudy crimson sheen of her tight dress, the skin of her throat and shoulders glowing with the lustre of cheap artifice, the sensuously vulgar fragrance of *Nuit d'Amour,* my knee pressing against her belly – and all was bathed in the soft, amber fireglow. We were like figures in an old daguerreotype, characters long forgotten and long disowned, left to our own singular devices for an eternity. I could smell her desire, and at once with the inner ear of my mind I heard a harsh, grating percussion somewhere in the middle distance, like the opening bars of an avant-garde tone poem. There were prickles on the back of my neck, but unlike the percussion I do not think this was the effect of my synaesthesia – I suspect it was sheer nerves.

We kissed, and kissed again, she apparently determined to force her long, hot tongue down the back of my throat.

'I can't breathe,' I managed to say.

She withdrew the tongue (it occurred to me that – braised, sliced and set in aspic – it would make a very nice salad meat) and whispered crooningly:

'It's love, baby, love. Don't you love me? Really love me?'

I slipped one hand up the length of a leg encased in a silky white stocking. The higher up I went the more humid it became, until –

'– oh, Orlando, baby –'

She pushed her face into mine again and the kissing was renewed.

'Love me, oh, love me!' she squealed between sucks and bites.

I reached up and pulled down the front of her dress, exposing one luscious globular breast, so ripe and full it was almost hard, the stiff little nipple standing up on its nut-brown aureole. Immediately she began massaging it with her left hand.

'Aren't I supposed to do that?' I said.

Then she popped the other one out and began to moan in a low, sing-song voice. I suddenly thought of Fuller's Hotel and old Mrs Butely-Butters, whose memories of desire-maddened afternoons in Kew Gardens with Stanley Baldwin had brought on her 'feelings' and whose money had enabled me to buy *Il Bistro*. Was the tart presently with me on the sofa also a sexual autolatrist? Knowing my father, she might well have had no choice in the matter.

But no –

'Down there,' she murmured, between verses of her little love-song, 'do it to me down there – oh! –'

Gently, surprising myself with my own tenderness – or

could it have been stealth? – I tugged at her knickers and drew them down over her thighs. I caught a damp blast of *Nuit d'Amour* yet again, this time commingled with the sour-sweet nursery smell of talcum powder.

'Yes, yes, Orlando, yes –'

I laid the palm of my hand on her plump *mons veneris* and pressed down firmly. Then, suddenly alarmed that the sedative I had given her in her wine might be soon taking effect – for I wanted her in the sweetest, most delectable swoon of pleasure before she succumbed – I withdrew my hand and checked the time by my watch.

'A few minutes,' I muttered, not intending to say it out loud.

She ceased her crooning and lifted her tousled head.

'What? A few minutes for what?'

'Minutes – just a few – I can't hold back much longer Lydia – I'm on fire. I'm burning up with mad desire –'

The head fell back onto the arm of the sofa with a little thud.

'My baby really loves me,' she said.

Less than a few, surely!

I replaced my hand on the hot, hairy *mons* and began pressing again. For good measure I inserted my thumb and moved it to and fro in what I was sure must be an excruciatingly delicious manner, but after twenty seconds or so it began to ache.

I heard her give a little sigh.

'Oh.'

'Oh what?'

'Nothing. Honestly, it's nothing.'

'What? For heaven's sake *tell* me, Lydia.'

'I don't want to hurt your feelings Orlando,' she said – in my experience the inevitable prelude to doing precisely that – 'But, well, aren't you a bit on the *small* side, baby? If you know what I mean. I know they say that size doesn't matter, that some men hung like a fieldmouse can work wonders, but –'

'That isn't my cock, you stupid woman. That's my *thumb* –'

I pulled myself up onto my knees and yanked down my underpants.

'Now *that*,' I said, 'is my cock.'

She lifted her head again and I saw her satin-blue eyes widen in astonishment and delight. How had Master Egbert described it? – yes – my 'ripe young cock,' were his very words. Clearly, Lydia Malone was as impressed as Master Egbert had been – and Mrs Butely-Butters, come to that, except she would have called it my 'willie-wonkie.'

'Oh!' she exclaimed with obvious relief. 'Silly me.'

I pushed her head down again on the arm of the sofa and climbed on top of her, covering her body with mine. She took a series of shallow, rapid breaths and pushed her hard breasts into my face, a nipple into each eye, which I only just managed to close in time. I could have been blinded. Then she slumped back in a kind of swooning, sinking motion, and the glossy crimson lips parted.

No time left!

'I feel sleepy,' she said.

'You're feeling hot and sexy and full of love.'

'Sex makes you sleepy?'

'Relax baby,' I whispered, slipping into her tart's absurd celluloid patois. 'Relax, enjoy.'

I lifted myself on one elbow, leaned forward, and kissed her lingeringly. I tweaked the nipple of her left breast. I pushed my knee into her groin and rubbed.

'Mmmm, that's nice.'

'Nice?'

'Mmmm.'

'Do you feel good? Sweet?'

'Sweet as sugar,' she murmured.

Then she began to snore.

In a matter of minutes she was stripped and in the cold-store alongside my father; in a few hours she would be stone cold dead.

The Great Banquet

I had been brooding on Arturo Trogville's attack on my art for some time prior to the killing of my father and Lydia Malone, and now, free of their tiresome presence, I began to do so again. Neither Jacques nor Jeanne seemed to think that Trogville and his opinions were of any great importance, but I could not help feeling otherwise. Besides which, I freely confess, there was deep down in me a nagging sense of injustice which required the exacting of a revenge of some kind – a vindication, so to speak, of my skill in the face of prejudice.

Then the idea came to me – why not bring the whole pack of them together, the critics and their camp followers, and give them such a feast – a *free* feast! – such a display of my culinary craft, that further carping would be impossible? I would give them my *Roast Loin with Peach and Kumquat Stuffing* and a sensational *Rosette of Lamb Stuffed with Olives and Almonds*.

Roast Loin with Peach and Kumquat Stuffing

1 loin of pork 3½ lb (1.6kg), bone removed
2 sprigs of sage
Stock or white wine for deglazing
FOR THE STUFFING
1 onion, peeled and sliced
6 fresh kumquats, unpeeled
2 peaches, de-skinned and stoned
3 oz (85g) fresh white breadcrumbs
1 clove garlic peeled and crushed
Salt and pepper to season

Trim the loin and discard excess fat. Chop the peaches and kumquats together with the onion. Add the breadcrumbs, garlic, salt and pepper seasoning, and mix well. With a sharp knife slit the loin of pork along its length and open it out flat. Spread the stuffing over the meat. Then roll it up and tie it at intervals, making sure that none of the stuffing comes out.

Preheat the oven to 180°C/350°F gas mark 4. In a deep non-stick frying pan fry the loin – without oil – until is is sticky and browned. Put the sprigs of sage in a greased roasting tin and place the loin on top. Roast for about 2 hours, until properly cooked.

Remove the loin from the oven and keep warm. Remove excess fat from the roasting tin and deglaze it with the stock or white wine. Boil and strain into a gravy boat. Pour over the loin before serving. Carve at the table.

Rosette of Lamb Stuffed with Olives and Almonds

1 boned shoulder of lamb about 3–4 lb (1.35–1.8kg)
FOR THE STUFFING
4 oz (110g) fresh white breadcrumbs
1 tbsp olive oil
1 small onion peeled and chopped
10 stoned black olives
2 tbsp chopped almonds
2 cloves garlic peeled and crushed
2 sun-dried tomatoes, finely chopped
1 tsp mixed herbs

Preheat the oven to 220°C/425°F gas mark 7.

Blend all the stuffing ingredients and carefully place in the opened out shoulder. Fold the edges of the flesh over it, and secure with string in three places along the length. Arrange in a roasting tin and cook for 1½-2 hours, 30 minutes less for a more rare roast. Leave to rest for at least ten minutes before carving.

Arturo Trogville was the first to arrive, dragging a fat and ridiculously overdressed female in tow. Allow me, reader of these confessions of mine, to describe this nauseating creature who claimed the authority – founded not on training or talent, but on pomposity and greed – to judge the fruit of my labours:

Trogville is small in stature – about five feet six inches, I would guess – but, like most of his colleagues, he is overweight: flabby, paunchy, buttocky. The top of his head is completely bald – pale and shiny – but he allows the locks to grow long at one side and arranges these across the crown to give the impression that he is not quite as bald as he looks. His eyes are small and dark and far too close together. Gingery bristles protrude from his ear and nostrils, and he wears a scrubby little salt-and-pepper moustache; it is almost as if he is attempting to compensate for the lack of hair on his head by growing it everywhere else on his ugly face. His gait is light and mincing, his voice displeasingly querulous; it is the kind of voice which does grave justice to *Maud* or *The Last*

Rose of Summer in village halls at fund-raising amateur concerts.

That is (*was*, I suppose I should say) Arturo Trogville.

'Nice to see you again, Crispe.'

'I'm so glad you could come. The evening would not have been the same without you.'

As I took his plump, moist hand in mine, my synaesthesia suddenly switched into overload, and somewhere in the landscape of my mind I heard a tuba farting an *andante-doloroso* in – so I hazarded a guess – F minor.

'Flattery won't get you anywhere, Crispe. You'll have to read the Sunday papers to find out what I might or might not think about tonight.'

I smiled sweetly.

'It'll be something special, I can promise that.'

The glittering cow hanging on his arm bared her teeth momentarily.

'Let me show you to your table,' I said.

Oh, such a great banquet it was! Quite apart from the *Roast Loin* and *Rosette*, I gave them *Mousseline of Dover Sole and Asparagus, Timbale of Smoked Salmon in a Dill Sauce, Salmon Tarts, Fresh Tagliatelle with Oyster Mushrooms, Seafood Parcels with a Lime and Spring Onion Sauce* and *Goat's Cheese Ravioli with Herb Butter.* For the desserts they had *Loganberry and Bardolino Sorbet, Caramel Crèmes, White Peach Mousse Brulée, Raspberry and Vanilla Cream Tartettes, Wholemeal Bread Ice Cream* and *Bitter Chocolate Soufflé.*

Their heads went down and they guzzled like the pigs they were.

The Nightmare at Il Bistro

Everything had started so well and I had no reason to imagine that everything would not end well – indeed, I was already envisaging the extravagant praise that would undoubtedly be heaped upon my culinary endeavours in the weekend newspapers and journals. Alas, it was not to be. It was about half-past ten, just as coffee was being served, that I began to sense something wrong; it was an irritatingly elusive feeling, like catching a glimpse of something out of the corner of an eye, like being aware of another presence when you are certain there is no-one else in the room A vague unease, an uncomfortable premonition of something – but what? On the surface of things all seemed well: both the *Roast Loin with Peach and Kumquat Stuffing* and the *Rosette of Lamb Stuffed with Olives and Almonds* had been rapturously received; the conversation was flowing comfortably; the candles, low, cast the room and everyone in it in a lovely, mellow, opalescent glow pinpricked with *scintillae* of white light reflected on glass and silver . . . and yet – yet! – I knew that there was *something* amiss. Or shortly would be.

'Can you feel it?' I whispered to Jeanne.

'Yes. And I do not like it.'

I closed my eyes for a moment and tried to make my mind receptive to its synaesthetic powers, but I quickly opened them again when the only image I saw was a human face twisted and distorted by a huge mouth, gaping wide and ready to scream.

'Neither do I,' I said.

Just at that moment, as I was walking away from Jeanne, something – a swift, sly movement – caught my attention: the hand of a man was up to some mischief or other under cover of the tablecloth. I moved a little closer. I knew the man in question – it was old Henry Futtock from *The London Towner* – and he was someone who, ever since he had written an appreciative comment about my *Trippa al Vino Bianco*, I had always regarded as slightly less disgusting than the rest of the critical ratpack.

'Everything to your satisfaction, Mr Futtock?' I asked politely.

He looked up at me with a cunning smile and said:

'Oh yes, yes indeed. I'm having a *frantic* time of it!'

He lifted the tablecloth and at once I saw what he intended me to see: the stiff, leathery prick protruded from the front of his trousers and he was rubbing it briskly with his right hand.

I leaned forward, placed my head close to his, and hissed in his ear:

'Put it away, for God's sake.'

'Why should I?' he said with a giggle.

'You'll upset the others.'

'Oh, I hardly think so.'

Then he lifted the tablecloth a little further, and I saw to my amazement and dismay that Henry Futtock's prick wasn't in his *own* hand at all, but that of the man sitting beside him. In confusion I fled to Jacques, but it seemed that he had encountered a similar situation.

'Table seven – look –'

'Oh God. And table four –'

A low, throaty snigger came from a secluded corner somewhere, followed by a brassy laugh. Then a tiny scream, only half-smothered, of shocked delight. At every table something was going on: fumblings, gropings, pinches and squeezes . . . snatched kisses, lingering kisses, kisses administered and received in unexpected places . . . fingers probing, eyes fluttering, thighs opening with experienced stealth, languorous and inviting.

Then, quite unexpectedly, someone flicked a spoonful of chocolate soufflé across the room; it struck a fat, dowdy-looking woman full in the face, just below her left eye. She laughed in an absurdly coquettish manner and offered her cheek to her neighbour, who began scraping off the mousse with his tongue.

The chaos that ensured with unimaginable swiftness was indescribably shocking; it was so sudden and so violent, so obvious that it would be stopped only by burning itself out, that I was reduced to the status of a helpless onlooker, unable to stir, huddled in a corner like a frightened child. The twins, I noticed, bore a look on their faces that I can only describe as horrified bewilderment. Like me they stood motionless and passive. Tables, chairs, plates, food, *people* – everything and everybody in the room – was strewn about in anarchic disorder. It looked like the result of an act of uncreation. The sly, subtle whisperings over wineglasses and

112

the even more sly explorations under tables had given way at first to mere boldness, then to hilarity, and finally to this orgiastic frenzy.

There was the noise: the noise was earsplitting – screaming, yelling, groaning, screeching, cries of vile pleasure and shouts of pain, hoots of triumph and moans of submission. The crack and splintering of wood as chairs shattered, the brittle singing of broken glass, the *whitchz!* of clothes ripped from bodies.

There was the smell – oh, the smell! It was the thick, miasmal odour of unrestrained animality, of a thousand and one illicit desires so long repressed by common-sense and convention, now rising up from the lightless night-black depths of the psyche like malarial smog from a prediluvian swamp.

It was a cacophony that stank.

I saw two women squatting beside an upturned table; they had taken off their blouses and one was licking the nipples of the other, her head thrown back, her face contorted in a spasm of sexual agony.

A young man lay motionless on his back, his trousers down around his ankles; someone had pulled his testicles out of his underpants and now they hung defenceless against the squeezing, rubbing, pummelling hands of those who crawled by.

Two men were fighting over the same woman; wearing only her panties she sprawled on the floor, her stomach streaked with bright blood. As they flailed and thrashed, I saw her hand go down between her legs, and she moaned lasciviously.

Several couples were actually having intercourse, either oblivious or uncaring of the people who were crouching and watching, whispering encouragement, suggesting techniques, touching themselves and each other in those private, vulnerable places that only embalmers and gynaecologists should know.

I saw one naked man mount another, crying words of love, of unashamed passion; then, as penetration was achieved and their hairy, overweight bodies began to pump in unison, I realised to my horror that one of them was Arturo Trogville. Moments later, I caught sight of the glitteringly vulgar companion he had brought with him: she was topless, writhing beneath a musclebound youth who had his mouth glued to one of her breasts and his hands underneath her buttocks. He lifted her body to meet his every manic thrust.

A single, full-throated roar ascended from the *canaille* and turned back upon itself to shatter, like a wave in a tempest breaking on the rocks of a hostile shore – a fearsome, bestial roar of insatiable appetite.

I heard the voice of Jacques in my ear, urgently sibilant:

'Let us leave before it is too late – *please* –'

Oh, God! What have I done? Look – that's Trogville over there, being well and truly buggered –'

'This is not passion – it is violence!'

It did not take long for that to become only too obvious: groans of desire and cries of satisfaction gave way to murderous screams; mouths that had kissed and sucked now began to bite; caressing hands became vicious fists, and the bitter odours of fear and fury rose up from the tangle of undressed bodies.

'We must stop them, Jacques – they will kill one another!'

'But what can we do?'

'Oh, this is a nightmare!'

A half-naked woman came staggering towards us, her arms raised imploringly, her hands bloodied and torn; someone had thrust a dessert fork into her left breast – it dangled there shiny and absurd, like a long silver nipple.

'We have to get out of here,' I said.

The woman collapsed at our feet; immediately, a merciless hand reached out and grabbed an ankle, dragging her back into the melée.

A voice screamed out above the din:

'What's happening to us?'

It was the voice of Arturo Trogville. He had managed to pull himself from beneath his partner in buggery and had staggered clumsily to his feet. Tears glittered at the corners of his wild eyes.

114

'He's crying,' I hissed to Jacques.

'Why – look – they are *all* crying –'

Indeed they were. Sobbing, shuddering, wailing and shaking, they wept unrestrainedly, uncontrollably. Some had begun to cover their nakedness, brazenly denying complicity in either love or loathing; others screamed vile accusations; a few stood silent and ragged, their eyes full of incomprehension. The floor was slick with blood and semen.

Jacques placed his lips close to my ear and whispered:

'For God's sake – while there is still time –'

Time there was, but only *just*. Jacques, Jeanne and myself ran through the kitchen and made our escape through the side door – I locked it with my own key from outside, and as I withdrew it with a trembling hand from the lock, I heard the mob begin to pound on the unpainted metal. It shook with the force of it.   Had they apprehended us, they would have torn us to pieces.

***

Report of Doctor Enrico Balletti to the Chief Medical Officer of Regina Caeli Prison
1st December 19—
(Translated from the Italian)

He speaks to me again and again of this repulsive 'philosophy' of his. Whenever he expounds its metaphysic he becomes increasingly possessed by an inward – what shall I call it? – an inward passion, a fury, an insane devotion that almost physically burns him up – his face strained and flushed, his voice urgent, his breathing rapid and shallow. Nurse Petti, coming unexpectedly into the room during one such session, was quite shocked.

'Is he sick, doctor?' she asked.

I could not bring myself to answer; of course he is sick! His whole being is overpowered by a huge and terrible sickness of soul. Naturally, Nurse Petti has not read all the grim details of this case, and neither would I wish her to do so. One would need the spiritual constitution of an archangel to be able to immerse oneself in such horrors and remain sane, and this, I know, she does not have; the real tragedy is, neither do I.

It appears that he has written down a great deal of his philosophical speculations, but he refuses to let me read them, just as he continues to refuse me access to his so-called confessions. This is a great pity: firstly because my task would be a great deal easier (if not more tolerable), and secondly because I would not have to sit and endure his sickening ramblings. I shall continue in my efforts to persuade him to change his mind.

It is, I am informed, the new philosophy of the age; although, just as Augustine believed of Christianity, Crispe believes that his principles and practice have always been present in the world – indeed, that life itself is a single, continuous act of absorption – and that he, its latter day prophet, is merely rediscovering and restating what the world has lost sight of. He quotes Plato, who said that all knowledge is an act of remembering, and loves to compare himself with that particular Greek. Naturally, this disgusts me, but there is very little point in allowing myself to be drawn into a debate – how can one reason with madness? – which I am sure he would like to happen. It sometimes seems that he is baiting me, implicitly challenging me to refute the theses he proposes; it is a challenge I always silently refuse. Is this cowardice on my part? No, Luciano, I do not think so. It would be all too easy, in the name of decency and common-sense, to leap into the fray and destroy the logic with which he invests his arguments, but this is precisely what he wants me to do – put myself in the absurd position of having to defend that which needs no defence because its truth is absolute: namely, that murder is a moral evil. It would be equivalent to asking me to defend the proposition that water is wet.

Apart from himself – his own vocation and 'genius', that is – and these twins he calls Jacques and Jeanne, Crispe also apparently believes in God. That's more than I do, anyway. However, his conception of the Supreme Being is marked by a perversity of such magnitude, it really would be better for everybody if he believed in nothing at all. Having once been a Creator, God is now an Absorber – an Absorbent, to be more precise. It is the fate and destiny of every

116

existent to be absorbed into an existent greater and more powerful than itself, until everything has been absorbed into the Divine Absorbent. Crispe claims that the natural law inherent in what has been created confirms this – the fly is absorbed by the spider, the fieldmouse by the owl, the gazelle by the lion, and so on; throughout the created order the law remains constant – the lesser and the weaker being absorbed by the greater, the stronger.

He claims that the natural state of all beings is to be in competition.

'The very fact that you are sitting in this chair means that I can't sit on it,' he says to me. I do not point out the obvious fact that no-one can sit on two chairs at the same time, and therefore there is no element of competition. Then he seems to read my mind.

'And if there were only one chair in the room, we would be in direct and immediate competition,' he says.

The Divine Absorbent, it would seem, has remedied this lamentable state of affairs by introducing the idea and principle of creative absorption. This monstrous lunatic insists that if the stronger absorbs the latter consciously and with full understanding, and – furthermore – as a creative act, then it becomes a movement of love – creative absorption equals love. He cites sexual intercourse as an example of this.

'The two become one in a spasm of carnal fulfilment,' he says. 'Naturally, it is the woman who is stronger, and it is she who absorbs – takes into herself – the man. The essence of intercourse is precisely this: a making one of the two.'

I want to scream at him: 'You insane bastard!' but I do not, Luciano. I do not.

The woman is the stronger! I find this phrase highly significant: of course she is the stronger, because she has always been the stronger! No-one – certainly not his father – could compete with his Highgate queen. Her psyche absorbed his (I hate using that phrase) as a sponge absorbs water; he existed only for her, and through him she lived another life which was not hers – a life she appropriated in order to extend the span of her own, which was facing termination. Now, it would seem, she lives on, since the son has elected to perpetuate – in actual reality! – the mother's capacity to absorb.

117

Oh, Lord, Luciano! What a revolting case this is! Pray, to whatever God you believe in, that my professionalism will be strong enough to withstand the onslaught of this monster.

Enrico Balletti.
Report registered by Luciano Casti, Chief Medical Officer.

VII

All Roads Lead to Rome

It was Master Egbert who came to our rescue. That gross, gifted, shameless buffoon, whom I had never thought to see again, was on the telephone the morning after the fiasco at *Il Bistro*.

'Master Egbert!' I cried. 'What on earth – ?'

'I heard about your spot of bother, my lovely lad,' he said. 'I should think everybody on the circuit has heard about it by now. I won't ask for details.'

'And I won't provide them. But I have to get out.'

'So I assume.'

'Well?'

'I want to make you an offer. For old time's sake, you might say.'

'Egbert – Master – don't imagine for one moment that we can pick up where we left off. Things have changed.'

'Is that all you think of me, a sexual opportunist? I'm hurt, Orlando, deeply hurt.'

'Rubbish. I'm just telling you, that's all.'

There was a pause, and I heard an exaggerated theatrical sob on the other end of the line. Then:

'Do you want to hear my offer or not?'

'Of course I do.'

'Well, why don't we meet?'

I hesitated.

'Do you really think that would be a good idea?' I said.

'Certainly I do. Only my wickedest dreams have mitigated the pain of your absence, Orlando. Oh, you did such naughty things to me in my dreams.'

'I can't be held accountable for that'

'Neither can I. Where shall we meet?'

'I'll come to Fuller's Hotel.'

'When?'

'As soon as possible.'

'Why then, this very day is convenient as any other –'

'It's not a matter of convenience, Master Egbert – I'm in trouble if I stay here – it was my own fault, I should have understood, should have realised –'

'Come this afternoon – that would be perfect. I'll have Flavio Fulvio make us a special batch of his cream horns. We shall consume them with a pot of peach oolong.'

'I can't – I mean – I've got to be back here at *Il Bistro* tonight.'

'You mean you don't want to sleep with me. Is there anyone quite so ruthless as a disenchanted lover?'

'I don't mean that exactly, Master. Yes I do.'

'You shall be returned chaste and unmolested on the seven forty-three from Bristol. I assure you my offer is one you –'

'Can't refuse?'

'One you won't wish to. Besides, there is another light in my life now.'

'Oh?'

'His name is Sven, and I'm moving him on to salads next week.'

'Ah, then I can guess his fate.'

'You blue-eyed bastard,' Master Egbert said.

Then the line went dead.

Fuller's Hotel had not changed. Indeed, neither had Master Egbert – he was as round, rich, ripe and ridiculous as ever.

'Orlando, dearest boy!' he cried, throwing his arms around me, nearly suffocating me with the smell of stale sweat and the acrid tang of onions.

'I never thought I'd be back here,' I said, extricating myself from his embrace the moment his meaty hands began to wander, to explore and squeeze.

'Did either of us? Oh, let me look at you, Orlando!'

Inevitably, he looked at me a little too long and too lingeringly below the waist.

'Behave yourself,' I chided.

'Don't be angry with me,' he said petulantly. 'It's been so long, and you are as lovely as ever you were.'

'I'd rather we got down to business, Master Egbert.'

He wagged a fat forefinger.

'Say "please".'

'Please.'

'Very well, then. Have a cream horn. Flavio Fulvio baked them only this morning, as I promised you he would. Dear Sven is keen to learn from our Flavio, but I told him he'll have to be patient. A little more attention to *my* horn, I think, before he gets his hands on the cream variety.'

I bit into the sweet, sugared pastry, and vanilla cream oozed onto my chin.

'Can I lick it off?' Master Egbert said.

'No. *Business*, please.'

He sighed and shuddered.

'Ingrate.'

'What is this offer, precisely?' I asked.

'If, as you tell me, you need to get away – well, Orlando my boy, I have just the place for you to go. You'll adore it.'

'What place? Where is it?'

'It already has a substantial reputation, which I am sure your particular gifts can only enhance –'

'Where is it?'

'– I don't doubt that for one moment, or I wouldn't be making the offer in the first place –'

'Where is it?'

'In Rome.'

'Rome? Rome, Italy?'

'Of course. A small but stylish *ristorante* called *Il Giardino di Piaceri*. Just off the Piazza Farnese. It even possesses its own roof garden. Think of it: balmy nights, a Mediterranean moon, the scent of bougainvillæa –'

'And who is the owner of this paradise?' I asked.

Master Egbert looked at me rather slyly, his eyes shining with secret amusement.

'Who do you think?'

'I really don't know, Master. And I've no time for games –'

'Me,' he said.

'You?'

'And why not? It's an investment for my old age.'

'How old are you now?'

'Sixty-four, and I don't intend to drop dead with a frying-pan in my hand.'

'More likely the cock of a young apprentice.'

'Try not to be too much of a bastard, Orlando. As I say, I regard it as an investment. The trouble is –'

'Trouble?' I said.

'Yes. The chef I've had there until now suddenly took it into his head to go all *nouvelle cuisine* on me, and you know how I hate that. He started painting plates with a smear of *coulis* and charging my customers a fortune. They wouldn't have it, and I don't in the least blame them.'

'Until now, you said?'

'Yes, I kicked him out. *Ergo*, I need someone to take his place. That's you, Orlando. You'll never regret it, I promise – you'll have a completely free hand – you know that I have complete faith in your abilities –'

'But I wouldn't be the proprietor?'

'You surely don't expect me to make you a gift of the place?'

'No – no, of course not.'

'Well then, what? True, you wouldn't be the proprietor, but does that matter? The place would be yours in all but name. I wouldn't interfere, I'm kept too busy here at Fuller's. I wouldn't *want* to interfere. Oh come, Orlando, I'm offering you a unique opportunity! God knows why – you never did anything for me, except let me have the use of your – admittedly succulent – body.'

'An opportunity to do what, exactly?'

'To make money. For *me* first and foremost, but for yourself too, if you work hard.'

'I know all about hard work, Master.'

'I don't doubt it. I want you to go over there and undo the damage that idiot Stradella has inflicted on my little paradise. Put things right. Get the customers back again. Oh, you know what I'm talking about.'

'Yes, I think I do.'

'Well? Will you do it?'

I hesitated. Then I said:

'I – well – I'll have to think about it.'

Master Egbert threw up his arms in exasperation.

'What the hell is there to think about?' he cried.

'It isn't just myself I have to consider,' I said slowly. 'There are two other people living with me at *Il Bistro*.'

'Boys or girls?' Master Egbert asked, his eyes widening.

'Both.'

'Ah!'

'And before you get any disgraceful ideas, allow me to say that they live *and* work with me. *For* me. I am their employer.'

'And nothing more?'

I did not reply.

'You can't deceive me! I know you. Oh, boys and girls come out to play, with little Master Orlando –'

'Don't be disgusting. It isn't like that.'

'Ah, but it *is* like that, precisely like that, isn't it?'

'Rubbish.'

'Well, if you can't live without them, take them with you.'

'Suppose they don't want to go?'

'As their employer you will simply tell them that all three of you are moving to Rome.'

'But if they don't agree –?'

'Get rid of them and hire someone else.'

I half rose from my chair.

'I don't think I could do that,' I said. 'Jacques and Jeanne are extremely useful to me – you just don't understand the situation –'

'My, you really *are* smitten, aren't you? With both of them?'

'I'm not smitten – don't be crass. It's nothing to do with being smitten. Oh, what's the point? All I can say is this: if they don't go, neither do I.'

'Then you're a fool.'

'I'll be late for my train,' I said, confused and upset.

'And your answer to my offer?'

'I told you – I'll have to consult the – my – Jacques and Jeanne. I'll call you tonight.'

Master Egbert shrugged.

'The choice is yours,' he said, rising from his chair and kissing me juicily on the mouth – I only just managed to prevent the hot, hungry tongue from slipping in.

'That's the point, Master Egbert – the choice isn't mine, not all mine, anyway.'

He put a fat hairy hand down between my legs and squeezed my crotch.

'I'll be waiting for the call,' he said.

I fled from the room, knocking a cream horn from the table and squashing it underfoot.

To my complete astonishment, the twins thought it was the perfect solution to our problem.

'I can't believe what I'm hearing,' I said. 'After all these years at *Il Bistro*, everything we've worked for –'

'We can work for everything again.'

'And what about the room in the basement? All your beautiful things, your wonderful treasures –'

'Treasures can be transported. There will be new treasures to acquire.'

'And I assume,' said Jeanne, ever the pragmatist, 'that *Il Giardino di Piaceri* also possesses a basement.'

'As well as a roof garden,' Jacques added.

I shook my head.

'I still can't believe it. No argument, no fuss, no protests?'

'Believe me, we cannot remain at *Il Bistro*. What happened –'

'What happened cannot be dismissed so lightly,' Jeanne said. 'It was fantastic, incredible –'

'Yes.'

'Do you know the *power* your art wields? Neither Jacques nor I understand it, but it is there.'

I, on the other hand, understood it only too well.

'I had not thought it to be of such a magnitude, I confess.'

Then I thought:

But still – if I can do that – how can it not excite me? How can it not inspire me?

I said:

'There is some rather – well – rather *special* meat of mine in the cold-store. I'm afraid it would have to come with us.'

'Of course. Meat, as well as treasures, is transported every day.'

'Flesh,' I said quietly.

'Yes, flesh.'

Oh, my beloved flesh! The *raison d'être* of my life, the meaning and purpose of my alchemical art.

'Very well,' I said slowly. 'It shall be done.'

The twins regarded me solemnly.

I Indulge in Unspeakable Pleasures

Late that night I got up from my bed and went to the little chest-of-drawers that stood behind my bedroom door; opening the top drawer carefully, I ran my fingers through the cool, lavender-fragrant garments that were there – yes, my mother's intimate garments that I had kept with me since the day she died. I had taken them from her room, hidden them in a secret place, and had brought them with me to *Il Bistro*. I guarded them as a shaman guards his talisman, as a nun guards her virginity – with a fierce, proud loyalty and devotion. Whenever I succumbed to the burden of my labours and fell into melancholy or depression, I would open the drawer, breathe in that cool, consoling perfume, and run the satiny, silky stuff through my fingers.

I did so now, closing my eyes and switching on my synaesthesia; in my mind's eye I saw a meadow of rich, viridian grasses, flecked with tiny wild flowers glittering in the sunlight like a hundred thousand brilliants. I heard with my soul's ear the sound of gentle strings, rising up in perfect harmony to a tender, undulating melody. A warm breeze caressed the boughs of fruit-laden trees. Was this, then, the heaven in which her spirit presently wandered? Oh –

Then, quite unexpectedly, and altogether breaking the mood of rapt stillness into which I had fallen, I heard a

125

disgusting, throaty noise from an invisible tuba playing at the very bottom of its range, like a grotesque fart; no doubt this was due to the influence of my so-called father who – I shuddered at the knowledge, but was obliged to confess it – had clearly left his own dirty psychic vibrations on my mother's underthings. Even repeated washing had apparently failed to extirpate them entirely. I selected a pair of lace-trimmed white silk knickers, lifting them from the drawer with great care, and took them with me down to the kitchen.

My beloved was waiting for me, just where I had left her outside the cold-store, patient and kind and shimmering with tiny trickles of perspiration as the heat from the ovens warmed and melted her chilled fat. I stripped myself naked and knelt before her, leaning forward to touch the rich, dark, crimson flank with my forehead.

'I love you,' I whispered, and I swear she trembled as I spoke. 'I trust you totally, as I trust no-one else. My entire art is yours, my philosophy a tribute to your meaning and purpose. My genius springs from your existence, my recipes are a litany of praise to your glory – you are my muse, my inspiration, my *daemon*, my delight and joy. What, oh what would I be without you, my sweetest love?'

I kissed her, and kissed her again, again; my lips were suddenly slick with her fatty fluids, and the smell of her meaty sweat burned my nostrils. Now I was hugely erect, shuddering, shivering. I unfolded the silk knickers, lifted the great carcass, and pulled them over its lower half, drawing them carefully across the slippery flesh. The white against the crimson – the colours of semen and blood, the primal liquids of life – fascinated me, and for a few moments I lost myself in a strange, mystical reverie; they say that the old German mystic Jacob Boehme fell into a similar state whilst gazing outwardly and contemplating inwardly the gleam of polished metal, letting loose the stream of spiritual knowledge that was to become the material for his esoteric theology. Well then, even as I knelt there, rapt in an inner stillness, I knew that, in a similar fashion, knowledge of a high and rare kind was flooding my soul – I could neither define nor categorise its content and object, but I *assimilated* it, soaking it up as a sponge soaks up water, through that elusive faculty we call intuition. I saw and I understood the fabric of dreams, the tissue of myth, I beheld the texture, in its perfect wholeness, of my own ineluctable uniqueness, which appeared to me as a great, effulgent circle of quivering flesh, numinous and awesome.

My beloved lay there in her knickers.

'I dress you only that I may have the exquisite joy of *undressing* you,' I murmured. 'You are irresistible to me. I desire you – oh! – how I desire you –'

As that old idiot Balletti once said to me:

'*È una furia, quest' amore per la carne.*'

And how right he was.

I placed my hands upon my darling's flesh and slid them down the length of her gorgeous flank. Gently, solicitously, I moved beneath the elastic of her silk knickers – which were rapidly becoming stained with grease and blood – and pushed my fingers into the crotch. Then I pulled the thin silk away to expose the succulent privacies beneath. I buried my head there and, extending my tongue, yielded myself up to unspeakable pleasures.

The Whore That is a City

Rome! The Eternal City. City of time past, present and to come. Rome, birthplace of an empire which imposed civilisation with the cruelty of tyranny. City of culture, of military glory, city of sanctity and clericalism, of ruins and revelations, city of emperors, popes, artists and lunatics; not for nothing was a small village on the Tiber chosen by the gods to rule the world. Oh, Rome, one must either love you or loath you, for there is no in-between – it is impossible to be indifferent to this sprawling, legs-apart, raddled, overpainted yet still overwhelmingly seductive whore of a city. Jung remarked that he always wondered about people who visit Rome casually, as they might London or Paris; for he believed that, affected to the depths of one's being by the spirit that broods within the heart of this beckoning *donna fatale*, one might turn a stone or round a column and suddenly, shockingly, be caught unawares by a face that is at the same time both incalculably old and instantly recognisable. Archetypes dwell there, he knew, and on the two occasions he attempted to arrange to visit the city, some mysterious happenstance prevented him from doing so; in 1949 he was struck by a fainting fit in the queue to book train tickets.

I for my part had long ago been smitten in my soul by the diseased charms and narcotic delights of Rome – as with the ulcers of venereal love or the sick lassitude of addiction, I had languished in the heats of desire for her embrace ever since coming upon a picture of the Colosseum in *The Reader's Digest Book of Ancient Monuments* at the age of twelve. Neither the images nor the archives nor the known contribution to human history of any other city has either before or after so enthralled and seduced me, and I am still at a loss to explain it more precisely than this: some secret chord deeply rooted in the fabric of the psyche is touched and sounded by the antique glamour of Rome, and its effect is either the sweetest consonance or an indescribably harsh dissonance – one is at once and forever either a helpless lover or an implacable foe; I am decidedly the former.

Italy like France, takes food seriously, but unlike France, never self-consciously so: the purpose of even the greatest and most noble of culinary endeavours is, for the Italian, first and foremost to fill the belly – only secondarily is it to entrance the palette or uplift the spirit. The cuisine of Rome more than any other city of the peninsula expresses and is founded upon this pragmatic philosophy. Do not mistake me: the homely, uncomplicated, bright, substantial character of Roman cooking does not prevent it from being amongst the most diverse and adaptable in the world – there are, for example, at least twenty-five different kinds of risotto indigenous to the area between Rome and Naples – but the emphasis is always on immediate satisfaction rather than prolonged novelty.

Roman chefs are skilled practitioners of culinary understatement, quite capable of transforming the most basic ingredients – tomatoes, bread, herbs and oil, for instance – into something utterly wonderful, possessing all the characteristics of a great classical dish, the chief of these being freshness; moreover, because Italians prize this above all else, they consider that the most treasured key to culinary excellence is seasonality – if it is not properly in season, it will not be served.

Without a doubt, it was the principles of *honesty* and *immediacy* that Master Egbert's protegeé at *Il Giardino di Piaceri* had surely flouted, subjecting his customers to a prolonged exercise in gustative discovery which, beloved by the French, is essentially alien to the soul of the Roman gourmand; it was this error of judgement which was now my task to rectify, and I determined I would do so in the shortest time possible, restoring that which had been abandoned, building up what had been torn down and, in the process, strengthening both my own reputation and Master Egbert's bank balance.

Il Giardino di Piaceri
The three of us were enchanted by *Il Giardino di Piaceri*.

'It is beautiful,' cooed Jeanne.

'Perfect,' Jacques said.

'I believe,' I whispered, 'that we shall be happy here. Master Egbert, it seems, has done us a great good.'

Later, as you will come to read in these confessions, I had cause to revise that opinion.

Master Egbert had told me that *Il Giardino di Piaceri* had been in the same family for generations before he came to acquire it, and it was not difficult to believe this as I looked around me at the pale ochre walls laden with sketches and paintings – once exchanged by impoverished artists, no doubt, for a bowl of pasta and a litre of rough country wine; the main door was panelled in glass and the kitchen opened directly onto the dining area, as in so many city *trattorie*; the tables were covered in plain, homely white linen and the chairs were of bentwood; on a shelf a foot or so below ceiling level, running the whole way round the room, there was displayed a collection of glazed pottery bowls and majolica plates.

The roof garden was splendid, boasting a well-tended grape arbour that canopied approximately half of the eating area; on a warm, moon-rich Roman night, one could easily imagine romantic love flourishing here, old friendships being renewed, confessions given and received – or indeed any activity of the human heart which mellow wine and starlight facilitate. There was something magical about it, something beneficent, promising camouflage, protection, kindliness and intimacy. Below was the Piazza Farnese, where lone night wanderers could gaze up at the astonishing ceiling on the second floor of the Palazzo Farnese – the French Embassy – whose considerate staff were in the habit of leaving the lights on for this very purpose.

'One of my most special creations,' I said to the twins. 'Something to give them a taste of the wonders to come. Something to obliterate all recollection of the fancified frippery that brought ruin to this splendid place.'

'No doubt you will rise to the occasion,' murmured Jacques.

'We have the knowledge!' I cried. 'All we need do is apply it.'

And so we did.

Early the following morning, while the flesh I had acquired for the evening opening was marinating nicely in its own savours, I went out and crossed into the Campo di Fiori with the intention of buying a quantity of salad leaves – some fresh *rughetta* in particular; even at ten o'clock the flower, fruit and vegetable market was still bustling, although it had opened for business shortly before dawn. Now, other vendors had set out their stalls and were screaming the praises of their wares in competition with the grizzled old men and their ripe Neapolitan peaches:

'*Coraggio, ragazze! Guarda, son' perle!*'

Enamel kitchenware, copper pots, pans, stewing-pans, jelly moulds . . . meltingly soft blue cheeses from local farms, and cheeses as hard as rock, goat's cheese, sheep's cheese, cheese of dubious provenance with no recommendation other than its pungent odour . . . garish plastic accoutrements for kitchen and bathroom – bright scarlet buckets, collanders, sieves, garlic presses and toilet roll holders . . . American-style jeans, tee-shirts, boxer shorts . . . and everywhere the morning smell of an ill-washed humanity, pressing in on itself, still elated enough by the new day's sun to surrender to cynicism and acknowledge that a genuine bargain is like the end of a rain-bow – just a nice idea.

I made my purchase from one of those toothless old crones garbed in ancient widow's weeds, who sit, impassive, behind their featherweight mountains of salad, stripping stalks until their fingertips bleed. She measured out the green leaves in a battered tin scoop and weighed them on an antiquated pair of scales, using those little brass weights that one only sees these days in junk shops. Oh, but they were fresh! They smelt of southern hills and the sea and dew-laden fields.

'*Tante grazie signora, arrivederla.*'

At that moment, carrying my plastic bag of salad, I turned away from the old woman and, my gaze drifting aimlessly in the middle distance, I suddenly received a sickening shock: across the *Campo*, just a little behind and to the left of brooding, doomed Giordano Bruno clutching his book of hermetic her-esies, I saw – I *thought* I saw – I knew I saw, *must* have seen and couldn't be mistaken – the paunchy figure of Arturo Trogville. His flabby, pasty face was turned directly towards me.

'Trogville!' I cried.

And at once he was gone.

***

Report of Doctor Enrico Balletti to the Chief Medical Officer of Regina Caeli Prison
14th January 19—
(Translated from the Italian)

Flesh is his Highgate queen. Of course! Therefore, since she represents – indeed, embodies – all that flesh means to him, he strives to become one with her through the consumption and 'absorption' of vast quan-tities of the stuff. By cooking and eating his esoterically prepared meat, he thinks to be made one with his mother, because she is them.

Whenever he took flesh into himself in whatever revolting manner, he took into himself his Highgate queen. This, of course, is both a metaphorical and an actual substitute for sexual intercourse – and we are back once again to the Œdipus complex. As you know, I had toyed with that possibility in the beginning.

Do you see how simple it all is, Luciano?

1. He harbours sexual desire for his mother, which he suppresses with the utmost severity, and with feelings of horror; so successful is this suppression, he actually imagines that the very idea belongs to other people – people like myself, Luciano – who have been depraved by unspeakable Freudian excesses. He projects what he cannot admit – as we all do, to a greater or lesser degree.

2. Somehow, in some way I do not presently comprehend, his mother becomes a symbol of flesh – all flesh, no matter what the variety. I am sure his untimely separation from the maternal nipple is of absolute significance here.

3. By consuming his disgusting meat dishes, he consumes by proxy the flesh of his Highgate queen, and becomes one with her; this oneness is a substitute for the orgasmic union attained in sexual intercourse. Hence, in a very real sense, his suppressed desire is fulfilled. As a matter of fact, I do not think that for him this experience is by proxy at all, since his mother does not merely represent or symbolise flesh – she has become flesh.

Where do I go from here? I will have to think long and hard, Luciano. Certainly, Crispe still revolts and disgusts me, but I am slowly coming to terms with that, humiliating though such an admission may be. Yesterday I could not bring myself to touch the veal in white wine that the canteen served us for lunch. I am seriously considering the idea of giving up meat altogether. Since meeting Orlando Crispe, my taste for it has diminished. (Can you blame me for that, Luciano?) If this maniac has by some grotesque chance hit upon a philosophical truth – namely, that all existents by nature of their very extension within the space-time continuum are in competition – then it behoves us to cultivate more and more not the cruelty of absorption but the graceful art of sharing. If this beastly competition theory holds any truth, then we must learn to marshall and conserve our spatial resources, to respect the territorial rights of others, to change the methodology of our science *from analytic dissection to intuitive holism. God help me, Luciano, I'm beginning to sound like a New Age mystic! Yet the fact remains — the monster Crispe and I probably agree on a principal thesis, whilst diverging absolutely on the course of antithesis and synthesis.*

These twins of his begin to sound like a pair of opportunists willing to do almost anything in his service if the recompense is adequate. At any rate, he refuses to speak about them in detail. What else can one expect, but that a criminal should have about him other criminals?

Enrico Balletti.
Report registered by Luciano Casti, Chief Medical Officer.

VIII

Larger Than Life

I first set eyes on Heinrich Hervé when he came one evening to *Il Giardino di Piaceri* with a swarthy, thick-set young companion; Heinrich was wearing a fedora and a voluminous black clerical cape, complete with baroque clasp – this, I was later to learn, was an habitual attempt to disguise his bulk. A vain one, I might add, since – cape or not – it was perfectly obvious that he was grossly overweight. He carried an ebony cane topped with a lion's head of blanc-de-chine.

The pair of them made their way to one of my most private tables, tucked away in a corner far from the kitchen doors, where the light was mellow and the shadows were enticing. When I say they 'made their way', please do not imagine that this was done in a discreet or even *reasonable* manner – far from it; Heinrich invented obstacles where there were none, he excused himself to people who were sitting five or six feet away, he dropped his cane at least twice and stooped to retrieve it with the greatest possible fuss and bother. In short, he made himself ridiculously obvious to everyone else in the restaurant. It is a commonly held belief, I know, that grossly fat men can be surprisingly light on their feet or possess an agility and grace belied by their corpulence, but I consider such a belief to be quite unreasonable, the result of a misplaced romanticism, a sentimental faith in the rare kindliness of nature – the effects of obesity are haemorrhoids, varicose veins, excessive perspiration and fallen arches, not agility. Certainly, Heinrich Hervé was neither light on his feet nor graceful in his movements: he bullied the space he moved in, grunting and snorting, pushing and puffing, flailing his arms and shifting his great body first to one side then the other as though the world and everything in it stood in his way. Were it not for the gold-rimmed spectacles that glinted challengingly in almost any light, he would have looked a little like

Herman Goering; certainly, he possessed the same inflated temperament.

'A modest enough establishment,' he cried in that rich, fruitily theatrical voice I came to know so well. 'But it will serve our equally modest needs for one evening, I do not doubt.'

'Monsieur has a reservation?' said Jeanne, approaching the table.

'*Reservation?*' echoed Heinrich thunderously, making it sound like an anti-social disease.

'Yes, Monsieur, a reservation.'

'But the place is half-empty –'

'It is half-*full*.'

'Bah!'

'Then Monsieur has no reservation.'

'Certainly not. My dear young lady, I have just this moment come from the *Teatro Cherubini,* where I gave a recital of German lieder to a specially invited audience of discriminating connoisseurs who – I add immodestly but with perfect truth – detained me for no less than *seven* encores. Seven! Even a professional artist such as myself – for that is what I am – is not often called upon after a completed programme for such a further expenditure of intellectual, emotional and physical energy. Therefore, my dear young lady, I am drained – *exhausted!* – in mind, soul and body. I am hungry and thirsty, as is Angelo, my companion. Please allow us to be seated and to have our supper. I have no doubt – since my instincts tell me the food will be unremarkable – that this should present no great challenge to the management.'

'Monsieur may be seated,' Jeanne replied in a dignified manner.

'Thank you. And now kindly do me the courtesy of bringing the list.'

Jeanne bowed and headed towards the kitchen.

'Who *is* that man?' I asked her, stopping her at the door.

'I do not know, Maestro. But I do not think I care for his manner.'

'That's good enough for me,' I said.

Heinrich's 'modest' supper consisted of *Salade Danicheff*, *Civet de Lapin à la Française*, *Petits Soufflés Glacés aux Abricots*, *Sorbet au Champagne* and, to accompany his coffee, *Chocolate Chestnut Pavé* decorated with individual bitter chocolate leaves. He finished with several glasses of *amaro*. Lighting up a slim Turkish cigarette that had an absurd silver-wrapped filter, he blew smoke out of the side of his mouth and leaned back expansively.

'I predicted that it would be unremarkable,' he said to no-one in particular. I later learned that this was a habit of his – even without an audience, or an audience who cared to listen, Heinrich would speak anyway. And *sing*.

'Where is that girl?' he boomed, waving his cigarette in the air. Jeanne materialised immediately.

'Yes, Monsieur?'

'I would like to speak with the *Maestro di cucina* if you please.'

'Monsieur Crispe –'

'Crispe? *Crispe?* Incredible! Fetch him at once!'

'I'm here,' I said, walking over to the table.

Heinrich looked at me with a peculiar combination of surprise and satisfaction.

'You are Crispe? The chef at this establishment?'

'The chef and – and – the proprietor, yes.'

Pace Master Egbert.

He extended a plump, hairless hand. The fingernails were long and had been discreetly buffed; on the index finger he wore a huge amethyst set in scalloped white gold, and there was a smaller ring adorning his little finger.

'Allow me to congratulate you!' he cried effusively.

'Thank you.'

'I had anticipated a – what shall I say? – a tolerably acceptable meal, which indeed it was, but had I known that the *Maestro di cucina* was an Englishman, I should have expected much worse. In view of the inevitable limitations your race imposes upon whatever natural talent you have, I am obliged to say that you have wrought nothing short of a small miracle. Hardly raising the dead – but – yes, resuscitating the severely weakened, at least.'

I eventually managed to work out that this was a compliment – of a sort.

'Monsieur is too kind.'

'You have been trained in the classical French tradition?'

'Not particularly. Much of what I create is French – some is Italian. When in Rome, you understand.'

Heinrich's flabby mouth fell open; a plume of sweet-scented blue smoke wreathed out and drifted across my face.

'*Create!*' he thundered. 'You call yourself a creator?'

'Of course.'

'Then you must surely be a true artist, if I may say so. One who instinctively and unerringly grasps the nature of his calling – oh! – the soul of a chef, the heart of a poet, the vision of a painter, the emotional power and exquisite technique of a singer such as myself – it is all the same. One must fully *comprehend* the vocation before one can completely surrender to it.'

I had the distinctly uncomfortable feeling that it could have been myself speaking.

'Let others cook their dishes,' he said with a grandiose flourish of his cigarette, 'but let Crispe *create* them!'

'You're too kind,' I said, appreciating the content of his little speech, but only too well aware of its gross theatricality.

'And now I shall sing for you.'

'Sing?'

'But of course! It is the least I can do –'

'After such a modestly acceptable meal, you mean.'

'Ah, Crispe, do not tease me!'

Then quite unexpectedly and much to my dismay, he kissed me on both cheeks in the continental manner, his fat little lips leaving two wet rings on each side of my face. With a struggle, I resisted the temptation to wipe them away with my sleeve. I caught a whiff of *Notte di Donna,* an expensive fragrance favoured by wealthy Roman matrons.

'But there is no pianoforte,' he said.

'No. This is a restaurant, Mr –'

'Hervé. Herr Heinrich Hervé.'

The name rolled off his tongue like a rich, resonant recitation.

'Herrr Heinrich Herrrvé,' he said again, obviously relishing the sound of it. Yet there was more than relish here – there was also expectation; I think he expected me to have heard of him.

'Ah yes,' I murmured. 'Hervé. I think – yes – yes.'

This seemed to satisfy him.

'I shall send you tickets for my recital next week. I am singing for the *Amici di Germania* – a small private society here in Rome to which I have the honour of belonging.'

'How kind.'

'And now I shall sing. Without the pianoforte. Angelo – my case!'

And sing he did.

He began with Nordqvist's *Till Havs,* crooning in a powerful bass-baritone with a querulous vibrato that grew increasingly noticeable as he turned up the volume, until, as the melodic climax approached, one couldn't be sure whether he was on the note or just slighty off it – the latter, I suspect. *Till Havs* was followed by *Svarta Rosa,* a clutch of Schubert songs including *Die Fiorelle, Ständchen* and *Die Böse Farbe,* then Tosti's *Ideale* and – with stunning incongruity, *Abide With Me.* He concluded with *Old Man River.*

The few diners who remained (one or two had hurriedly finished their meal, paid the bill and departed during the performance) seemed to be dazed; a man sitting near the kitchen doors made a half-hearted attempt to raise applause, but there was no response. Angelo, Heinrich's 'companion', whistled through his teeth. I had no doubt that the acquaintance between the two of them had begun and would come to an end in the space of this single evening, with the exchange of bodily fluids and cold cash.

'An impressive performance, yes?' he said, without a trace of shame.

'Unique, I would say. I've never heard anything quite like it.'

Since Heinrich could not conceive of anyone actually disliking his performance, he took this as a compliment.

'Thank you Crispe, my dear friend.'

Dear friend? In so short a space of time?

'Call me Orlando.'

'Orlando! So English cathedral, so Tudor!'

'It was my mother's choice.'

Quite absurdly but with disturbing accuracy he murmured:

'Your mother was a genius.'

'I've always thought so.'

'And I shall sing for you *every* evening, my dear Orlando.'

'What?'

'Yes. Here in this place, I will create a sensation.'

'I don't doubt that for a moment –'

'Think of your customers!'

'I am.'

'You will of course install a piano –'

'Look,' I said, 'there can be no question of your singing in my restaurant –'

Then, all at once, Herr Hervé's attitude changed – subtly I admit, even though subtlety is not one of his chief characteristics, but definitely and perceptibly. I cannot quite find the words to describe it, but it was like one of those unexpected moves in a game of chess that suddenly turns a loser into a winner. The flicker of a smile played about his lips and his spectacles glinted purposefully.

'May we speak privately, my dear Orlando?'

'We *are* speaking privately,' I said. 'Almost everyone else has gone, and it isn't my place to tell your – friend – here to go or stay.'

Heinrich grasped me by the elbow and drew me apart with a little flurry of theatrical gestures of confidentiality. He placed his face close to mine.

'Let me tell you,' he began, 'that some time ago I was in London to give a recital of songs at the Wigmore Hall . . .'

'Oh?'

'Yes, indeed. After the performance – you may have read the spectacular review of it in *The Telegram* –'

'You mean *Telegraph*.'

'Just so. After the performance, I decided to pay an unannounced call on an old friend of mine – Mr Gervase Perry-Black.'

'Ah.'

'You may have heard of him. He is the author of several well-regarded –'

'Yes, I know.'

'To my surprise, my dear Orlando, I found him in a most distressed state – he had been *physically assaulted,* can you imagine? Assaulted, I learned, in a *restaurant.* More than that –'

'I don't want to hear any more,' I said, feeling the sweat drip down my temples and underneath my collar. My stomach was churning.

'He was reluctant to speak about his ordeal,' Heinrich went on. 'Indeed, he seemed anxious that *no-one* should come to hear of it. Nevertheless, since I *am* such an old and dear friend, he felt able to confide in me. I tell you, I simply could not believe the story I heard. You understand me, *cher* Orlando?'

Oh, what was the point of a denial?

'I think so,' I murmured.

'And now here I am in *your* little establishment – and quite by chance! It is a most extraordinary coincidence, is it not?'

'It certainly is.'

If it was *a coincidence, that is . . .*

'Hearing your name – oh, I knew I had heard it before, as soon as that stupid girl spoke it – why, hearing the name of Orlando Crispe brought the whole episode back to me.'

'Why didn't you tell me straight away?'

Heinrich shrugged.

'You hadn't yet told me you wouldn't permit me to grace your restaurant with my singing.'

He was quite shameless.

'You hadn't asked.'

'Naturally, since this story was told to me in the strictest confidence, I have no intention of repeating it to anyone, ever. As I have told you, I am almost disinclined to believe it; perhaps my friend Gervase was drunk and fell down in the street, perhaps he is ashamed to admit it.'

'Yes, that seems a very probable explanation,' I said lamely.

'An explanation,' Heinrich said, 'that I hope I will not have cause to reconsider.'

'I'm sure you won't.'

He kissed me again on both cheeks. I shuddered.

'And I will sing for you my dear Orlando, yes? And for your customers also. I have told you – I will create a sensation!'

Then he looked at me and added:

'One way or the other, that is.'

The choice, of course, was mine.

Putting his arm through that of his swarthy companion, this fat, talentless, vulgar blackmailer left the restaurant in a cloud of sweet blue smoke and the discernible fragrance of Nina Falloni's *Notte di Donna*.

After that he came every evening on the stroke of eight o'clock.

The Serpent in Eden

In spite of this, *Il Giardino* rapidly became something of a private Garden of Eden of mine – I began to build up an excellent clientele and worked hard to reverse the damage inflicted by the idiotic Stradella and his *nouvelle cuisine* novelties; in particular, I seemed to be popular with well-placed clerics from the Vatican, who came for discreet dinners with their boyfriends. Most of them finished eating before Heinrich began to sing. The only blot on the landscape was Arturo Trogville. Almost a year had passed since I *thought* I had seen him in the *Campo* market, and now, on a fine May morning redolent with the sweet promises of the coming summer, we found ourselves standing face-to-face in my restaurant. He breezed in through the door with an infuriating insouciance, full of smiles, for all the world as though we had parted only the day before, the best of friends.

'Well,' I said, 'what is it you want of me?'

He tut-tutted mock remonstrance.

'Now then Crispe, is that any way to greet an old colleague?'

'You are no colleague of mine.'

'We're in the same line of business,' he said, trying hard to keep the sneer out of his voice, but rapidly losing the battle as he continued. 'That's partly your trouble old boy, just like I said in my first review – *pretension*. You're a cook – what's wrong with that? Why not say you're a cook? You cook, I eat what you cook and then write about it.'

'You wouldn't even begin to understand what I am,' I answered with commendable dignity.

'I don't think you understand yourself, do you?'

'Why are you here in Rome? To persecute me?'

'Now there's some I know as would call that paranoia –'

'Hardly likely; most individuals of your acquaintance have difficulty with words of more than two syllables.'

'My, we *are* touchy, aren't we?'

'Why are you in Rome?' I asked again.

'As a matter of fact – not that it's any of your business, of course – I'm on an extended holiday. Sort of a working sabbatical, you might say. Taking it easy, by and large.'

'Oh? Need the rest, do you? Been ill, I hope?'

His face darkened.

'I haven't been quite right since that hellish evening at *Il Bistro*,' he muttered. 'You'll remember that, I take it? I certainly do. I'll never forget it.'

Then, abruptly changing moods, he sauntered to the door.

'Nice to have made your acquaintance again,' he said. 'I expect I'll see you tonight.'

'What?'

'I generally get peckish about nine o'clock – I might just pop along and see what you have to tempt me, eh?'

'No chance,' I said. 'I'm afraid we're fully booked.'

'I'm sure you'll find room for me.'

'As I said, we're fully booked.'

He went out whistling.

He *did* come back that evening, much to my chagrin; it turned out that he had booked a week before in the name of 'Martini' – or, to be precise, a woman calling herself Martini had reserved a table for two, and she turned up with Trogville as her guest. I could hardly refuse to admit him.

'I told you I'd see you tonight, didn't I?'

I could not bring myself to reply, but snapped my fingers at Jacques who showed them to their table. The woman was of the type that Trogville generally preferred: overweight, over-

142

painted, vain, with hopeless aspirations to pedigree. She was, Trogville informed me during the course of the evening, Mrs Lily Rose Martini, the widow of Alfred Martini, a clerk at the American Embassy who years ago had fallen into the Trevi fountain incapably drunk and had drowned; Mrs Martini lingered on in Rome, involving herself in various kinds of charity work, living in a swish little apartment off the *Corso Vittorio Emanuele* provided by the Embassy, and was presently engaged on an assiduous quest for a replacement for Alfred. There were hundreds just like her in the city, and not enough expatriate males to go round.

'I don't think I fancy the full menu,' Trogville hissed to me as I passed, 'but I wouldn't mind a nibble at the *hors d'oeuvre.*'

'Are you referring to the food or to Mrs Lily Rose Martini?'

He winked at me in a revolting manner.

'Chiefly the latter,' he said. 'Now then, what about some service around here?'

I was not deceived, not for a moment – the veneer of saucy bonhomie was perilously thin, and beneath it, I knew, raged a maelstrom of anger and the desire for revenge.

Indeed, three days later, a vitriolic review by Trogville appeared in *Expat-Eat* – a home-grown but essentially influential monthly restaurant and eating-out guide for English speaking expatriates.

No Place like Home
by Arturo Trogville

If you were thinking of trying *Il Giardino di Piaceri* instead of your usual eatery by way of a change, I'm sorry to have to report that you'd probably be in for a disappointment; a companion and I did just that only the other evening, and came away chastened by the knowledge that change is not always for the better.

Il Giardino has built up something of a reputation for itself since Orlando Crispe took it over; admittedly, its alleged pleasures have been known chiefly to a discreet group of *cognoscenti* (including a certain archbishop notorious for his gourmandising, one hears), but one has constantly been catching snippets of tantalising gossip, and rumours have abounded in the city. On the principle that nobody likes to miss out on a good thing, and taking to heart the advice of the Buddha to *find out for yourself*, I went along full of expectation and hope. Alas, what I found out for myself is that the 'pleasures' supposedly on offer at *Il Giardino* to those in the know, are either too esoteric for my taste or they simply don't exist, only nobody wants to stand up and say so for fear of being labelled a gastronomic moron. I strongly suspect the latter – a case, one might say, of the emperor's new clothes.

Many of you will know that Orlando Crispe came to Rome from London, where for some years he was proprietor and chef at *Il Bistro;* the circumstances of this modest little restaurant's closure remain something of a mystery, as does Maestro Crispe's drop in status from employer to employee: for I have heard (but cannot yet confirm) that *Il Giardino* is owned by none other than the flamboyant Egbert Swayne, under whom Crispe served his apprenticeship and for whom he now works. Well, the names and places may have changed to protect the innocent, as they say, but the style remains the same: *pretentious.* Years ago in my first review of *Il Bistro* I said that pretension was the hallmark of Orlando Crispe's cooking, and neither I nor my companion were offered anything last Friday evening to make me change my mind.

I wish I could say that the pan-fried calf's brains on sage and thyme *bruschetta* were delicately crisp on the outside and creamily pink within; or that the baked loin of blue-fin tuna with sweet pickle sauce was done to just that perfect degree of juicy rareness – you know how dry tuna can be if it isn't; or that the apricot and pistachio tart managed to avoid the fatally glutinous sweetness so common with nearly-made-it desserts; I wish I could say every one of these things, but in all honesty I can't.

In this critic's opinion, Orlando Crispe should concentrate less on flippant and pretentious names for his creation – *Ocean Symphony,* for heaven's sake? – and more on the basic techniques of his craft. I have heard on the grapevine that Maestro Crispe is enjoying life in Rome – that indeed he has not the slightest regret about moving from London; if he truly feels this way then I am glad for him, but speaking as one who eats for a living rather than one who cooks for the same purpose, I must say frankly that there's no place like home.

It was the first attack of a series: a fortnight later a slightly different version, equally damning, appeared in the Italian weekly, *Il Piatto d'Oro,* then another in *Eating Out in Rome* and *The American Review;* three more times he had the brazen cheek to dine at *Il Giardino,* always coming as the guest of someone who had reserved a table for two, always full of smug satisfaction, knowing that *I knew* a fresh onslaught would appear in print and that there was nothing in the world I could do about it. It was maddening, sickening, frustrating almost beyond endurance. And it went on for months.

You may wonder why I did not do to Trogville what I did to my father and Miss Lydia Malone, but this would be to misinterpret the complex circumstances that surrounded their final demise. My vocation is to create, not to destroy – I had not, in any case, *planned* the murder of my father, which was the result of a passionate and uncontrollable outburst of anger; admittedly, the killing of Miss Malone was premeditated, but it sprang from exigence, not simple malice – it came about through necessity, not a surfeit of hatred. I was never at any point (of this I am sure) in any physical *danger* from Trogville, but I *loathed* him with all my heart, all my mind, and all my soul. Loathing makes an unworthy motive for murder – certainly one which is far beneath the high principles of my alchemical art. Besides, with Trogville being a fairly well-known character on the circuit, I wasn't so sure that I could get away with it.

Meanwhile, the twins and I got on with life as best we could – a life, I might say, full of keen study, development, inspiration and development, as far as my culinary endeavours were concerned. Having grasped the principle that *psychic* vibrations can be imparted to and captured in a particular dish – and, further, that these vibrations are transferred to the one who consumes it – I set to with a will, creating my own exotic masterpieces of ingenuity that not only surprised and delighted my clients, but actually *changed* their state of mind, their mood, their psychic condition. Can you imagine it? They went home uplifted, often in a state of exaltation, over-powered by sexual desire, yearning for love, melancholy, thoughtfully sombre or manic, just as it pleased me to have them do so! Oh, the twins were so right – the sheer *power* that my skill was capable of wielding was incalculable!

The Thursday Club

The Thursday Club was Jeanne's idea really, but all three of us were enthusiastic from the beginning. It came about in a casual kind of way, as most good ideas that are practical enough to be turned into a reality seem to do.

Il Giardino was now succeeding beyond all our original

145

expectations – most evenings the place was full, ringing with cries for extra portions of this and second dishes of that:

'*As a personal favour, Signor Crispe – Maestro – will you not oblige us with just a forkful more? I must have more of this outstanding vitello –*'

'*Sumptuous! It arouses in me such pleasure, such satisfaction!*'

'*– for Christ's sake bring the whole joint out, will you? This is superb –*'

'*Who has taken my plate? Ah! I had not finished! There was still some juice left – that heavenly juice –*'

One particular Thursday evening, it happened that a certain foreign prelate came to dine, and was so impressed by my *Manzo Bollito con Sugo del Divino Amore* that he requested me to make it available for him the following Thursday, when he would come with a friend from the Danish Embassy.

'I am sure,' he said, 'that *Il Dottore* Hornbech will discover as much delight in your skill as I have done, *Maestro* Crispe.'

'Your Grace is too kind.'

'*Allora, arrivederla, e tante grazie.*'

Heinrich Hervé, taking a break between songs to fill his belly with a plateful of my *tagliatelli con funghi porcini*, sidled up to me with an eager look on his fat face.

'Did I hear the Archbishop mention the name of *Dottore* Hornbech?' he hissed, spraying me with half-masticated slivers of pasta.

'Yes, you did.'

'Hornbech of the Danish Embassy?'

'Yes.'

'He will come here to this establishment?'

'Yes.'

'To eat?'

'I cannot imagine that he will come to hear you sing,' I said.

'But this is unbelievable!'

'Oh?'

'Clearly, my dear Orlando, you have not heard of *Dottore* Hornbech –'

'As a matter of fact, I haven't.'

'Oh, but he has the finest collection of 18th-century jade in

Europe! He is an acclaimed expert – a collector of many years experience – oh! – how I would adore to see those treasures –'

Then, the look of eagerness being swiftly replaced by one of naked greed, he went on:

'I will sing for him. Yes! You will introduce us when he comes to dine –'

'I will certainly do no such thing.'

'You will introduce us and I shall sing for him. Perhaps – *ach, nein!* – I hardly dare to think of it! – perhaps he will invite me to see his collection – perhaps even offer me a little something as a gift, a *complimento* to my voice, you understand . . . '

'Heinrich, please go away. I'm busy.'

'I would do anything for one of those pieces . . . '

You could do worse than have a word with the twins, I thought. *That's their speciality.*

'Just one piece – or maybe two – I *must* have one –'

'Just go,' I said.

Heinrich shuffled away muttering to himself and, a few moments later, I heard him launch into *Old Man River.*

It was as we were closing up for the night that Jeanne made her suggestion.

'What?'

'But yes Maestro, why not?'

'A club, you say?'

'Exactly, a club. A discreet little club for selected members, with a special menu. One evening each week *Il Giardino* could be open only to this club. The cost of admission would be high, of course.'

'Naturally. The higher the better.'

Jacques said:

'You know what people of wealth and pretension are like – tell them that your little club is exclusive, and they will move heaven and earth to get into it.'

I looked at him in astonishment.

'Good heavens,' I murmured, 'I think you may have something there.'

'The club would dine on Thursdays,' said Jeanne.

'Why Thursdays?'

'Because today is Thursday and this evening has been such a success. It is *fate,* is it not? It is never wise to contradict fate.'

'Really, Jeanne? I had no idea you were superstitious.'

'Oh yes,' she replied, suddenly serious. 'Profoundly so. It is the only way to be.'

'The Thursday suppers.'

'The Thursday *Club.*'

'Wonderful!' I cried. 'Let us name our venture precisely that: "The Thursday Club".'

Word of the Thursday Club soon spread – although I had not actually intended that it should do so – at least not so swiftly or so widely – and I began to receive applications for membership from all kinds of weird and wonderful organisations: *Società Gabriele d'Annunzio, La Confraternità dei Fratelli della Rosa Crocefissata, Yanks Away From Home, Bunny Club II, Amici di Pico della Mirandola, Sarah Leander Fan Club of Italy, Babylonian Boys Inc., and Suore della Notte* to name but a few – this last being a group of high-ranking Vatican clerics who liked to get together and dress up in drag, away from the inquisitorial eyes of their curial masters at the Holy Office. It was the *Suore della Notte* who inspired a creation of which I have always been especially proud:

Noisettes de Curé Aujourdoi

8 thick cutlets taken from the rib
1 glass good dry white wine
2 tbsp fresh chopped coriander
½ pt chicken stock
3 oz (75g) unsalted butter
Black pepper

I first cooked and served this simple dish to His Eminence Giovanni Cardinal Pulcelli, who headed the Commission for Interfaith Reconciliation at the Vatican.   Melt the butter in a deep pan and brown the cutlets over a high heat, turning once. Remove them from the pan and keep them warm.

Deglaze the pan with the white wine, adding the coriander and a pinch of black pepper. Pour in the chicken stock and simmer for five minutes or so. Return the cutlets to the pan and cook in the liquid until it thickens. Serve in a warm metal dish.

The Thursday Club advertised itself – that is to say, its devotées spread the word of its pleasures by discreet whispers and subtle innuendo – and before long I was being approached by private individuals who wished me to create a dish that was, so to speak, tailor-made for their purpose, cooked according to their particular requirements for the evening. Thus:

'I have heard, Signor Crispe – naturally, a man in my position does hear such things – I approach you not only as a great artist Signore, but also as a man of the world – it is a delicate matter of which I speak –'

'An affair of the heart, perhaps?'

'Ah, the Signore has such insight! Alas, the lady in question does not return my devotion with the same degree of – of *passion,* Signor Crispe –'

'Please, leave it to me, Count. I think I may be able to do something to remedy that.'

'You will earn my undying gratitude, Maestro . . .'

'And a great deal of money also, I trust.'

'Yes, yes, that too.'

Indeed, those who came to me with these personal requests were individuals to whom – since they had so much of it – money did not greatly seem to matter, and I rapidly amassed a small fortune. In cases such as that of the Count in question, I generally found that my *Noisette à la Crème au Coeur de Passion* did the trick:

Noisette à la Crème au Coeur de Passion
1 small saddle of flesh boned and split into 2 loins and 2 fillets
1 clove of garlic peeled and crushed
5 fl oz (150ml) double cream
5 tbsp vegetable oil
1 sprig fresh thyme
Freshly ground black pepper

Before preparing the noisettes, place the flesh in a large freezer bag. The cook should remove his clothing and position himself on his back on a comfortable bed, his head resting on a firm, supporting pillow. Music should then be played which will arouse feelings of a tenderly erotic nature – it is not the dark urgency of lust that is required here, but the gentle ache of gradual arousal. The choice of music will of course vary from individual to individual; to speak personally, I have always found that Rodrigo's *Concierto de Aranjuez* does the trick.

The freezer bag containing the flesh should then be placed over the genitals and resealed at the edges. The bag needs to be fairly large, since an erection (but *not* ejaculation) is desired; indeed, without it, the final dish will lack the pungency it should properly have. The cook then allows himself to doze off – at least two hours are required.

Upon awakening, the bag should be immediately removed from the genitals and the flesh set aside. The condensation which will have gathered in the bag should be very carefully collected and deposited in a small glass dish. Be patient – the more condensation collected, the better. Split the bag and garner the droplets with the blade of a knife, if necessary.

Back in the kitchen, prepare the noisettes. Use a sharp knife to slice each loin into 6 noisettes, each about 1¼ inches (3cm) thick. Tie the fillets in three or four places with string and cut into 4 slices. Set aside.

Mix together 2 tbsp of the oil, the crushed garlic, the thyme and the condensation previously collected from the freezer bag. Cook over a low heat, stirring continuously, for about 6 minutes. Add the cream, two tablespoons of cold water, black pepper to season, and simmer gently for about 15 minutes, or until thickened to a sauce-like consistency. Remove the sprig of thyme.

Heat the remaining oil in a deep frying pan and add the flesh, browning thoroughly. Cook until medium rare. Serve on warm plates, and spoon the sauce over.

But now it is time to tell you of the momentous event which – I still consider – marked the beginning of what was to prove my downfall. I refer to the ultimate fate of Herr Heinrich Hervé.

***

150

Report of Dr Enrico Balletti to the Chief Medical Officer of Regina Caeli Prison

(Translated from the Italian)

17th November 19—

I have called my philosophy 'Sacrificialism' — an antidote to the murderous heresy of Absorptionism, spewed forth by the monster. Life and death are met in deadly combat, as the scriptures truly say! Mors et vita: *for my speculations, agonising as they have been, Luciano, concern themselves with life, while the monster — with his obscene metaphysic — is none other than the Master of Death.*

I would never have imagined — could never have done so! — how my encounter with the monster would change my life; yet he and his fatal art have picked up my soul as though it weighed less than a feather, shaken it out like foil, turned it inside out and left me an image-in-reverse of what I once was. All that I used to hold so dear: the supremacy of the intellect, the absolute integrity of science, the comprehensibility of the mechanism of human behaviour, the triumph of rationalism over pseudo-mysticism — all gone, gone, gone, all of it and every shred! I see now, with a radiance that is painful in its clarity, how essentially absurd *the psychological posturings of my life have been — the truth is so much simpler than Freud or Adler or Skinner or Bertorelli-Fitch would have us believe. The truth is only this: every existent in this created universe — from the smallest blade of grass to the most massive leviathan, from the pure singularity of the amoeba to the stunningly complex virtuosity of the human personality — every existent, I say, is either good or evil. Grasp this one basic fact, Luciano, and you have the meaning and purpose of life in the palm of your hand!*

The monster is of course a particularly revolting manifestation of evil. Indeed, I now believe that he is possessed by an entity far greater, far more potent in its capacity for evil than his own rather self-conceited, little Œdipal self. I have been in touch with Don Luca Bandieri, an unfrocked priest once attached to the clergy house of Santa Maria in Trastevere, who indicated to me that the devil possessing the monster Crispe — (oh, I have written that dreadful name!) — may be known by its infernal title to a colleague of his who to all intents and purposes is an unremarkable curate in a suburban parish, but who in fact is a gifted exorcist, presently editing a grimoire for the Vatican. I contrived an appointment with this particular individual, and he has told me the possessing entity's name, but I dare not set it down here. I am in constant touch with him by telephone. He has given me certain – objects – with which to protect myself. I used one of them yesterday, when I was obliged to interview the monster.

Sacrificialism is our only hope of survival, believe me, Luciano – for it is truth! To the precise degree that Absorptionism is a pernicious lie, Sacrificialism is the truth. Since all heresies contain a kernel of truth (which is precisely what makes them so insidious), so does the monster's philosophy outline certain principles whose validity is undeniable – however, the implications he extrapolates from these principles are utterly false and twisted.

It is, for example, a certain fact that, spatially at least, all existents are in competition with one another – where you sit, I cannot, by virtue of the fact that you sit there, not me; from this observation, the monster concludes that the weaker of us should give way to the stronger – and, moreover, that the stronger has a moral right to ensure, by force if necessary, that the weaker does so. You see the perversion, Luciano? You grasp the essential distortion? – quite apart from the fact that he derives an 'ought' from an 'is', which itself is a philosophical invalidity. Since all existents are in competition, the destiny of the weaker at all times and everywhere is to yield to the stronger – be absorbed by it, subsumed into it, substance into substance, accident into accident. The monster goes on to insist that if some kind of creative expression can be given to this absorption, it becomes an act of love.

But why, Luciano, why should the truth not be the precise reverse of this, as indeed I believe it to be so? Why should not the destiny of the stronger be to yield to the weaker? Or, of an even more profoundly mystical, paradoxical nature, why should not the two co-operate? And this is where the Catholic Christian concept of divine revelation enters the picture, Luciano: for has not God himself said: 'The first must be last?' and 'The greatest must be the least?' If only I could persuade you of the truth I now so blindingly perceive!

We must cease to eat flesh. We must cease to slaughter millions of innocent creatures for our own gastronomic pleasure – and believe me Luciano, pleasure is all it is, for we do not need to take flesh into ourselves to survive. What of the grains, the pulses, the grasses and the fruits of this earth? Have we so glutted ourselves on flesh – thick and bloodily crimson – that we have forgotten the delights of the gentle green children of the soil? I toss and turn in my bed at night Luciano, unable to shut out the terrible cries of infants torn from their mothers – is she any less a child because she is a lamb, and her mother a sheep? Or a calf and a cow? I tell you, the very skies are rent with the lamentations of the bereaved, the suffering, the needlessly dead! 'A cry goes up from Ramah – Rachael weeping for her children, and she will not be consoled, because her children are no more.' I know it now Luciano, I know it!

Flesh-eating is murder.

Do not imagine for one moment that I have returned unreservedly to the faith of my childhood, Luciano – far from it! Indeed, what I have espoused – almost involuntarily I admit, but with a great and illuminating joy – is a philosophy far older than the teachings of Holy Mother Church, a teaching which was most certainly on the lips of the gentle Nazarene, whatever papacy and magisterium may have said to the contrary. I have embraced an older, wiser, truer faith Luciano, which is known as 'Gnosticism.' To be precise, I have made my own the most central principle tenet of Gnosticism, shared by all the ancient Gnostic sects: the principle of Dualism. I have already described it for you in this report – every existent is either good or evil, and draws its goodness or otherwise from a transcendent absolute. These two absolutes are ceaselessly at war one with the other, and our terrestrial existence is their field of battle. Here, I pass on the teaching given to me by Don Luca, who has been degraded and stripped of his priestly powers by the Church he has served so faithfully for most of his life, and which is prepared to stop at nothing in order to prevent him from disseminating the truth he discovered for himself.

I need hardly add, Luciano, that the evil absolute brought forth from itself all flesh – for flesh, material form, is the immediate instrument of separation and division, of that existential competition the monster

153

makes so much of. Flesh is, always and everywhere, the antithesis of love. Trapped as we are in this fleshly realm, it is our task to bring down into the darkness as much of the light as we can; above all, this means a refusal to submit to the law of competition inherent in earthly life, and a devoted adherence to the spiritual practice that I have called 'Sacrificialism.' This is like spitting in the face of the demonic creator of flesh.

The world is full of angels and demons, Luciano! They are everywhere! We move among them as a fish moves through river-weeds, but we are blind to their ubiquitous presence — which is our chief tragedy. The angels ceaselessly call us toward the transcendent good, while the demons, hungry for an experience of the flesh which their spiritual constitution by its very nature denies them, prowl around like wild beasts, seeking victims, on the look out for human beings to possess and control. We must be ever vigilant! As I said earlier in this report, I have actually been told the name of the vile entity which possesses the soul of the monster and impels him to commit his perversions; to know the name of the creature is to have a certain power over it, and because of this I am now less afraid than I once was.

Cease to eat flesh, Luciano! Cease to do murder in the name of gastronomic snobbery! Embrace with me the principles of Sacrificialism! I could easily arrange a meeting for you with Don Luca, if you are interested — just to hear him speak about what he knows is an experience of conversion in itself — a true μετανοια! I know this Luciano, because I have had the experience myself.

We must destroy the monster — no, no, I will not write down that name again! — listen, they speak to me now, his loathsome incubi — let me do it, give me that privilege, for after what he has made me suffer, I deserve it — no, do not eat flesh, forbid all flesh — I will not! —

(Here the report breaks off)

Report Registered by Luciano Casti
Chief Medical Officer

IX

Heinrich and Friends

For some weeks Heinrich had been pestering me to attend one of the recitals he regularly gave to the *Amici di Germania* – a private 'cultural society' to which he belonged; by dint of evasion, excuse, prevarication and sheer lies, I had thus far been able to avoid what I knew to be the inevitable, but at last the sword of Damocles fell and I was quite unable to defend myself against the blow.

'I *insist* on it!' he cried, stamping his foot and making half-a-dozen tables shake.

'But Heinrich,' I protested feebly, 'I simply don't have the time – you know how busy we are these days –'

'Bah! And why do you think it is that you are suddenly so busy? Why do you think your restaurant is flooded with customers night after night?'

'I'm sure you're going to tell me,' I said.

'They come to hear *me,* of course! Me, Heinrich Hervé!'

My mouth fell open.

'You really believe that?'

'What other explanation can there be? Oh, it is true that you *are* an excellent cook – but my dear Orlando, there are *hundreds* of excellent cooks in this city, *dozens* of restaurants comparable in quality to *Il Giardino.*'

If only this fat buffoon had known the real reason, *his* would have been the mouth that dropped open, not mine.

'No, no, I have considered it for a long time,' he continued. 'There *is* no other explanation. It is on Thursdays that so many people come – this club, this exclusive little gastronomic society of yours – why? Because only on Thursdays do I sing my most popular number – Kartovski's *Roses and Moonlight.* There, my dear Orlando, *there* you have the answer to the riddle of "your" success!'

I was by now too tired and too stunned to answer.

Then Heinrich said in a lower tone of voice:

'Besides . . . I am sure you would not wish me to dwell once again on the tragedy of my old friend Gervase Perry-Black. Have you read his book *Live to Eat?* It is a masterpiece. It expresses my own philosophy entirely.'

I didn't doubt that for one moment.

'Which also reminds me: I have not quite forgiven you concerning the matter of *Dottore* Hornbech – still, I am sure there is time enough to make amends.'

'All right,' I murmured. 'I'll come.'

Heinrich clapped me on the back heartily.

'Bravo, my dear Orlando! I promise you, you will not regret it!'

But, in the end, I did.

It was with a heavy heart that I left the twins and made my way to the *Vicolo dei Romanzieri,* to the dark, sombre building with the shuttered windows that housed the offices, library and banqueting room of this shady confraternity. Had I known then the sequence of events this fateful evening would set in motion, tending inexorably towards its end like a syllogism towards its conclusive flourish of logic, I think my heart would have been as heavy as lead. As I made my way up the grubby marble staircase, I heard the sound of strident masculine laughter.

A door at the top of the stairs was opened and an elderly retainer peered out.

'*Nome?*'

'Orlando Crispe. *Mi ha invitato Signor Hervé.*'

'*È un amico di Signor Hervé, Lei?*'

'*Si può dirlo.*'

'*Come tutti gli altri.*'

'No,' I said hastily, 'not like all the others at all.'

The door opened wider and I was ushered in.

I was taken aback by the size of the room, which was in fact vast – quite obviously the ballroom in former days of what must have been a private palazzo; the ceiling was painted and gilded, the central section heavy with gold and blue stucco, depicting a Poussinesque mythological landscape – there were nymphs and satyrs and centaurs frisking about between the trees, and some kind of whimsical rape was taking place, as it usually does in mythological landscapes. The great windows (certainly not those I saw from outside) were draped in crimson damask, the polished parquet floor strewn with sumptuous oriental rugs, the yellow-gold blaze of light from the crystal chandeliers quite dazzling. Slim young men in white uniforms were gliding to and fro bearing trays of champagne. I managed to snatch a glass as one passed me. I heard, above the noise of fifty people talking at the same time, the strains of *Eine Kleine Nachtmusik*.

Heinrich approached enwrapped, like a gigantic outer planet in rings of interstellar gas, in an overpowering cloud of *Woman!* by Nucci. I noticed that he had applied a discreet touch of midnight blue shadow to his eyelids.

'Ah, Crispe!' he purred, his voice all dark honey and cream, 'so there you are. I've been looking for you everywhere.'

'I've only just arrived.'

'Never mind that now – there's someone absolutely charming I want you to meet.'

I was introduced to at least half-a-dozen individuals – including a professor of urinogenitology, whose handshake was disturbingly damp – none of whom could even remotely be described as charming; finally, I was dragged halfway across the room and introduced to a tall, blond man with a glass eye – at least I assume it was glass, for it never once looked directly at me, while the other one certainly did. And it was distinctly unfriendly.

'Crispe, this is my *very* dear friend Herr Otto von Streich-Schloss – Otto, say hello to Maestro Orlando Crispe, who is a genius.'

Naturally I could not deny the truth of this assertion, but felt highly embarrassed at having it made in such a patronising manner by a gross *buffone* like Hervé.

'Oh?' said Herr von Streich-Schloss, as if he couldn't have cared less what I was.

'If you ask him particularly nicely, he may make you some of his exquisite little *sasaties*.'

'He's a cook?'

'He's a *chef*, Otto.'

'I am an artist,' I said.

Herr von Streich-Schloss sniggered.

'Don't be naughty *mein taube*,' Heinrich chided. 'I speak the truth. I have dined frequently at Maestro Orlando's own little *ristorante*, which is not so far from here –'

'You have dined there every night for the past fourteen months,' I said. 'With rare exceptions.'

Heinrich waved a fat hand in the air dismissively and continued without acknowledging the correction:

'– and you must believe me when I tell you that this boy is *good*. Indeed, I am thinking of taking a small private party there next week, after my performance at the Palazzo Fabrizzi-Bamberg.'

'You didn't tell me this,' I said. 'How many?'

'Oh, not more than a dozen. We shall require the roof garden for our exclusive use, of course.'

'But that's impossible –'

'*Tchzah!* And how do you like our little *pied-à-terre*, my friend? We find it comfortable enough.'

'It's – frankly – it's not what I expected.'

'Oh?' said Herr von Streich-Schloss. 'And what *did* you expect?'

'I'm really not sure. I know nothing about the *Amici di Germania* –'

'The relationship between Maestro Orlando and myself is one such as can exist only between fellow artistes,' Heinrich said, lowering his voice in a confidential manner. 'A bonding of creative spirits. We have never spoken in any depth about the *Amici*, you understand.'

The eyebrow above Herr Streich-Schloss' glass eye moved up and down quizzically, but the eye itself remained motionless.

'We are a small group of like-minded amateur culturalists,' he said guardedly. 'We have certain interests in common. We meet regularly to discuss them.'

'Oh?' I said. 'What sort of interests?'

'Mainly those which relate to the history of the northern peoples. I myself, for example, am particularly drawn to the mysticism of the old Teutonic orders. But there – we do not proselytise. In fact, we are a *self-contained* society.'

'But not a secret one, not by any means,' Heinrich added quickly.

Otto von Streich-Schloss smiled sourly.

'No, of course not,' he murmured.

'Can anyone join?'

'Not exactly. One needs to be of the same –'

'The same blood?'

'The same enthusiasms,' Herr Streich-Schloss said firmly. 'As I have told you, we do not proselytise. Our sphere of influence is not of any magnitude.'

'What sort of influence would that be?'

Herr Streich-Schloss made a small, impatient noise.

'We like to flatter ourselves that we make our own contribution to national self-awareness,' he said. 'To help preserve what is distinctive about a particular people.'

'Which particular people – in particular, I mean?'

'As I have said, Herr Crispe – the northern peoples, by and large. In our view racial, cultural distinction – call it what you will – is of primary importance for the evaluation of the right of a nation to survive –'

'Survive what?'

'Let us say, rather, to emerge as a *leader* from the competitive struggle that naturally and inevitably exists between disparate peoples. You do not agree, Herr Crispe?'

Certainly I agreed, but then this half-baked theory was nothing more than a pale reflection of my own philosophy of Absorptionism – I had recognised it at once! – and, furthermore, was based not upon the principle of creative inspiration or the privileges of artistic genius, but shabby nationalistic snobbery.

'About the roof garden,' I said, turning to Heinrich, who was by this time beginning to look uncomfortable.

'Close it for the evening.'

'No. It holds at least thirty. If you plan to bring only a dozen –'

'As I told you Maestro, the party is to be private – strictly so.'

I began, involuntarily, to envisage something along the lines of Ernst Röhm's ill-fated boys-and-buggery *soirée* for thugs at the Hanslbauer Hotel on the Night of the Long Knives, and I shuddered; for although I am by nature (as all true artists are, I suspect) completely uninterested in political ideology, it had very quickly become clear to me that the *Amici di Germania* was a neo-fascist brotherhood masquerading as some kind of private cultural club. I did not care one jot what they got up to in their own time and on their own territory, but I would not have my restaurant become the scene of some internecine *putsch*.

'Maestro Crispe will not fail us,' Heinrich remarked to Otto von Streich-Schloss.

'We'll have to discuss it,' I protested.

Again, Heinrich waved his fat hand in the air; there was a silver ring with a large blue stone wedged on his little finger – it glittered and winked at me with a harsh, vulgar sparkle. As you shall soon learn, it would not be the last time this ring brought itself to my attention – I cannot resist telling you this. But patience! – you will see in due course.

'Yes, yes, certainly we shall discuss it,' he said. 'Ah, *gnädige* Frau Richtenfeld! A delight to see you, as always! And dear Alfred? Is he quite recovered?'

I moved away as surreptitiously as I could, clutching my empty glass.

Later in the evening Heinrich sang; indeed, he sang interminably. He sang – with an emotional tremulo in his fruity voice and tears glistening in the corners of his piggy eyes – nauseatingly sentimental songs of homeland and hearth, unremarkable *marches militaires*, ballads that related the heroism of saintly patriots, and a chromatic sub-Wagnerian hymn, dirge-like and doom-laden, in praise of love between comrades-in-arms. I hardly need add that he concluded with *Old Man River*.

'You have known Herr Hervé for some time?' a voice whispered in my ear as generously enthusiastic applause filled the great room.

I turned to find Otto von Streich-Schloss standing close by my side, so close that I could smell the champagne on his breath. It was quite obvious that he was inebriated.

'As a matter of fact no,' I replied.

'Hardly what one would call a – *discreet* – character, if I may say so without disloyalty. I am very fond of Heinrich, I assure you.'

'Yes, I'm sure you are. Discreet? About the *Amici di Germania,* you mean?'

'Not primarily, Herr Crispe. I refer to certain other interests that he and I share – as do many of our little confraternity.'

'Ah.'

'I do not mean that we all display the same degree of enthusiasm, of course –'

'Of course.'

'One must never forget the principal aim of the *Amici,* to which all else is secondary.'

'Which is what, precisely?' I asked.

He patted me in a friendly way on the shoulder.

'I am not so easily drawn in as that, my friend. You must speak to Heinrich if you wish to know more. Perhaps even to join forces with us? You are English, after all – of the northern races, like us. Ah no, the subject to which I obliquely refer is of a more personal nature – even though, as I have said, many of my brothers in the society display a remarkable fondness for its subtle mysteries. Indeed, I am by no means the most experienced devotée here –'

'Oh?'

'Perhaps this is not so surprising, Herr Crispe. We are, after all, a single-minded group.'

'Do you mean military-minded?'

'Maybe so. It has to do, I am sure, with the whole concept of – what shall I say? – of *ordnung,* the longing for efficiency, purity of devotion to the highest ideals, the cleanliness of the military mind focussed unswervingly upon the true principles of patriotism – the virtue of manly comradeship – love of –'

'Discipline?' I said.

I felt him shudder.

'Oh yes,' he said, his voice barely a whisper, 'love of discipline – oh, above all, *that!* Small wonder, Herr Crispe, that we are dedicated to discipline . . . as I am sure Herr Hervé must have explained to you.'

'As a matter of fact –'

'Or perhaps even – dare I say it? – *demonstrated* to you . . .'

He had taken the seat beside me, and now one hand was pressing on my left thigh, the fingertips digging in hard.

'When I was a young corporal,' he said, 'there was an officer in my regiment who really knew what discipline meant – really *knew*, I tell you! He was neither afraid to give it, nor – ah – to receive it. Somehow, in some way, he came to know that I too was a worshipper at the same shrine . . . I had never spoken to him of it, would never have dared to speak of it, and yet one glance – one look exchanged between us! – and immediately he understood. He understood and he offered me the benefit of his rich, deep experience. There grew up between the two of us a relationship of such profound intensity, such mental and emotional empathy – like that of an old, wise philosopher to his young pupil, that of an aristocratic master to his beloved manservant – and our joy was all the greater because none of the others knew, never once guessed. We would pass each other in a crowded corridor, in a public room, and not a single sign of recognition was ever given except that dark, depthless glance – oh, so swift, so secret that no-one saw its coming and going! It was like the blink of an eye, the intake of breath, there and gone in less than an instant.

'We very rarely exchanged words when we met in our special places at night – just a touch, a brief smile, and the ritual commenced without further ado. It was what we craved, what we ached for. First him, then me. Total submission to the will of the other, absolute obedience, the willingness to take what was given without a groan, without a murmur. We found parts where the marks would not show . . . we even discovered techniques which left no marks at all.'

'How terribly inventive of you.'

'I tell you we learnt our lessons well, he and I,' he murmured. 'After all, pain is so often a salutary experience, is it

162

not? Ah yes . . . the swift, sharp crack of well-honed leather on bare skin is frequently so much more effective than a mere verbal command could ever be . . . the sudden fire, the reddening weal on pale flesh will restore dedication to the highest manly ideals as nothing else can –'

'In your experience, you mean?'

'Yes, Herr Crispe, in my experience.'

'I thought that might be the case.'

'Pain is clean, is it not? Pain is swift, pure, simple, efficient. It does its job, it is incontestable, irrefutable, irresistible. Pain is as hard as steel, as uncomplicated as a primary number, as undeniable as a geometrical proposition. You cannot argue with pain, Herr Crispe – you can only – only *embrace* it . . . '

'As you have done, Herr Streich-Schloss?'

'Indeed, as I have done. As I *must* do.'

'And Heinrich Hervé?' I said.

He was whispering into my neck now, nuzzling me there, nibbling at the lobe of my ear. I caught a whiff of some disgusting cologne, medicated and astringent, like a haemorrhoid preparation. In view of what he had been telling me, it probably *was* a haemorrhoid preparation.

'Alas, dear Heinrich has neither the courage nor the stamina for truly *concentrated* or prolonged discipline. We occasionally take a room in a private hotel for the afternoon, but – to be frank with you, Herr Crispe – his tastes are less rigorous than mine. What shall I say? He prefers the *dolce*, whereas I am more inclined to linger over the main course.'

'A charming analogy, Herr Streich-Schloss.'

'When we get to know each other better, I shall permit you to call me Otto.'

'I'm touched.'

'Any little slip – the slightest, Herr Crispe, I assure you! – before that permission is given, and I am afraid you will be subject to an appropriate punishment. I am fair, but I am strict. I would not hurt you too much at first, not to begin with – pain is also like an old, rare wine Herr Crispe, to be sipped and savoured slowly, rolled around the tongue . . . it must not be taken down too quickly or in too large a quantity, for that way lies the madness of inebriation. I have a stitched leather strap – oh, such a beautiful little thing! – it has been my intimate companion for many years now –'

All at once I felt him draw quickly away, and a moment later I knew why.

'Maestro!' cried Heinrich, the vast shadow of his bulk preceded by a strato-cumulus of his expensive perfume. 'Where have you been hiding yourself? Has Otto been boring you with his regimental stories?'

'Not at all,' I said. 'Quite the contrary.'

'I am glad to hear it – Otto, my dearest friend, fetch us some more champagne, it is good for my voice.'

'You shouldn't drink so much, Heinrich,' von Streich-Schloss said irritably, casting me a curiously pleading backward glance as he slunk off. I wondered, briefly, whether one of those little nocturnal escapades with his sado-masochistic boyfriend was the reason for his unmoving glass eye.

'Such a hypocrite,' Heinrich observed, lighting up one of his small Turkish cigarettes. 'He is drunk himself.'

'Yes, I know.'

'Well then *cher maître*, it is all arranged.'

'What is?'

'Our private party at *Il Giardino di Piaceri*, of course. Had you forgotten? After my performance at the Palazzo Fabrizzi-Bamberg – there will be exactly twelve of us including Otto, and you will reserve the roof garden for us.'

'I told you, it wouldn't be worth my while closing it off for a small group like that.'

'And,' he went on, utterly oblivious to my objection, 'you will prepare something *very* special for my friends.'

'But it's quite impossible, Heinrich –'

'Give free reign to your creative genius, my friend!'

'Look –'

'No, not "prepare" but *create!* Let Orlando Crispe show the *Amici di Germania* what he is capable of. Already, I am on fire with anticipation!'

And he was off, like a giant planet following its wide orbit, to embrace the professor of urinogenitology.

Like Pigs at the Trough

In the end the *Amici di Germania* did not get the roof garden; I cannot claim, however, that this triumph was entirely my own, for throughout the day it had rained heavily and by seven o'clock it was quite obvious that Heinrich and his party would be obliged to dine downstairs in the restaurant. On the whole I think the meal was a success; I took care to avoid the proximity of Otto von Streich-Schloss, who kept eyeing me soulfully across the room, doubtlessly conjuring up a mental image of the wine-red weals his beautiful little leather strap might make on the naked flesh of my defenceless buttocks, given half a chance. Jacques took an instant dislike to him.

'Be careful of that one, Monsieur,' he said with touching solicitude.

'You mean Herr Streich-Schloss? I certainly shall.'

'He has the look of a hungry dog.'

'Then let us see what the art of Orlando Crispe can do about that.'

Professionally (if not personally) sensitive to the Germanic character of the company, I gave them terrine of *foie gras au Riesling* and marinated herrings with a warm potato and herring salad; this was followed by a choice of shoulder of pork braised with mustard, *choucroute garnie Alsacienne* and chicken casserole with Riesling accompanied by *grumbeerekiechle* and *choux rouges braisés aux pommes*. Dessert was two kinds of sorbet – strawberry and *au Marc de Gewürztraminer* – and I served *Kügelhopf* with the coffee.

Towards the end of the evening they became raucous on my cognac – all, that is, except Heinrich Hervé, who, quite to the contrary, grew sullen and withdrawn. He even refused to sing when they called for him to do so – a unique event, in my experience. Finally, most of them moderately drunk, they began to make their farewells, quit the table – Herr Streich-Schloss to my great relief being one of the first – and drift out into the rainy night; eventually, only Heinrich was left.

'You enjoyed my little offerings?' I asked.

He looked up at me sadly.

'A triumph, my dear Crispe. Not your greatest to be sure, but a triumph nevertheless.'

'Then why the long face, may I ask?'

'Tonight I must sleep alone,' he said. 'For the first time in many weeks there is no companion waiting for me. It is a terrible thing to sleep alone.'

'It happens to us all,' I said.

'You also, *cher Maître*?'

'As a matter of fact I nearly always sleep alone.'

'I had no idea!'

He seemed to be genuinely astonished. I cannot imagine why.

'The genius always walks a lonely way,' I said, talking more to myself than Heinrich. 'He must blaze his trail without the solace available to those of lesser gifts. He has no-one to trust other than himself.'

Heinrich suddenly brightened.

'Oh, it is true!' he cried. 'Even I cannot always be lucky in love. Come, Orlando, let us drink together, and make convivial conversation.'

Foolishly, I said yes, and he chose a particularly fine bottle of my *Chateau Neuf du Pâpe*. Heaven knows why I agreed, for I knew that Heinrich's idea of convivial conversation was nothing less than a monologue, delivered by him, on the subject of himself. We sat at a littered table in the semi-darkness, a single candle guttering in its scalloped silver holder.

Heinrich held his glass up to the yellow light for a few moments, then put it to his lips and slurped. He said casually:

'It could be better.'

'It is a very fine wine.'

'I'm used to the best.'

'I'm sure you are.'

He sighed, and his multiple chins wobbled.

'Which is precisely why I have been urging you to set your mind to your masterpiece, Orlando my friend. The dish you were born to create!'

'And you to consume,' I said.

'Ah, you are teasing me again. Think of it! A creation to stun the world – a combination of flavours and fragrances to tickle the nostrils of Jehovah himself – an innovation, a masterly stroke of pure culinary genius –'

'Heinrich, *please* –'

'You must name it after me, naturally,' Heinrich said.

'Since you strive so earnestly to be my inspiration –'

'Exactly. Is it not I who have stood by your side, encouraging and exhorting?'

'Oh, indeed.'

As a matter of fact, I had become thoroughly sick and tired of Heinrich's encouraging and exhorting of late; I had served him – and an endless series of 'companions' – one culinary novelty after another, but none of them had satisfied him

'Bah!' he cried. 'I have had *Poussin à la Crème* at the Chateau Lavise-Bleiberger; in Florence I very nearly died and went to paradise on account of Maestro Louvier's exquisite *sasaties*; I have shared *Rosettes d'Agneau Parmentier* with the Duc d'Aujourdoi –' and so on, as I have recorded for you at the start of these confessions. Even the testicles of an Alsatian dog failed to arouse a jot of enthusiasm.

To be quite honest, I do not know whether I can say with complete truthfulness that the idea of disposing of Heinrich and wondrously transforming him into dishes rich and rare occurred to me at that moment, as we sat drinking wine by candlelight; maybe a nebulous glimmering had wreathed its way into my mind, like smoke through a keyhole, some time before – or maybe not. Perhaps the thing was never really properly planned, or even premeditated. It may be that according to the inscrutable dictates of that Higher Will which expresses the intentions of the Divine Absorbent – and my own personal *dharma* – this day, this hour, this opportunity and – most importantly of all – this *motive* was destined, fixed clear and immutable in the warp and woof of my existence since the very beginning. At any rate, all circumstances coincided in a way that made the inevitable actual. It *happened,* and that is the simplest way of putting it. The catalyst, which acted with devastating immediacy, was

167

the notorious remark Heinrich made about my beloved Highgate queen.

We – perhaps I should say Heinrich – had been talking for some time about the sensation that my so-called masterpiece would cause. Then:

'What a pity she could not be here with us tonight,' he murmured, 'sharing the anticipation of our future triumph.'

Our triumph?

'Who?' I said.

'Your dear mother, of course.'

He poured himself another glass of wine. He was becoming drunk.

'I'm perfectly sure she *is* here, in spirit. She is always with me.'

'Yes, yes. I only meant –'

'I know what you meant.'

Heinrich leaned forward and laid a plump, pale hand on my arm.

'And your father – would you not wish him also –'

'No,' I said quickly.

'Surely your dear, dear mother would have wanted –'

His speech was becoming slurred.

'You sound exactly like him. That's the kind of thing he would have said.'

'Orlando, my friend – you cannot go on despising him forever –'

'Why not? My mother did. I don't know why she married him in the first place.'

Then he sniggered and – unforgivably! – said it:

'Maybe he had a twelve inch cock?'

Synaesthetically speaking, I heard the ugly clash of steel upon steel.

'Heinrich,' I said with a calculatedly tender solicitude, 'your glass is empty. Let me open another bottle.'

He looked at me with those little piggy eyes encased in puffs of baggy flesh.

'Good idea,' he said.

Then he slumped forward across the table.

Brief Encounter

The twins took some persuading – not, I think, on account of any moral sensitivity, but rather because a) they were (naturally enough) taken aback by my request, and b) they were concerned about its possible consequences. However, my unremitting insistence eventually paid off.

'But you *must* do it Jacques.'

'You do not know what you ask –'

'I know perfectly well what I ask.'

'Look at him! I never had any clients as fat as that.'

'Jacques –'

'Or as ugly. Let Jeanne do it –'

'I will not!' Jeanne cried, her eyes widening in horror.

'Don't worry Jeanne,' I said as soothingly as I could, 'Herr Hervé's tastes are of the other kind.'

'Only men?' Jacques said, hope dying in his voice.

'Exclusively so.'

'But –'

'Please, Jacques!'

We argued for another fifteen minutes or so, but in the end he agreed – as indeed I was certain he would. Both of them demanded a hefty financial recompense for this extra-curricular labour (that was something else I had been certain of) and I did not quibble when they named their price.

We stripped Heinrich naked and laid him out on the great bed in the twins' room. He reminded me just a little of Master Egbert Swayne, who was of similar proportions. Henrich, however, had very little hair on his body, whereas Master Egbert had been positively cilicious – hair everywhere, except where he wanted it most, on his head.

It took some time to bring him round.

'Oh – where am I? – Orlando, my friend? Where *am* I?'

Jacques, also naked and looking rather beautiful, stood by the bed.

'I am your angel, Monsieur.'

'My angel?'

Heinrich's eyes were already becoming ungummed and were beginning to feast themselves on the sight of Jacques' cool, glistening body. To be honest, I felt a little sorry for Jacques, but then – oh, then! – all true art requires its heroes.

'I have come to minister to you, Monsieur.'

'To minister to me? Ah – dear boy –'

Jacques passed one hand across Heinrich's right breast and paused to tweak the huge, thick, brown nipple.

Suddenly, he caught sight of me; I was standing in a corner of the room beside a massive candelabra that stood on the floor, supported by a base of engraved gold. God alone knows where *that* had been stolen from, and I didn't want to know.

'Orlando!' he cried. 'Is this *your* doing? Could you not bear the thought that I must sleep alone?'

I smiled, but made no reply.

'Oh, Orlando!'

Jacques climbed onto the bed and covered – very inadequately I must say – Heinrich's bloated body with his own.

'Watch us, Orlando,' Heinrich murmured in a low, coarse voice. 'Watch us do it – it will increase my pleasure – yes, watch while we do it – oh! – my angel –'

He pulled Jacques' mouth to his and began to move himself in an utterly nauseating way, imitating the nervous writhings of a virgin bride, his fingers fluttering coyly at Jacques' buttocks, his massive thighs shuddering.

'Love me, my angel – love me –'

I did not allow Jacques to suffer for long; as soon as Heinrich's eyes had closed and he began to moan, I approached the bed. Lifting his head with one hand, I removed a plump, silk pillow – he was quite oblivious of anyone or anything other than his own gratification. I nodded to Jacques, who raised himself slightly to one side. I placed the pillow with mathematical care over Heinrich's face and pressed down hard.

I heard a small, muffled groan.

'Press harder, Monsieur! Harder!'

I did so, for about half a minute.

'Harder! Why does he not struggle?'

'He's drunk, that's why.'

I thought I heard another groan – fainter this time – but it could have been my imagination. Then Heinrich's arm fell over the side of the bed, fat and pale and limp.

'There. It is done.'

Jacques sighed – with relief, I should imagine.

'Thank you Monsieur,' he said.

Prime Cuts

Cutting up and disposing of Heinrich Hervé's massive corpse was not the difficult task I at first imagined it would be; in fact, in the end, it proved to be rather easy. Since both Heinrich's appearance and character were exceptionally pig-like, I followed the joint markings for that particular beast, using a Revlon *Sunset Glow* lipstick to cover his pale, bloated body with the bright red lines that would show me where I had to cut. The two really weren't so very different – head, loin, chump, leg, belly, it was all there – except that I had to make do without the trotters, for even I blanched at the thought of Heinrich's severed hands and feet served up as *Pieds de Porc Grillé*, garnished with apple sauce and gherkins.

The French have a saying to the effect that everything of the pig is good to eat – in English we say 'everything but the squeal'; certainly, it is a fact that more of the pig than any other beast provides *prima materia* for the most exquisite delicacies – the heart and the liver, it is true, are coarser than the heart and liver of lamb, but on the other hand, what else but the pig could provide us with fat so versatile it is wellnigh invaluable? The head is used to make brawn; the cheek cooked, shaped and breadcrumbed to make *Bath chaps*; the intestines are one of the chief ingredients of chitterlings; the liver makes delicious paté, and even the ears can be singed, simmered, breadcrumbed and fried. The main roasting joints are well-known to everyone: leg, loin, chump, belly, spare-rib, blade.

And all of these, Heinrich Hervé yielded up. As well as the hands and feet, I discarded also the heart (since I imagined this would be particularly tough), the liver and the tongue (the latter I was certain would be poisonous); there was no tripe to speak of, and of course no tail. In turning at least *some* of Heinrich into rissoles, I used a great deal of flesh from the shoulders, mincing it finely; it was, I suppose, the equivalent of ground pork, which is usually taken from the shoulder or forequarter. The kidneys I found to be particularly succulent – a fact I attributed to Heinrich's regular consumption of some of my finest wines; and, needless to say, there was absolutely *limitless* fat. Back fat I stored to use for wrapping around lean joints of pork or beef, and for turning into lard; the translucent crumbly fat around the kidney was superb for making pastry, just as it is in the pig itself. Oh, could I reasonably have asked for more? I think not. Dead and dismembered, Heinrich proved far more useful to me than he ever had when alive.

The genitals were surprisingly very small – a little curl of a cock nestling on its fat pouch. What an irony: the only thing about Heinrich he would have *loved* to be huge, was tiny.

'What did he do with that, I wonder?' Jacques said, wiping his bloody hands on his apron.

'Quite a lot, I believe. Thank God he didn't have time to do anything with you.'

'My own sentiments exactly, Monsieur.'

My rissoles *Il Giardino di Piaceri* were a sensation – just the kind of sensation, in fact, Heinrich himself would have adored.

Rissoles *Il Giardino di Piaceri*
2lb (900g) fresh finely minced beef
2 oz (50g) fine white breadcrumbs
3 oz fine white breadcrumbs to coat the rissoles
2 small onions peeled and chopped
3 tbsp strong beef stock
4 oz (100g) finely minced pork
1 tbsp fresh chopped sweet basil
2 tbsp dry sherry
1 tsp soy sauce
Black pepper to season
Olive oil for frying

Mix all the ingredients together into a bowl except the breadcrumbs for coating, using the fingers to ensure that they are completely blended. Shape into 6–8 balls and flatten between the palms of the hands. Coat each rissole in breadcrumbs and fry in a shallow pan in the olive oil. Pat dry on a kitchen towel before serving.

Alas, alas, that Heinrich provided so much *prima materia*, or that I used it to create such a plethora of gastronomically esoteric succulencies! Every one of them was a supreme sensation, and yet *one* of them precipitated my downfall. Did I refuse to see the inevitable? I don't know; yet, with hindsight, I can clearly see that the chain of events which now rapidly overtook me *could* have been prevented when it was still not too late.

For now I must tell you that Heinrich Hervé was by no means the first person I killed and cooked: *that honour belongs to the man who called himself my father.*

X

Nothing But the Truth
I ate my father.

Oh, stated baldly like that it does sound somewhat *outré* I admit, but what would be the point of wrapping up the heart of the matter in pseudo-psychological or self-justifying preludes? A genius never excuses himself, and I will not do so here.

Yes, I ate my father. I also ate Miss Lydia Malone. Naturally I didn't eat every scrap of them – various bits and pieces travelled overland to Rome in transportable cold storage; these were used to create a variety of delicacies which I served to my customers here at *Il Giardino* – and very successful they were too.

I must add that the intellectual *release* this bestowed on me can hardly be described: it was like a torrent, a flood. They say that when the heretic Luther's bowels finally opened and his shit filled the privy to overflowing, so did the soul and substance of his theology well up unstoppably from his heart – the liberation of the mind following the unblocking of the arse. Well, in the same way, so was my psyche freed from the fetters of fear and repulsion; it was the unlocking of my creative genius.

It was also the direct cause of the fiasco at *Il Bistro*.

For I used some of my father and the left thigh of Miss Lydia Malone to make *Rosettes Stuffed with Olives and Almonds* and *Roast Loin with Peach and Kumquat Stuffing*. I did not at that time understand how carefully the power of my art must be controlled. I had also forgotten the state of anger and fury in which my father had died; the psychic vibrations in Miss Malone were too strong for them – hence the frenzy of promiscuous sex – then, when my father's flesh began to make its influence felt, passion turned into hatred and violence. Naturally, I have long since learned to dilute the vibrations, and thus modify their effect.

After the killing and cooking of Heinrich Hervé – he was transmuted into dishes wondrously rich and rare! – I felt obliged to inform the twins of these others, and of precisely what had caused the nightmare at *Il Bistro.*

'You fed your father to your cusomers?' said Jacques, his mouth falling open.

'Yes. And his tart. But I didn't know how to control the power, then. They were overwhelmed by it – the sex from Miss Lydia Malone and the fury from my father. It was too strong. It isn't like that anymore – I'm very careful, now.'

'Now?'

'Yes. There were others after my father but before Heinrich Hervé.'

'Others?'

'Please don't keep repeating everything I say. There have been – well – about half a dozen, I suppose. I haven't kept an exact account. However, now that you know, you will be able to assist me in my work. Particularly in the obtaining of raw material.'

'You expect us to *help* you?'

'Certainly. Why not? You helped me with Heinrich Hervé.'

Jeanne said:

'That was different. Besides, neither my brother nor I liked him.'

'You must understand, both of you,' I said, 'there is nothing *personal* in any of this – I serve only my art, my creative genius.'

'One cannot put creative genius in the bank, Maestro.'

'No. But one *can* put cash in the bank. Shall we come to an agreement, then?'

They looked at each other for a moment, hesitating. Then Jeanne said:

'Let's sit and talk.'

I shook my head impatiently.

'What is there to talk about?'

'Figures, Maestro,' said Jacques. 'Figures.'

The Agony and the Ecstasy

The supper given for the *Amici di Germania* had proved such a success financially, that I decided to offer them another evening *chez Orlando* – and this time, there would be no Heinrich Hervé to cast a shadow over the proceedings with *Roses and Moonight,* Tosti's *Goodbye, Praise Jehovah Mighty God* or the despicable *Old Man River.*

'The tips almost equalled the bill!' cried Jeanne delightedly, clapping her hands.

'Quite clearly,' I said, 'Herr Hervé's companions do not share his parsimony.'

'Oh, he was a niggard, that one.'

'Except,' I added, 'in death. In death he was profligate.'

'Let us hope that the *Amici* will be as generous a second time.'

'You can count on it, Jeanne,' I murmured.

For the raw material of my act of creation, I settled on Herr Streich-Schloss; after all, if what he had told me was true, and many of his companions in the society shared his predilection for – for *discipline* – they would surely eat themselves into an ecstasy on flesh which had been obtained from one who expired in an agony of pleasure derived from pain. True, their membership would be down by two, but this, I calculated, was a very small price to pay for the delights of my table. Neither did I for one moment imagine that Herr Streich-Schloss' absence would be commented on anymore than Heinrich Hervé's had been – which is to say, not at all so far; Heinrich, I knew, occasionally disappeared for weeks on end, off on some provincial tour arranged by his long-suffering Italian agent, Umberto Tamisi – the only times, I might add, when my customers were spared his interminable evening performances. Perhaps they would imagine that Otto von Streich-Schloss had gone with him – at any rate, I did not greatly care. What I most certainly *did* care, was that I should give them the most incredible gastronomic experience they had ever had in their lives – an edible exposition of the principles of Absorptionism, the genius of my philosophy made perfectly manifest by the genius of my culinary techniques.

Accordingly, I wrote to Herr Streich-Schloss at the head-quarters of the *Amici di Germania* inviting him to an evening of 'private entertainment', and he accepted by return post. Exultantly, I began to make my plans.

'It was most kind of you to think of me,' Otto von Streich-Schloss murmured as we sat together in my private study. It was seasonably warm, and through the open windows drifted the perfumes of a perfect Roman evening: garlic, *espresso* and geranium. The distant hum of boys on their scooters hunting for female prey was like the gentle buzz of late summer insects – unobtrusive, lulling, reassuring, fatal.

'Please do not look upon it as a kindness,' I answered.

'Oh?'

'See it more as a response.'

'A response, Herr Crispe?'

'Exactly.'

'A reponse to what, may I ask?'

'Well,' I said, choosing my words with care, 'I have pondered deeply on the observations you made to me concerning – discipline –'

'Ah . . .'

'And I have begun to feel since that occasion that maybe we have something in common, you and I. Your colleagues in the *Amici* and I, that is.'

Herr Streich-Schloss shifted in his chair, transferring the weight of his body from one buttock to the other. His legs, crossed, suddenly seemed to be very long, encased within the tight black military trousers.

'You wish to join our little confraternity,' he breathed, his face aglow with an inner enthusiasm. His good eye glinted like cold blue steel; the other was like the glaucous eye of a dead fish.

'That, yes. But also –'

'Also, Herr Crispe?'

'Also – I thought that you and I – together I mean – that we might ascertain the strength of my feeling.'

'Or *confirm* it, perhaps?'

'Exactly, Herr Streich-Schloss.'

'I knew it,' he said breathily. 'Oh yes, I knew it. From the first moment I saw you, I was convinced that our tastes would be remarkably similar. Do you mind if I smoke?'

'Not in the least. Please feel free.'

He extracted a slim silver case from his pocket and drew out a cigarette; he held it towards me on the palm of his hand.

'Thank you, no. I don't'

He lit up, inhaled deeply, then blew out a stream of silver-blue smoke from his nostrils.

'My instincts are unerring,' he remarked. 'And I had an instinct about you.'

'I'm flattered.'

'The moment Herr Hervé introduced us.'

'How is dear Heinrich?' I asked.

'I really don't know. I haven't seen him for some time.'

'Gone to fulfil engagements in other parts of the country, perhaps?' I said, seizing the opportunity to suggest a plausible reason for his absence.

'Perhaps. He does so at regular intervals.'

'Yes, I know. His disappearance is in no way – remarkable – then?'

'By no means.'

Herr Streich-Schloss blew a plume of smoke directly into my face.

'I think,' he said slowly, 'the time has come for you to address me more familiarly. You may call me Otto.'

'Otto, then. And you may call me Orlando.'

Herr Streich-Schloss smiled in a very off-putting manner: the kind of smile, I imagined, that constitutes the rabbit's last glimpse of life on earth before the snake pounces. Yet had Otto von Streich-Schloss the slightest inkling of the fate that awaited him, the discomfort would surely have been his, not mine.

'My dear Orlando,' he said, his voice unctuous with a commingling of forced humility and growing desire, 'I see now that my remarks that evening acted merely as a catalyst – a fertiliser, so to speak –'

'Oh?'

'– and that deep within, unknown and unguessed except perhaps in the ecstasy of forbidden dreams, you were always one of us. Ah, dear friend, is not such self-discovery the most exquisite of all, far outweighing in meaning and value all those discoveries of the nature of the world outside us that we are foolish enough to call 'scientific'? Is not the only true science the science of self?'

'I am sure what you say is correct.'

'Yes, yes, absolutely correct. To discover what one is, and to *live* it to the full. It is the way – the way of –'

'The way of the genius?' I suggested, somewhat piqued that this absurd pervert, carried away by the eloquence of his own pseudo-psychology, had stolen *my* conviction.

'Precisely so!' he cried, spraying me with spittle, 'the way of the genius.'

I noticed with a thrill of horror that there was now a considerable bulge in the front of his tight black trousers. Still, having planned this evening with a mathematical – not to say obsessional – care, I knew that I was prepared for anything.

'I rely on you to guide me,' I said softly.

He leaned forward in his chair, his whole body tense. I could almost smell the desire, the expectation. I did not dare switch on my synaesthesia.

'Ah, here we come to the heart of the matter, then. You are proposing a joint venture . . . '

'Am I? Yes, I suppose I am.'

'A lesson in the love of discipline . . . '

'Yes.'

'I will not fail you, Orlando, believe me. I will be your teacher in the art of pain willingly embraced, pain surrendered to in the purest docility.'

'Fair, but strict.'

'Yes, fair but strict. Oh, *strict,* I promise you. Your guide, your teacher, your mentor. Pain is like a shy virgin bride, Orlando: one cannot force delight from her, can in no way demand that she yield up her delectable sweetness – ah, no!

She must be coaxed by gentle degrees, reassured that her caress is welcome by means of a thousand and one little love-bites, fleeting touches of affection and esteem; for only when she believes that her beauty is desirable and truly desired, does she consent to union.'

His face darkened as he went on:

'There are those who would not understand our love for her,' he said.

'Oh?'

'Yes, it is true. There are many who would consider us – *unnatural* – for bearing such love towards her.'

'Heavens, you do surprise me.'

'The *Amici di Germania* is a bulwark against those who neither comprehend nor tolerate a love such as ours.'

'I'm sure it is.'

'But, Orlando – oh, what wonders await you! – when pain is convinced of her lover's devotion and gives her all, then as the impaled flesh of a bride overwhelms the aching groom with ecstasies of the most exquisite intimacy, so does pain, in the fulness of union, render up the last drop of her sweetness, melting away all hesitation, all doubt, all fear. She becomes the *Domina*, the Lady who cannot be denied, who permits no holding back, who demands, gives and receives delight of unimaginable intensity and duration.'

To my amazement, I saw tears trickling slowly down his cheeks – well, down one cheek anyway, since the glass eye was incapable of producing any. In the half-light of my little study, his face appeared transfixed, his features petrified by some indescribable emotion that held him as a pin holds a butterfly.

'I have loved her from my earliest years,' he said in a voice that was so low, so soft, it was barely audible. 'We have been companions – lovers – for so long I cannot now recall a time when we did not walk hand in hand, she and I. It has been a relationship of mutual devotion: I have given her an unswerving, unfailing loyalty in return for every unspeakable pleasure she has bestowed upon me. And more than this: she has given me friends along the way – fellow devotées, comrades in her service – and each one of them has been a joy to me, a delight and a discovery. Together we have administered the sacraments of her grace, performed the rites and rituals of her liturgy. Have you any idea how completely this binds two men to each other? They become brothers, lovers, complementarities – for between them are her extremities displayed: her awesome majesty and her unbearably tender shyness; their bodies – the very substance of them – become the means of her self-revelation. Two hearts beating as one, in a movement of the purest dedication . . . breast against breast . . . pain to pain in pain's honour . . . to her glory, drinking deep of her delight.'

He was casting a spell over me. The low, undulating voice whispering its perversions, the caressing tone uttering such obscenities . . . the twilight and the fragrance of the evening . . . they combined to lull me into a peculiar kind of peace, like a resignation that was quite lovely in its hopelessness. I was being cradled into acquiescence. I knew that I must break the enchantment now or be lost to it completely.

Summoning up every ounce of willpower, as if dragging myself awake from some deep, narcotic slumber, I said:

'There is just one thing.'

'Oh?' Herr Streich-Schloss murmured, the eyebrow above his motionless glass eye shooting up.

'Just a small thing. I think it better if your first lesson was – well – if your instructions to me were to be in the *active* mode.'

He nodded.

'I understand completely, dear Orlando. Pain, as I believed I observed when we first met, is ruthless in its immediacy, its purity of meaning and purpose. It brooks no contradiction. It is – I am sure you are right – best to be introduced to its unique succulence by a third party, vicariously, so to speak, rather than risk a face-to-face encounter for the first time. I shall not only be your teacher Orlando, I shall also be your model – not only high priest, but also sacrificial victim.'

'I knew you would see my point,' I said, not without a significant measure of relief.

Herr Streich-Schloss rose to his feet and held out one sweaty hand for me to grasp.

'Come my dear sir, it is time for our first lesson.'

'So soon?'

Then, casually, he looked at me and said:

'Incidentally, during the lesson you shall be Daddy.'

Daddy?

He was naked except for his glossy leather boots. His pale, quite attractively muscular body glistened with a thin film of sweat. He knelt in front of me like a supplicant before an idol, his head bowed, his hands joined. At his insistence, I was clad only in my underpants.

'I've been so naughty,' he said, his voice unnaturally high and schoolboyish.

'Why? What have you done?' I asked sternly. We had spent at least thirty minutes getting this tone exactly right – neither too awesome nor too pliant, the perfect blend of sympathetic understanding and unswerving rectitude.

'I've been naughty. Oh please, please Daddy, don't punish me!'

'You know that I *must* punish you, if you have been naughty.'

'Yes, I know. Daddy is always good but just.'

'Fair but strict,' I said, and I heard him utter a tiny orgasmic sigh.

'Oh yes, yes, fair but strict.'

Then he took one of my hands and placed it on his left breast.

'Tweak me there,' he urged in a parenthetical whisper, like an actor in a farce hissing an aside to the audience.

I grasped the hot little nipple, already stiff, between a fore-finger and thumb, and squeezed, twisting it as hard as I could.

He cried out in pain.

'Oh, Daddy! Daddy is tweaking, twisting, pulling until it hurts!'

'How have you been naughty?' I boomed.

'Harder Daddy, oh, harder!'

'Tell me precisely how you've been a bad boy . . .'

'I've been naughty and wicked and *oh* so *bad,* Daddy –'

'Then you *shall* be punished.'

'Punishment is terrible –'

'But good.'

'Oh, but very good!'

'Very well, you know what all bad boys must do, don't you?'

'Please, Daddy, please –'

'There's no use pleading, no use begging for mercy. You've been a bad boy, and for your own good you're going to suffer.'

'Please, please, please, please!' cried the naked and absurd Otto von Streich-Schloss, who was clearly in paradise; as a matter of fact, I was quite beginning to enjoy my own role, but at present I do not care to speculate on the precise implications of this – I prefer to think that I was simply entering into the spirit of the game, and for a very worthy cause at that.

Herr Streich-Schloss turned on his knees to face away from me, leaned forward on his elbows, and thrust out his buttocks; they were pale, mottled with blue and hairy in a blond, downy sort of way.

'Daddy is going to punish you now,' I said. 'Daddy doesn't want to, but he must, because you've been a very bad boy.'

'Yes, *very* bad,' whimpered Herr Streich-Schloss.

'Daddy is going to smack you.'

'Oh! Will it hurt?'

'Certainly it will hurt.'

'Will it make me cry?'

'Without a doubt it will make you cry.'

'Do I have to be punished now?'

'Indeed you do.'

'With no clothes on?'

'Completely and totally nude. Not a stitch to cover you. All bad boys must take off every scrap of clothing to be punished. Daddy has to see *everything.*'

Otto von Streich-Schloss' upside-down face peered at me beneath one armpit. He was grimacing and touching himself furtively between the legs.

In the absence of his stitched leather strap, he had selected from the kitchen a steel spatula with a thick wooden handle, which he thought most suitable for the job, and it was this instrument I now brought down on his left buttock with considerable force; the high-pitched, sharp, clean *zist-tttinngg!* sounded really rather loud in my small study, and the deep crimson weal, spreading like a blush, was perfectly discernible in the dying light of the early evening. I lifted the spatula high, thwacked him again, then again.

He was burbling, chortling, muttering to himself in a baby voice, growing more excited each time I struck his backside.

'Yes, yes, yes!' he crooned, 'Daddy must punish me again, again – oh, yes –'

'Daddy is punishing his naked boy!'

All at once, I found myself quite involuntarily transported back to the scenario of my own childhood punishment – the one and only time my father had hit me, with that obsolete cricket bat. It was extraordinary how powerful, how *real* the resurrected memory was, played out now in my mind's eye in every little detail: I could smell the leather of the chair, feel the draught on the backs of my legs, hear my father's laboured breathing as he brought the bat down on my naked backside – and above all else, the sound of my beloved mother's nervous scream. I was caught, enmeshed like a fly in a sticky web, in that vivid time-trap. The harder and faster I struck Herr Streich-Schloss, the harder and faster my father seemed to strike me, even though in actuality his blows were feeble; the more shrill and panic-stricken his cries became, so did the screams of my Highgate queen, although at the time I think she had uttered only one. Like Proust's rusk, my steel spatula had become a technique of interior time travel.

Then, once again aware of my father's crab-like hand moving at the back of my balls, in a likewise fashion I reached forward and grasped Herr Streich-Schloss' scrawny, dangling scrotum. I squeezed it gently.

'Oh yes,' I muttered. 'A lovely pair . . . lovely . . .'

Then I set about beating him with a furious energy, bringing the spatula down alternately on each buttock.

'You bad, bad boy, you wicked, monstrous child!' I screamed.

'Oh, God, Daddy is punishing me – punish me hard, oh Daddy, oh *please* –'

'You unspeakable bastard, you filthy, despicable creature!'

'More, Daddy, *more* – harder, harder – oh Daddy – oh yes, yes –'

At that moment I felt a light, warm spray on my face – it was blood. Herr Streich-Schloss had hauled himself upright on his knees, his breathing swift and shallow, his speckled shoulders heaving. Blood, claret-bright, ran down the backs of his legs. I saw that he was quiveringly erect.

'Oh Daddy!' he cried aloud. '*Now, yes, its's coming – oh! – now!*'

Before he was actually able to climax, I struck him hard across the side of his head with the wooden handle of the spatula, and he collapsed immediately.

As he did so, I thought:

Manzo Gordiano dei Piaceri del Dolore.

Manzo Gordiano dei Piaceri del Dolore
1¾ lb (800g) prime flesh taken from one who has expired of pain's pleasure, cut into 8 large chunks
4 fl oz (120ml) olive oil
2 shallots, finely chopped
FOR THE MARINADE   ¾ bottle of Chianti
2 tbsp red wine vinegar
1 onion, finely chopped
2 cloves garlic, peeled and chopped
1 sprig fresh thyme, fresh rosemary
1 bay leaf
1 small piece orange zest

185

Mix together all the ingredients for the marinade and leave the beef-flesh in it for at least 24 hours. After this time, drain the meat, vegetables and herbs, and retain the liquid.

Fry the meat for a few moments on both sides in the olive oil. Add the shallots and the chopped vegetables and herbs. Fry for a few more moments then transfer to an ovenproof casserole dish and cover with the marinade liquid. Cook in a low oven at 150°C/300°F, gas mark 2 for about 3½ hours.

This dish I served to the *Amici di Germania,* and it was a sensation, as I had fully expected it to be, given the manner of Herr Streich-Schloss' expiry and the proclivities of the confraternity.

'Maestro Orlando!' cried a bull-necked, bald-headed fellow ecstatically, 'it is a taste of heaven! More, more! Bring us more!'

So I did, and they ate with ferocious appetites, lips slick with juice, succulent meaty fluids snaking down their chins, eyes thyroidal and cheeks flushed as they wolfed down the fleshy delights of a remarkably transmuted teutonic pervert.

'Such a pity Otto could not be with us,' someone said eventually.

A voice across the table observed:

'He has gone with dear Heinrich, off on a tour of the provinces, I believe.'

'Ah, dear God, what he has missed here!'

I allowed myself the satisfaction of a discreetly smug smile.

Slowly, by degrees of perceptible acceleration, the madness began to possess them: they ceased to plead for more *Manzo Gordiano* and fell back in their chairs, bloated in body and satiated in soul with the emotional fever my creation had both ignited and fuelled; tiny moans escaped from their open mouths, bubbles of saliva appearing and bursting on their lips; palpebral fluttering was the only movement visible on their florid, transfixed faces. Then, as the endogenous debilitation subsided, giving way to an upwelling that swiftly burgeoned from a quickening interest, through appetite, to an aching hunger and finally ravenous desire, they began to touch each other across the tables – fingertips contriving appointments, hands snatching and grasping, eyes concluding assignations. Several of them scrabbled at their collars, pulling loose their ties, unfastening buttons; their voices rose, querulous, fruity with nervous anticipation; then they started to shout.

'I think,' I remarked to Jacques, 'that our guests are ready to leave. I imagine that they are eager to pursue their own private – *activities* – for the rest of the evening.'

Indeed they were, practically fighting to get to the door. Some of them were already holding hands, clearly paired-off for the worship of the goddess of pain.

'Maestro, how can we thank you?' screamed one, pumping my hand in his own, sweaty and fat.

'Your pleasure is tribute enough,' I said modestly.

This was true, but I was also delighted when – the last of them gone – I saw that the tables were covered with bank-notes, as thick and crisp and uplifting to the senses as a blanket of snow covering a winter landscape. In the practical matters of this world, even a genius – by temperament and talent far removed from its mundanity – needs to be as wise as a serpent.

Pearls Before Swine

And yet, in the end, you must know that my primary concern was not about money, despite Egbert Swayne's rantings over the telephone – no, as a genius, it was naturally for my reputation in the eyes of the general public; if this was to be protected from the assaults of Arturo Trogville, I knew that I could no longer put off a face-to-face encounter.

He lived in a little jewel-box of an apartment in the Via di Orsoline, the rent doubtlessly paid for by one of his obese paramours, since I could not imagine that his salary as a restaurant critic covered what it must have cost to maintain such an enviably secluded place – and, oh, how shabby his character and habits were by comparison! He knew absolutely nothing of refinement or discretion or harmony of proportion, yet this lovely building exuded all three virtues. Within the foyer – whose security door someone had conveniently left open – all was coolness, shadow and peace; I did not, however,

187

imagine that these same qualities would be waiting for me behind Trogville's own door, which I now rapped on firmly, decisively, with my knuckles.

'It's you,' he said, gruff and surprised. 'What the hell do you want?'

'To talk to you,' I answered.

'I don't think we've got anything to say to each other.'

'I disagree.'

He hesitated for a moment, then opened the door wide to admit me.

'All right,' he muttered, 'you'd better come inside.'

The style within was minimalist and redolent of discreet wealth, as the finest minimalism invariably is – less than the finest merely gives the impression that one cannot afford much furniture. The base-tone colours were black, white and gold.

'Like it?' he asked, a sneer in his voice.

'Yes. Must have set you back quite a bit.'

He shook his head.

'Not me, old boy. Didn't set *me* back a single cent.'

It was precisely as I had guessed: Trogville was presently a kept man, which at his age was disgusting.

We sat in square, black suede armchairs, facing each other.

'I won't offer you any liquid refreshment,' he said. 'I don't imagine that you'll be here for long.'

'No. I'll say what I came to say, then go.'

'What you have to say to me, I can't think. Unless –'

'Unless?'

'Unless it's to offer an apology.'

'An apology?' I cried. 'What the hell have I got to apologise for?'

He leaned forward in his armchair and stared at me intently. The tiny tufts of gingery hair protruding from his nostrils quivered.

'For that night at *Il Bistro*,' he said in a strained voice.

'It was years ago.'

'It's been with me in my nightmares ever since, you callous

bastard! It was hell on earth, that madness, that – that cacophony, that bestiality –'

'Don't exaggerate,' I said, trying to sound casual.

'Exaggerate? Dear Christ, it would be impossible to exaggerate what went on there! Do you know what happened to me?'

'I didn't see everything, naturally – I can't explain any more than you can –'

'Didn't see? *Didn't see?* You filthy liar!'

'Look, Trogville – I came here –'

'I'll tell you what happened to me: I was buggered by a total stranger, that's what happened! And you tell me not to exaggerate –'

'It wasn't entirely my fault.'

'What did you do to us, Crispe? Just tell me what you did to us, and I'll be satisfied.'

'I don't know what I did – anyway – you wouldn't begin to understand even if I tried to explain. How can I explain, when I hardly understood it myself at the time?'

'Oh, you understood all right, I'm no fool.'

'I'm sure you aren't.'

He leaned back in his chair and sighed.

'So you haven't come to apologise, then?'

'I'm sorry that those – those things – happened, but I'm not sorry because they happened to you. I'm sorry in a general way, not in particular. I can't apologise. I won't do so.'

'I didn't imagine you would.'

'I want you to stop writing these vile reviews of my restaurant and my cuisine. They're doing no end of damage – well, not so much to my trade, since I'm packed out every night, but to my reputation. They are chipping away at my reputation.'

'That is precisely their purpose,' Trogville said with a hideous smile.

'I had a call from Egbert Swayne recently, and he was furious. It's his restaurant, after all. He threatened to come out to Rome and – well –'

'And what?'

'– see you himself.'

'I'm not susceptible to threats, Crispe.'

'I'm not threatening you. Look – I came here in the hope of being able to have a reasonable conversation with you –'

'And I came to Rome in the hope of finding out the truth,' Trogville hissed.

'The truth?'

'The truth of what happened that night at *Il Bistro*. Sooner or later the same thing is going to happen here, and I want to be around when it does.'

'You're wrong, Trogville,' I said. 'It isn't the same – everything is – well, everything is different now –'

Trogville shook his head.

'No,' he said. 'You're the same – you're the same arrogant, conceited bastard you always were, up to the same old tricks –'

'And you are the same old swine,' I cried, instantly regretting my loss of equilibrium, which I knew put me at a disadvantage. 'Pearls before swine! I don't know why I bothered to come. I didn't want to. I was urged to.'

I got up from the armchair and began to pace around the room. I thrust my hands in my trouser pockets for fear that I might start to wave my arms around and make a spectacle of myself, and – as I did so – my fingers encountered a little square packet – a paper packet of something – some stuff or other –

'Why Maestro Crispe,' said Trogville in a voice unctuous with imitation solicitude, 'I do believe you should have that liquid refreshment after all. You appear to be quite agitated.'

'A whisky will do, if you have one,' I murmured.

Then at once, and with absolute certitude, I knew two things: first, I knew that the little packet in my pocket contained a narcotic powder of the kind that I was in the habit of administering to my 'raw material' in order to induce unconsciousness before the dismemberment procedure; second, I knew that I would use it on Trogville.

Oh, how easy it was! I simply tipped it into his glass of whisky when he disappeared into the kitchen to get some *acqua minerale*, and stirred it vigorously with a fingertip. By the time he had returned, it had completely dissolved – tasteless, odourless, swift and efficient, as I knew from long practice.

He added the water to both glasses.

'A pity we can't drink to a beautiful friendship,' he said. 'Still, down the hatch.'

He sipped, nodded approvingly, sipped again and smiled.

'Don't imagine that it's simply revenge I'm doing this for,' he said, 'although God knows, when I think of what happened to me, that would be motive enough. No, not just revenge – as I said a moment ago, it's the truth that I'm after.'

'Truth has many facets, Trogville. It is rarely simple.'

'Then, by Christ, I want to know them all! Firstly, I want to know exactly what was in the food you served us that night – some sort of hallucinogenic drug, was it? Secondly, I want to know *why* you gave it to us –'

'Look, I didn't give you *any* kind of hallucinogenic drug – the very idea is completely absurd –'

'What happened to us was far from absurd!'

'Don't forget that *Il Bistro* had to close – do you think I *wanted* that? It was *my* restaurant, *my* living –'

'You must have misjudged the dose. Something went wrong.'

'Oh, this is ridiculous!'

'And thirdly – thirdly – I want to know – oh – I want to know why I suddenly feel so peculiar –'

He began to lean forward in his armchair, his head slumping down onto his chest. His shoulders heaved and his breath grew increasingly laboured. Sweat beaded his forehead.

'Oh Christ, I think I'm going to be sick – I feel faint – please, help me – oh, help me up –'

His glass fell from his hand and the remains of the doctored whisky dribbled out onto the parquet floor.

'What's the matter with me – what –'

He managed to raise his eyes, the pupils high up, half under the eyelids, the whites glossy and veined.

'What have you done to me? You bastard – you bloody swine –'

Then he was silent.

I don't know why I stripped him, but I did. Stretched out on the floor his body looked so flabby and ineffectual – what could his mountainous mistresses ever have seen in this? It was mottled with little stains and patches, some pink and others yellowy-white, like the body of an ageing model who poses for 'life studies' at some provincial art college in order to eke out a meagre pension. So harmless now he seemed, limp and absurd, shapelessly spreadeagled, the grubby dough left over after the first batch of bread has been baked. His penis, curled beneath a nimbus of sparse gingery hair, glistened damply. As I stared at him I suddenly felt the first quiverings of an incongruous sexual desire, and a deep, shocked shame at once rose up from within my bowels to meet it, like antibodies in the blood roused to attack and repel an alien invader.

I found the courgette on the draining board in the kitchen, where I had gone to rinse out our glasses and replace them in the cupboard; returning to the living-room I stood quite motionless for some moments, gazing down on Trogville and feeling rather like Tosca contemplating the lifeless body of Scarpia. Except that Trogville was far from lifeless – indeed, he had begun to snore – and I knew that within a few hours he would regain consciousness. I placed one foot beneath his right side and pushed him over so that he was lying on his stomach; then, with a slow, mathematical precision, I bent down and inserted the courgette into his arse.

'It should have been me,' I whispered.

That was the last time I ever saw him.

Some time after my departure and before he had awoken from the effects of the narcotic, a third party entered the apartment and murdered him. Despite what everyone says, you know that it was not me: *I did not kill Trogville.*

The Long Arm of the Law
As I made my way back through the darkening Roman streets, I was possessed by a sense of calm and contentment. To tell the truth, I would have liked to rape Trogville for myself, pushing my rigid cock up into that tight arse rather than the courgette

– and this would have been not so much a matter of sexual pleasure, but rather the sweetness of revenge – but there really hadn't been enough time for one thing, and – if I am to be perfectly honest – I was not anxious to provide him with another motive for continuing his assaults on me in the restaurant guides. I most certainly did not wish to give Master Egbert a reason for coming over to Rome.

At exactly four minutes to three o'clock – the moment is etched on the fabric of my psyche and forever will be! – there came the unwelcome sounds of clenched fists hammering on the door of the restaurant. I pulled on my dressing gown and went downstairs.

'What is it?' I cried. 'Can't you see we're closed? Do you know what time it is? How dare you disturb me at this hour –'

'My name is Andrea Colliani, Signor Crispe. I am the Chief Inspector of police for the *centro storico*. Please open the door.'

There were five of them – Andrea Colliani, his deputy Enrico Maroni, and three heavy, thick-set toughs who were there, without a doubt, in case there was trouble.

I ushered them into the restaurant.

'What is it? What do you want?'

'You will forgive the lateness of the hour Signor Crispe, but our business is urgent.'

'Oh? What business can be so urgent that you must awaken an entire household –'

'You are not alone, Signor Crispe?'

I hesitated. Then I said:

'My assistants are upstairs, sleeping.'

'Then let them be – for the moment.'

'Kindly state your business, Signor Colliani.'

He was tall, slim, and rather attractive in a saturnine way; he held out one hand and showed me something that glistened and winked on the smooth palm.

'Have you ever seen this before, Signor Crispe?'

Oh Christ. It was Heinrich Hervé's ring! It was the ring he had been wearing – the ring I saw on his fat finger – at that fatal gathering of the *Amici di Germania*, when I had first met Herr Otto von Streich-Schloss.

'No,' I lied.

'It is a ring, Signor Crispe.'

'Yes, I can see that.'

'A ring that was brought to us by a certain Herr Albert Richtenfeld.'

'Am I supposed to be familiar with that name?'

'You tell *me*, Maestro.'

'Well then, I am *not* familiar with it.'

'Herr Richtenfeld belongs to a – a *private society* – here in Rome, called the *Amici di Germania*. You have perhaps heard of it?'

'Yes, I have several times provided supper for the *Amici*,' I said.

There was little point in denying it.

'Can you guess where this ring came from?'

'No.'

He regarded it for a moment with a curious look of distaste.

'I am sorry to say that it came from the bottom . . .'

'The bottom? The bottom of what?'

'The bottom of Herr Richtenfeld, Maestro – the *sedere,* the *culo.* You understand?'

'Ah. Only too well,' I said.

'It came from Herr Richentenfeld's bottom the morning after he had dined at this restaurant.'

(God damn that bloody ring.)

'I cannot imagine how that might have happened,' I said with complete truthfulness – after all, the twins and I had been so careful during the dismemberment process; furthermore, I had discarded Heinrich's hands and feet. How, then –?

'Nevertheless, it *did* happen.'

'What are you implying?' I cried, genuinely agitated now.

'I am implying, Signor Crispe,' said Andrea Colliani, 'that the ring was in something that Herr Richtenfeld ate at this restaurant.'

'That's utterly monstrous!'

'Yes Signore, it certainly is. The ring itself belongs to Herr

194

Heinrich Hervé, also a member of the society. Herr Hervé cannot at present be located.'

'He's a singer – of a sort,' I said as casually as I could. 'He's often away on tour.'

'But not this time, Signor Crispe.'

'Oh? How can you be so sure?'

'We have checked, believe me. Herr Hervé's agent assured us that he has no engagements outside the city for at least six months.'

'I know nothing of Heinrich Hervé's movements, of course,' I said.

'Of course. But you do *know* Herr Hervé?'

'Yes, I do. He was in the habit of singing here in my restaurant every night.'

'*Was?*'

'Is, then. He hasn't turned up for a while of late.'

'Every night?'

'Until recently, that is.'

'Can you offer any explanation as to how Herr Hervé's ring should find its way into Herr Richtenfeld's bottom?'

'Certainly not. Although . . . the members of the *Amici di Germania* are addicted to a certain kind of pleasure, you know . . . '

'Yes, I know.'

'I suppose it's possible that in the rough and tumble of their little games . . . need I be more specific?'

'The idea also occurred to me, Signore, but Heinrich Hervé has been missing for a considerable period of time; Herr Richtenfeld kept the ring for some weeks before bringing it to us, you understand – it is inconceivable that it could have remained in his bottom since the disappearance of Herr Hervé.'

'Why did he keep the ring for so long before bringing it to you?' I asked, my mind desperately casting about for an avenue of escape from the net that I saw was rapidly being drawn in.

Andrea Colliani shrugged.

'It is true that he was puzzled by its sudden appearance –

that much he has already told us – but puzzlement must have given way to suspicion only after Herr Hervé's absence became prolonged. By themselves, the facts of Herr Hervé's disappearance and the ring's somewhat unusual materialisation were probably not sufficient to arouse his curiosity, since each *can* be explained as a separate incident – but put together, any likely explanation takes on a much darker, more sinister aspect, Signore.'

'Do you *know* that this is the case?'

'Herr Richtenfeld will doubtless make a statement to that effect later.'

'Later?'

'At present he is in a somewhat – what shall I say? – Herr Richtenfeld *sta con le spine sotto i piedi*. He is most anxious that the society he represents should not become involved in any public scandal. I calculate that his sense of duty will overcome the fear of scandal as soon as he is presented with the possibility – indeed, the likelihood – of an immediately *personal* involvement not merely in public scandal, but in criminal proceedings. Herr Richtenfeld is keen to assist the workings of justice Signor Crispe, or he would not have brought the ring to us in the first place.'

'You have it all worked out scientifically, I see.'

'Thank you Signore,' said Andrea Colliani, completely oblivious to the sarcasm.

'I am sorry that I cannot give you an equally scientific explanation.'

The Chief Inspector sighed.

'You see, Signor Crispe, whatever way we turn, whichever avenue we explore, we are always led back to your restaurant.'

'Oh?'

'Yes, Signore. It is like a spider's web, you understand? So many threads, so much twisting and turning, so many complicated patterns – but all joined together at the centre. *Il Giardino di Piaceri* is the centre of my investigation, I find. The centre of the spider's web of circumstances and events.'

'And what do you propose to do about it?'

'I propose, Maestro, to search these premises.'

'Not without a warrant you don't,' I said firmly.

'I have one.'

'Ah.'

'Would you be so kind as to accompany me, Signore?'

And we rose together, Andrea Colliani's hand on my arm.

They did not find anything of Heinrich Hervé, since he had been completely enrissoled, but they did find the bleach-white shinbone of my father, from which I had long ago made some very potent stock and which I had kept as a kind of memento. They also discovered the head of Miss Lydia Malone – pickled, in a jar. I wish to God I had thrown it away.

They questioned me endlessly about Heinrich Hervé, about the *Amici di Germania,* and my wretched father. They were also extremely interested in the head of Miss Lydia Malone – and, inevitably, where the rest of her might be. They were obsessed with details, with ridiculous periphera, never once grasping the meaning and purpose of the whole; had they done so, even for a brief moment, they would have immediately understood my genius. Their questions were repetitive, uninformed, incongruous and tedious in the extreme.

Thus:

'How is it possible that you remain so calm, Signore? Do you not feel any guilt, any shame? No horror at the magnitude of your crimes?'

'Certainly not. I am an artist, not a criminal.'

And:

'Was the woman's flesh sweeter, you insane bastard?'

'That depended on how it was cooked.'

'Oh, you beast!'

Or:

'Who were your accomplices? Name them, and we'll go easy on you. Tell us who made you do it, who first suggested it.'

'No-one made me do it, no-one suggested it. My work is the fruit of my genius.'

'Was it Hervé's money you were after?'

'Don't be vulgar.'

And even:

'Did you fondle her before you cut the woman up? Did you knead her full, hard breasts? Rub them slowly? Did she moan with pleasure even in her drugged sleep?'

It is, I assure you, an inherent trait of Italian males to perceive the opportunity of carnal arousal in the most unlikely and incongruous of circumstances – read in the right tone of voice, you could turn them on with a telephone directory. Thus, professing their shock and repulsion at my so-called 'acts of criminal perversion', they nevertheless contrived to find my calm, reasonable explanations of these acts, repeated *ad nauseam*, sexually stimulating – they pressed up close to the chair on which I sat, rubbing their weighty thighs against my shoulder, surreptitiously squeezing their crotches (sometimes even each other's, I noticed), whispering their ridiculous questions in my ear like lovers crooning amorous intentions.

'Did she cry out when you had her?'

'Tell me, tell me again how she moved in her sleep –'

'– don't imagine we don't know the pleasure you took in this –'

And once:

'Did you have sex with your father before you chopped him into pieces, you maniac?'

Oh, it was all so dreadfully wearisome.

'The night we arrested you, you told us that your assistants were upstairs asleep,' Colliani said.

'But it's true – they were.'

'Yet we found no-one.'

'I cannot explain that. Maybe they've gone back to England – there's nothing for them here. Not now.'

'Our inquiries in London have not yet begun in earnest, Signore.'

'So they *have* begun, then? I thought they would, sooner or later.'

'But we do not look for these twins anymore. We don't need them, Signor Crispe – we have you. *Finito.*'

Two weeks elapsed, after which time I was told that before very long I would undoubtedly be formally charged with the murder of Heinrich Hervé. I was also informed that a further two charges of murder would be brought against me in connection with my father and Miss Lydia Malone, after consultations with the British police had been concluded. They apparently neither knew nor suspected anything of Otto von Streich-Schloss or the others I had used as the raw material of my creations since coming to Rome.

Then, to my complete bewilderment and complete disgust, they added the name of Arturo Trogville to the list – complete bewilderment because I never knew he was dead, and complete disgust because they actually considered me capable of such a commonplace crime. Clearly, my genius was quite beyond them.

Nor Iron Bars a Cage

I was consigned to Regina Caeli prison to await my inevitable fate. I did not once protest my innocence but, rather, tried to provide the most intelligible explanation first, of the philosophy of Absorptionism and second, of the meaning and purpose of my alchemical art; but it was hopeless – I would have had more success explaining the principles of Euclydian geometry to a monkey. You can, I am sure, imagine my mental exhaustion and distress. They sent that Freudian idiot Balletti to me, they pumped me full of tranquillizers, they invaded my austere cell and bombarded me with their absurd questions whenever they were in the mood for a little sexual stimulation. They refused to listen to me when I persistently and strenuously denied that I had been involved in Trogville's death.

I, more than anyone else, was deeply shocked by his murder. I continued to be angered by the suggestion that I was capable of such a thing – a deed of naked, malicious revenge pure and simple. After all that I have told you about myself, I beg you to consider: am I by nature a vindictive person? I pointed out to them again and again that my so-called 'victims' were my *prima materia*, that the transmutations I worked on them were acts of creative love – *love*, not malice. The very fact that they considered me capable of a mere common murder shows how little they understood of what I was trying to tell them – little?

Nothing! They understood absolutely *nothing*. Even the killing of my so-called father ultimately constituted a reconciliation. They said I was mad.

The murder of Trogville continued to puzzle me right up to the moment when – well, when – but no, of this I shall write soon enough. Meanwhile, I might say that it was the news of Trogville's murder which inspired me to set down these confessions of mine, in order that the world should know not only my innocence in this matter but, more importantly: i) my art, and ii) my genius – both of which placed me above the categories of good and evil, right and wrong, lifting me to a dimension that transcends the moral conventions of a world of lesser, petty men.

Dr Balletti did not arrive for several of our sessions scheduled for the end of the month, and two days later I was given the news that he had suffered a severe nervous breakdown – a complete collapse, in fact. Naturally, I was blamed for this.

'But I didn't do anything!' I protested.

'Enough that you exist,' they answered.

His reports to the Chief Medical Officer – none of which I ever saw, of course – had apparently become increasingly incomprehensible, full of ramblings about demons and sacrifices and unfrocked priests; well, I suppose in a way I was sorry for Balletti (and still am, to tell the truth) since he never did me any personal harm, but I could have told them from the beginning that he was mentally unstable, only they wouldn't have listened, so I didn't bother. When I recall all those burblings about breasts and nipples, I shudder. And they call *me* mad?

XI

Into the Light

In my lifetime, I have received two great shocks – incidents which have left such an indelible impression on the fabric of my psyche that I expect them never to be fully erased by the passage of time. True, they may become so deeply buried that their after-effects are minimal, but the original power of their impact will remain forever in the *nidus* of my most persistent memories. I do not refer to the nightmare at *Il Bistro* – that was not so much a shock as a little death, marking – and *causing* – an irreversible transition of my life from one stage to another, both inwardly and outwardly.

The first was when I was told that my beloved Highgate queen was dying – to say nothing of her actual death and the tissue of monstrous lies my father expected me to believe about the circumstances surrounding it. The second happened only yesterday afternoon, and I am still trembling from its impact; this second shock however was *not* unpleasant – quite the contrary – and the precise details of it I now relate.

At half past two, I was informed that I had a visitor.

'I can't imagine who in the name of God would want to visit *you*,' said Fantucci, the corridor guard, a surly misanthrope who constantly scratched his balls and picked his nose – not necessarily in that order, and sometimes even simultaneously.

'Please have the kindness to show my visitor in.'

'What am I, a butler?'

'No-one in their right mind would hire you as a butler, not if they intended inviting their guests for a second time, that is.'

I said this in a deliberately deferential tone of voice, so that Fantucci, whose intellectual powers were limited, would not be able to work out whether it was an insult or not. He lingered momentarily at the door, then slunk off, muttering to himself.

Oddly enough, I suddenly found myself agreeing with him:

who *would* want to see me – Orlando Crispe, parricide and cannibal? Could it be the twins? My heart leapt at the possibility.

But it was not the twins.

'Hello Orlando.'

It was Master Egbert Swayne. This was not the moment of the second great shock, you understand – that came a short while later, as you will learn for yourselves.

'Egbert!' I cried, jumping up from my chair. 'Is it really you?'

'In the flesh Orlando, in the flesh!'

And there was still a great deal of that commodity; he stood with his arms stretched, beaming, his vast bulk creating a shadow the size of a partial eclipse in my little cell. We embraced affectionately, and even though he pulled me a little closer and a little tighter to himself than I cared for, I was still delighted to see him. Ironic really, when you consider that not so long ago I wanted to keep him as far away as possible.

'You can let go of me now Master Egbert,' I said, struggling against his vice-like hold.

'Oh, let me look at you!'

He held me at arm's length.

'You've lost weight, Orlando . . . are they feeding you properly? Still, it brings out the contours of your divine musculature in a *most* attractive way . . .'

'Same old Egbert.'

'Same lovely Orlando. Ah, what a pretty pass things have come to.'

'Yes,' I said sadly. 'They have, rather.'

We sat together on the edge of the bed; I sank into the well in the mattress that his vast body created all around itself.

'Why have you come, Master?' I asked, believing at that moment that I knew quite well why he had come.

'Aren't you pleased to see me, then?'

'Of course I am – you *know* I am –'

'Isn't that enough for you?'

'Not really,' I said. 'I want to know *why* you've come.

202

Nobody visits someone accused of the crimes I'm accused of without motivation of a less than altruistic kind.'

'Cynicism does not become you, Orlando.'

'It's about *Il Giardino,* isn't it?'

'What?'

'There couldn't be any other reason. You've come to berate me for cocking-up your source of retirement income.'

'Is *that* what you think? I'm hurt –'

'Rubbish. The only things that hurt you are an empty belly and a red bank statement.'

'What's happened to our *friendship,* Orlando?'

'It's still there. I'm just being realistic, that's all.'

'If this is reality, then give me fantasy!' he cried aloud, throwing up his arms to heaven and poking me in the eye with an elbow in the process. What an old ham.

'I'm sorry if I sound bitter,' I said, 'but can you honestly blame me?'

He sighed and was silent for a moment or two. Then he murmured:

'No, I can't. However, do me the courtesy of allowing me to tell you the *real* reason for my visit.'

In spite of what he had said, I still expected a lecture about duty, responsibility and commitment, and I allowed my thoughts to wander as he began to speak.

'I'm dying, Orlando.'

'We all are. We're dying the moment we're born. Who said that?'

'I've no idea.'

'Was it that fool Heidegger? No, not him –'

'Are you listening to me?'

'Of course.'

In fact, I wasn't listening to him much at all.

'There's nothing I can do about it, nothing whatsoever. Oh, I've seen the best specialist there is, but it's hopeless. Well, a man in my position can't help but look back on the course of his life with a certain amount of regret – regret and, yes, shame. You see all the things you did which you *knew* you had to do at the time, but which in retrospect don't appear quite so – I mean – quite so well done, if you take my point. Things you did, things you didn't do – and I tell you, it is surprising how the tiniest details suddenly take on a desperate significance.'

'Oh?'

'Such as debts unpaid . . .'

'Debts?' I said, still not really listening.

'Oh, I don't mean money, in spite of your heartless remarks. I mean debts of – well – debts of *honour*. Truth, for example. In the end, you owe people the truth; certain people, anyway . . . you couldn't go round telling everyone the truth all the time, that would be a terrible thing. But *you* are one of those certain people, don't you see, Orlando? The fact of the matter is, I owe you the truth. And I've come to give it to you.'

'What?'

'Have you heard a word of what I've been saying?'

'Of course I have.'

'What *did* I say, then?' he demanded.

'Something about debts of honour – oh, I don't know – something about truth. You said that – you said –'

'I'm dying, Orlando . . .'

He had told me he was dying. Had he really said that? What in Christ's name *had* he said?

I was sitting bolt upright now, looking at him intently.

'I *thought* I heard you say you were dying –'

'I owe it to you to give you the truth, Orlando – and the truth is, I owe you quite a lot, one way or another. Initially, you will doubtless despise me, but that can't be helped; in any case, I'm convinced it will take very little to make us friends again – a stolen kiss, a tender caress, and everything will be forgiven and forgotten. Or do I make too much of the place I once held in your affection and esteem? I hope not.'

He paused to wipe his eyes against the back of his hand, but I did not see any tears – he never could resist a theatrical gesture when there was an opportunity for one.

Then he said quietly:

'You see Orlando, I killed Trogville.'

Now *that* was the precise moment of the second great shock.

Somewhere deep inside me – buried far too deep for words, or even for non-rational sounds, somewhere in the profoundest fathoms of my bowels, a distant nuclear detonation occurred. I was faintly aware of it, and waited in terror for the deadly after-blast of the radioactive firestorm. What actually happened in the immediate realm of physical reality was that I fell off the bed. It was some minutes before I was able to pick myself up again. Oblivious, Master Egbert went on:

'I did not in the first place intend to do so – but then, if the road to hell is paved with good intentions, how much swifter and more direct runs the road that is paved with the absence of evil ones? No, I didn't intend to kill the little bastard, but when I saw him lying there on the floor of his apartment, all naked and mottled and helpless, I simply couldn't help myself. It was, I might say, just too good an opportunity to miss. So I removed the courgette you had stuck up his arse, gave him a thorough buggering, then replaced it. It was the courgette, you see, that gave you away; until I saw that, I had no idea who had reduced him to the state in which I found him. Only you could have dreamed up that little flourish!

'He hated you, you know. Yes, I know you know, but what you don't know is *why* he hated you. This may come as something of a surprise to you, but he hated you because of me – or, rather, he hated me through you. The fact is, Orlando, Trogville and I had been lovers for years. Are you shocked? Are you confused, dazed, stunned – even just a little? Well anyway, it's true. Our affair had begun long before you first came to me to serve your apprenticeship; we met at a party to launch Gervase Perry-Black's book *Live to Eat*. It certainly wasn't a case of love at first sight, but – well, when you look as I look, you have to take your pleasure where you can. He made it clear that he was what is known in the trade as a 'chubby-chaser' – you must surely have noticed that all his lady friends were more than generously endowed? So it was an arrangement that suited both of us, you might say.

'He knew at once that I was having sex with you. One could keep nothing from that all-seeing bastard! He was immediately consumed by an overpowering jealousy. I told him that I meant nothing to you, that you allowed me the delights of your body simply in order to advance your career – that indeed, you were also humping a repulsive antique called Butely-Butters for the same purpose – and that I would be cast off the moment your apprenticeship was over, but he would have none of it. I also told him that I had no intention of giving up those delights while they were on offer.

'That first review Trogville wrote for *Il Bistro* was a hostile one not because you deserved it, but because it was written in a paroxysm of jealousy; anyway, in attacking you, he was attacking me. Such was the spite of the man. I do not know exactly what happened that strange night at *Il Bistro* and I suspect nobody ever will, unless you choose to reveal it – and I know you won't, not now, not with so much water under the bridge; besides, it was a long time ago. Unfortunately however, it served to inflame Trogville's insane hatred of you. Please get it clear in your mind: whatever happened to him that night did not *cause* his hatred – it simply worsened it – and this remains true, whatever he might or might not have told you.

'I was more than sorry when he followed you to Rome, Orlando, but there was little or nothing I could do about it; I had hoped that, given your absence from the scene, his thirst for revenge would die a natural death. It was for this reason I offered you *Il Giardino* – well, not entirely, I admit, because I was also convinced that you would make a success of it. When his onslaughts began in earnest – despite the reputation you swiftly managed to build up – I knew it would not be long before I would have to come over and speak to him myself. And in the end I did come over, only you never knew it. I could not allow his jealousy to ruin me, Orlando! I'm growing old, and I was anticipating a long and comfortable retirement; if I had permitted that little shit to bring down *Il Giardino,* I would have only the workhouse to look forward to in my autumn years.

'After I had buggered him and replaced the courgette, I went into the kitchen, found a big carving-knife, and cut out his heart with it. I left him lying on his back, the bloody heart on the palm of one hand. Then I returned to the kitchen, washed the knife, replaced it, and departed. As I told you earlier, I did not at first intend to kill him; I had planned to reason with him if such a thing were possible – even to blackmail him by making our relationship public, if necessary. Then, when I saw him lying there – well, the opportunity was too good to miss, and the impulse was too strong to resist. I was back in London that same evening.

'I was delighted when I heard that they would be charging you with his murder! Forgive me Orlando, but what difference could it possibly have made? You were going to be charged with murdering Heinrich Hervé anyway. I do not pretend to understand or approve of the path you chose to take, but I want you to know that I am sorry you were caught. Once caught, however, what did it matter how many they said you had killed? One or four – where's the difference in terms of the sentence you will have to serve?

'Now, of course, all that's changed. As I told you – I'm dying, Orlando.'

'Of what? Treachery?'

'Don't be unkind to me –'

'Unkind?'

'Can't you see I'm trying to make amends?'

'Amends?' I screamed; then the firestorm struck, and I began to rage and foam like a mad thing, a thing possessed. How long it went on, I do not know; I was vaguely aware of words – terrible, obscene malignities – pouring out of my mouth, but what their import was apart from malediction, I do not know. My limbs became uncontrollable, flailing like the limbs of a man eaten away by some dreadful neurological decay. Once or twice I felt my head come into contact with the walls of the cell, and I heard Master Egbert screaming. It was, in brief, an *orgasm* of blind fury, and I presume you know how impossible it is to stop an orgasm once it's started – it just has to expend itself. Mercifully, my synaesthesia switched on

of its own accord, and unable to cope with the overload, all I saw was a great, depthless sheet of black – blackness – that swiftly descended and enfolded me about with the mercy of unconsciousness.

When I came round, I was on the bed again. Master Egbert was making me sip water from my toothmug.

'There,' he said in soothing, nurse-like tones, 'there. You'll feel better after that.'

As matter of fact, I felt completely drained.

'What happened?' I said, managing only a hoarse whisper.

'I think you lost your temper with me.'

'Can you blame me? Oh – God – my head is *splitting.*'

'You bashed it against the wall – twice. Do take care dear boy, you may have given yourself slight concussion.'

'Why should you be so solicitous?' I said bitterly.

'I told you – I've come to make amends.'

'Have you indeed?'

'I told you just – well – just before you had your little turn.'

'Is that what you call it? – ow! – my *head!* –'

'Can you not find it in your heart to forgive me?'

'No.'

'After all, they arrested you for Heinrich Hervé's murder first, not Trogville's. They simply added him to the list later. I had nothing to do with Hervé's death.'

'That's beside the point,' I said, swinging my legs over the edge of the bed and sitting upright. Master Egbert's hand was on my thigh. I brushed it off.

'What do you mean?'

'You come here, bold as brass, admitting that you've been fucking Arturo Trogville for years, that his attacks on me had nothing to do with my cuisine but were in fact vicarious attacks on you, you tell me your first instinct was to sit back and let me rot away in this filthy prison – and *now* you have the gall to ask why I find it hard to forgive you?'

'Well of course, if you want to put it like that –'

'What other way *is* there to put it?' I cried.

Master Egbert sighed a long, exhausted sigh. Then he said: 'Must I keep on saying it, Orlando? I'm dying.'

'So am I. A lot more slowly than you. Do you realise how old I'll be by the time I'm likely to get out of here? First, that's if they *let* me out, and second that's if they don't have me transferred to a lunatic asylum.'

'It's very rare, apparently – Langford-Beckhausen's disease. Quite inoperable. Dr Moisivich-Strauss told me I've got about a month or two at the most.'

I was about to make a cruel and cutting reply, but a thread of affection for the old bastard snaked its way out of some secret chamber of my heart and put more kindly words into my mouth.

'I'm sorry,' I said. 'I wouldn't have wished you that.'

'No, well, there we are, there's no use regretting what can't be changed. Oh, I've come to terms with it, dear boy. It isn't so bad. My life has been rich and full.'

'But not particularly long. You aren't *old* Master Egbert.'

'No – but I'm reasonably content.'

He put his hand back on my thigh, and this time I left it there.

'And as I said,' he went on, 'I've come here to make amends.'

'How?'

'Well, with only a couple of months to live at most, I'm not going to see a great deal of prison life, am I?'

I looked at him, puzzled.

'Prison life?' I echoed. 'Why should *you* see prison life?'

He was unable to resist the dramatic effect of a long pause. Then he said:

'For the murder of Arturo Trogville.'

'What?'

'You heard me.'

'I heard, but I don't understand,' I said.

'I'm going to confess, Orlando.'

'Confess? You mean –'

'Yes! I'm going to confess to the murder of Arturo Trogville. I'll be dead before I'm even brought to trial. Don't you see, it's the perfect solution!'

I shook my head.

'It won't help me in the slightest,' I murmured. 'I'm in here for the murder of Heinrich Hervé too.'

'Then I'll also confess to that.'

'And my father – and Miss Lydia Malone –'

'And to those.'

I was rapidly becoming excited now.

'There have been quite a few others, of course – Otto von Streich-Schloss for one – but the police don't know anything about those –'

Master Egbert blinked several times.

'Others?' he said.

'Oh yes, naturally. I had to have a continuous supply of raw material for my work, you see –'

'No, Orlando – no – I don't want to hear about them. Let's just stick with Heinrich Hervé, Arturo Trogville, your father and his tart. By Christ, that's enough.'

'And you would really and truly confess to killing all four of them?'

'Yes. I told you – I'll be dead before they can bring me to trial.'

I leapt off the bed and screamed a scream of pure, naked joy.

'But listen to me Orlando, listen! You must tell me *all* the details of what you did – after all, they aren't just going to take me into custody and let you go simply on my say so. They'll question me – and thoroughly. I have to give convincing answers. Trogville will be easy enough, naturally, since I *did* kill him. But the others . . . you'll have to prime me well, Orlando.'

'They'll get their dirty little rocks off all over again,' I said.

'What?'

'They get turned on by their own questions. It's disgusting.'

'Oh? I might actually *enjoy* that bit – you know how stunning Italian policemen are. I remember once, when Arturo and I were on holiday in Venice –'

'Do you mind?'

'Only happy memories . . .'

'You're incorrigible, Master Egbert.'

'And I'm also your saviour, Orlando. Don't forget that.'

'I'll prime you on every last little detail,' I said. 'Then let them question you all they like, it won't make any difference. I'll be back at *Il Giardino* within the month.'

He coughed.

'Ah. As to that,' he said 'I don't really think it would be feasible.'

'Why on earth not?'

'Well for one thing, I've installed Henry Batt there in your stead.'

I was stunned.

'Henry Batt? But he's an idiot, an amateur, a brewer of stews —'

'Don't be too critical dear boy, he does have his good points. He'll do well enough, believe me — there's nothing like a juicy scandal to pull in the punters. After all, there must surely be a certain *frisson* attached to being unsure not of "what" you're eating, but "who", wouldn't you say? No, I'm sorry that it has to be so, but you can't possibly go back to *Il Giardino.*'

'Where, then? Where shall I go?'

'There's another little place I have in mind . . .'

'Oh?'

'I assure you dear boy, it is *delightful*. A first-class reputation, too. Just the sort of establishment where you can begin again.'

'Yours?'

'Of course.'

'Manager or proprietor?'

Master Egbert shrugged.

'Well,' he said with a little sigh, 'I shan't be needing it anymore. So — proprietor, I suppose.'

'Where is it?'

'In Switzerland — just outside Geneva. *Le Piat d'Argent.* Two stars, but you'd have that bumped up to three in no time.'

Oh, what choice did I have? And, after all, it didn't sound so bad, much as I would miss *Il Giardino*.

I suddenly noticed that Master Egbert was regarding me with a sly look – a sort of secretly *triumphant* look.

'Naturally, I shall want something in return for all of this,' he said slowly. 'I may be dying, but I'm not daft.'

Equally slowly – and with more than a little apprehension – I asked:

'What, exactly?'

'A night of love . . .'

'A night of love?'

'Yes, with you. Well not a night exactly, but we have an hour to go before visiting time is over. I can think of a great many games to play in an hour, believe me. It'll be just like old times.'

'No!' I cried. 'Absolutely not!'

'Is the prospect so terrible?'

'Yes.'

'Am I so unappealing?'

'Ditto.'

'Is a lifetime in prison preferable to an hour of passionate sex with me?'

This time, I could not honestly have said yes.

'Look – Master Egbert – those days are *gone,* don't you see? You *know* why I slept with you before, and you must surely realise that it wasn't love or because I found it irresistibly exciting.'

'Oh, God! Was it utterly loathsome, then?'

He looked so pathetic sitting there on the edge of my bed – a great, blubbery, quivering baby whale with an expression of dignified hurt on his fat face.

'No,' I said, 'perhaps not. But I – well – I don't know if I *can* be passionate with you, not here, not now, not anymore.'

'Oh, don't worry about that,' he cried, suddenly cheering up. 'I'll have passion enough for both of us, you see if I don't.'

I stood looking at him for a long time before saying anything. Then, at last:

'All right, I'll do it.'

'You'll never regret it, I promise you –'

'God, the times I've heard that.'

'Angel!' he cried.

Within seconds his trousers and underpants were off, and he had his rapidly stiffening cock in his hands, pointing it at me like a gun.

'You don't believe in wasting time, do you?' I said.

'Time is the one thing I don't have much of.'

That was true enough, anyway. I began to undress.

Then:

'I'm ready.' I could not quite disguise the heroic tone in my voice.

However, under such circumstances, plunging into those oleaginous anal depths was like walking out into the light.

***

From Commendatore Alberto Signorelli to Gianni Caspi, Superintendant-General of Police 13th April 19—

Caspi,

I write to confirm arrangements for the release of Orlando Crispe. Colliani tells me that Egbert Swayne's confession to the murders with which Crispe was originally charged has been thoroughly investigated and that there can be no doubt of its veracity.

I am as stunned as I am sure you are. I need not say how badly this whole affair reflects on the service. I shall ensure that Colliani's handling of the case becomes a matter for urgent enquiry. As you may know, I have never had any real confidence in that man's abilities – I was the only member of the board who voted against his promotion. But there you are – what can you expect of an avowed Socialist?

If Crispe decides to sue for wrongful arrest, matters will be made infinitely worse; neither can we expect any co-operation from the press – I fully anticipate front-page headlines by the weekend. It is incredible how block-headed Colliani and his team have been. I am very angry Superintendant, and when I am angry, heads always roll.

Swayne has been formally charged. The best thing we can do now is to see to it that the trial is over and done with as speedily as possible.

Commissioner Sir Digby Strutton-Phipps has been most helpful – he is as anxious to forget this fiasco as we are; I have written to him on your behalf, expressing our gratitude.

That is all I have to say. Please give my regards to Sylvia.

Yours, etc.,
Signorelli, Commendatore.

***

Reunion
Le Piat d'Argent, Switzerland

I am writing this in my little study here in my private apartments above the restaurant. How much cleaner the air is here! The view from my window is of a broad green valley encircled in the distance by snowy mountain peaks – then, where the shimmering hairline of the horizon kisses the metallic blue sky, more snowy mountain peaks, and more. It is rather like living on top of an iced cake. I can also see the great lake from here. How I miss the tripartite odour of my dear Rome – coffee, garlic, and the heady perfume of sexual appetite! Here, I smell only melting snow and melting cheese. Synaesthetically speaking, Switzerland is also less interesting, expressing itself in the eye and ear of my mind as a series of blue-grey parallel lines accompanied by a repetitive diatonic triad on muted horns. Still, I musn't be ungracious.

And so the curtain opens on the final act:

There they were, the twins, waiting for me at Termini station. I had not thought to see them again; neither was I in the mood for an emotional reunion. To have abandoned me when I was arrested and now to seek me out again after my release – was this the service they offered? I cannot pretend to have been anything but deeply disappointed with the pair of them from the moment it had become clear that their silence would last as long as my incarceration. Oh, I had held out against the inevitable for as long as I could – I had kept on hoping that somehow, in some way, they would contact me without compromising themselves – but no. They were mercenaries, that's all they were. What other explanation could there be?

Jacques rushed to embrace me, but I pushed him roughly aside.

'Maestro?' he said, confused and somewhat taken aback.

'I think the less we have to do with each other, the better,' I said.

'What? I don't understand . . .'

'That makes two of us,' I snapped.

Her face a mask of consternation, Jeanne asked:

'You are angry with us?'

I shook my head.

'No,' I replied, 'anger is not the correct word.'

'But –'

'Outraged, disgusted, bitter, betrayed – any of those would be more accurate. Take your pick. Angry? No, not angry, Jeanne. I've gone beyond anger.'

I picked up my suitcase.

'What are you two doing here, anyway? Did you really think I would welcome you with open arms?'

'We are going with *you*, of course. To Switzerland.'

'How the hell do you know I'm going to Switzerland?'

Then I threw my head back and laughed aloud, and I saw one or two people glancing at me curiously; madmen and drunks – to say nothing of pimps, tarts, pickpockets, the dispossessed and the merely despairing – are common around the area of Termini station, but I was too well-dressed to be any of these. I began to wonder whether they might not have recognised me from the weekend issues – there had been a particularly unflattering photograph in *Venerdi*, accompanied by the memorable headline: *The Cook and the Cock-Up*. In this case, absolutely nothing is lost in translation.

'You are certainly not coming with me,' I said.

'But *why* not? Where else would we go?'

'You may go wherever you please, Jeanne. That is no longer my concern.'

'You need us,' she insisted, 'for your work – your *art* –'

215

Something snapped in me then, and I whirled round to confront her face to face.

'Yes!' I cried. 'Yes, I needed you once before, but you abandoned me!'

'Abandoned you?'

'Where the hell were you when I was languishing in that shit-hole of a prison? Nowhere! Gone, fled, disappeared, off to save your own precious skins. I could have rotted to death for all you cared. And now, when the horror is over, now you come running back, all smiles and embraces, expecting me to be overjoyed? Well frankly I'm *not* overjoyed. I'm deeply hurt.'

Jeanne regarded me long and thoughtfully, her clear grey eyes searching my own. Eventually I lowered my gaze, unable to bear that penetrating and somehow strangely innocent scrutiny any longer. She said softly:

'You truly thought that my brother and I had abandoned you?'

'What else *could* I think, Jeanne?'

'Did we not make an agreement? We promised to serve you in return for a suitable recompense . . .'

'You think that because we offer our services for money – but – everyone works for money, Maestro. What else is there?'

I pulled myself up to my full height.

'There is the way of the genius,' I said haughtily. 'The genius exhausts himself for love of his art. But you wouldn't know anything about that.'

'Maybe not. But I tell you, we have kept our part of the agreement. Even if we *had* been inclined to break it, it would not have been possible.'

'Why?'

Jeanne said:

'Consider: we know what your work is, what your art demands. We have been accomplices to it. We have provided you with your *raw material*.'

It was true. They had.

Jacques went on:

'Even so, my sister and I did *not* feel inclined to break the agreement. We have remained loyal. We have kept it not out of fear, but out of honour.'

'Then why didn't you get in contact with me? A letter, a note, a word – anything to let me know you were still with me –'

'We had other things to do.'

'Oh? Such as?'

Jacques stared at me. Then he said:

'Such as arranging for your release, of course.'

'What?'

I felt my suitcase slip from my grasp and drop to the ground.

'You mean to tell me that Egbert Swayne isn't dying at all?' I cried.

We were sitting at a filthy table in one of the coffee bars in Termini station; the train for Leonardo da Vinci airport was due to leave in twenty minutes.

'No, not at all. He is as healthy as you or I. Does he *look* like he's dying?'

'Certainly not. But I still don't understand – he told me he'd been to a first-class specialist. Moses somebody-or-other.'

'Dr Moisivich-Strauss of Harley Street,' Jeanne said.

'Exactly – *what?* – you know this man?'

'He was once a client of ours – in the days of Jean-Claude Fallon at *Il Bistro*. Perhaps I should say a client of Jacques.'

'You took a photograph?'

'But of course. Several, in different positions – one of them quite extraordinary. Dr Moisivich-Strauss was a most energetic man.'

'The photographs had been taken at his request,' said Jacques. 'You know how our system worked.'

'Only too well.'

'But this time – this time we found ourselves obliged to use it against him. It is something that has never happened before. He was very angry! But – *pouff!* – what could he do?'

'And Egbert Swayne?'

217

'He knew us well. He knew Jacques *very* well.'

'Oh, don't tell me –'

'Yes. How should it not be so?'

By now I was completely in a daze.

I murmured:

'But – I mean – he never said – he gave me the very distinct impression – when he first suggested that I should move to Rome and I told him that you two were working at *Il Bistro* and had to be consulted – *the bastard!* – and now you're telling me he'd already *met* you, already knew you? –'

'Had you never guessed, Monsieur?' asked Jacques.

'Guessed? Of course not! I'd never even thought – dreamed – it would simply never have occurred to me. Why, you were different worlds, alien planets with your own separate orbits.'

'Orbits that frequently collided.'

Then, it suddenly hit me with the force of a fist in the face:

'Then – you mean – *he* was a client too?'

'Yes. He came one afternoon to call on you, but you were out. Jacques opened the door to him. It began immediately. Master Egbert could not resist the charms of Jacques.'

I nodded slowly.

'Yes,' I said, 'I can well imagine that. Oh Christ, what a fool I've been!'

'No, not a fool. Egbert Swayne was very insistent that you should not know of his visits to Jacques.'

'I'm quite sure he was.'

'He told us that you would not like it.'

'And he was right,' I said.

Jeanne went on:

'A short time after you had been arrested, my brother and I went to Fuller's Hotel to seek out Master Egbert. We told him that his sessions with Jacques could be recommenced in complete safety now that you were in prison. You see, he had always been a little nervous – he could never be certain that you would not discover his secret –'

'The swine!'

'So Jacques began to visit him twice a week at Fuller's Hotel – *Il Bistro* was out of the question, you understand.'

'Oh, completely.'

Jacques said:

'On one of these visits I remarked to him that he did not look so well. I appeared concerned and I attempted – unsuccessfully, you comprehend – to disguise it. Then, suddenly, he was concerned too. During the course of the next visit I told him he had lost some weight – ah, what a triumph of cunning that was!'

'How?'

'Reflect, Maestro: Master Egbert knows that if he *has* lost weight, it is not due to any effort on his part – *pah!* – such a thing would be inconceivable, and that it must therefore indicate the possibility of illness. On the other hand, he is *flattered!* You see his dilemma? He does not wish to admit to himself that he might be sick, but his immense vanity refuses to deny my insistence that he has lost weight.'

'Jacques, you clever boy!'

'I had no doubt that his vanity would triumph, and so it did. I had no difficulty at all persuading him to see a doctor. But not just *any* doctor you understand – no, a *specialist*. I told him that only the best opinion was good enough –'

'The opinion of Dr Moisivich-Strauss, God bless him!'

'Precisely so. I accompanied him to Harley Street, and Dr Moisivich-Strauss told Master Egbert exactly what he was instructed to tell him –'

'That he has Langford-Beckhausen's disease, and only two months to live.'

'Yes.'

'And Langford-Beckhausen's disease doesn't exist?'

'No.'

'Better and better!'

'He emerged from the room crying – weeping and sobbing. It took a very long session with me before he found any kind of consolation. We had a drink together and he became very sentimental, very – I cannot – I do not know the right word in English –'

' "Maudlin" will do,' I said. 'He was always prone to that.'

'He also became very sexy, but he could not do anything because he was too drunk. He began to talk about his life – about all the bad things he has done – oh, I cannot tell you how boring that was! Complete *ennui*. But then I took the first opportunity to slip into his mind the idea that there was a way to make amends –'

'The exact phrase he used to me, the hypocritical bastard,' I said.

'At first he was not sure – he was still too fond of himself to agree – but I continued to suggest it to him, especially when he was inebriated, and little by little it took hold within his heart. In the end, he was convinced that the idea was *his* – oh, was Jacques not astounded at his nobility of soul? Did Jacques not consider him a truly wonderful man? Did Jacques not know that even the saints have not done as much as he proposes to do?'

'Yes, that sounds like Master Egbert.'

'Would it not truly be an *honour* for Jacques to penetrate him just one more time – and would he please rub a little harder, a little faster? –'

'Even more like him.'

Jacques sighed.

'And there you have it. The great self-sacrifice of Master Egbert Swayne.'

'The deception won't last forever, you know.'

'Alas, no.'

'After a couple of months he'll begin to wonder why he's still so fat. He'll wonder why Langford-Beckhausen's disease hasn't yet carried him off. It can't last longer than a year, Jacques – I guarantee he'll have asked for a second opinion long before then. And the second opinion will tell him that there's no such thing as Langford-Beckhausen's disease.'

'But,' said Jeanne, 'what can he do? *Rien!* He can tell them he has changed his mind and wishes to deny his confession – but what would be the result of that? The Italian authorities have already been made to look fools once, remember – they would never take the risk of this happening a second time.

Another release, another arrest, another trial, another public scandal? Oh no, it is inconceivable. And if they transfer him to an asylum for the criminally insane, no-one will listen to a word he says in any case. They would simply say that he is raving mad. One way or the other, Master Egbert Swayne is incarcerated for the rest of his life.'

I got up from the table and started to laugh. I laughed so much, I pissed myself.

***

Here at *Le Piat d'Argent* I continue my work. Oh, if my beloved Highgate queen could see me now! The twins and I have resurrected the Thursday Club, and the discreetly wealthy of Geneva – of the whole of Switzerland, indeed – are beating a path to my door. There are plenty of them I have to say, but we remain fussy about whom we admit – we can afford to be. My little establishment will soon obtain its third star, I'm sure of that; only last night I had the influential food columnist Sturges M. Wildeblood – an acidic old queen of an expatriate who writes for *New Century* – grovelling in gratitude at my feet. He had dined sumptuously on the tender flesh of a classy rent-boy picked up by Jacques and marinated by me in the most exquisite juices of carnal desire. No wonder old Wildeblood nearly had an orgasm with the first forkful.

Flesh! I surround myself with it, I luxuriate in it, I shape it, mould it, dissect it, transform and adore it! I never cease to develop my alchemical art – honing and refining my techniques, constantly discovering new methods and means, giving myself over unreservedly to its certainties and possibilities. Oh, could there be any flesh-eater in the world happier than Orlando Crispe?

Tonight I shall prepare a very special dish for a very special client – a certain Minister of State well known for his extra-marital activities, who has recently been elected President of the Thursday club by the other members. This is a singular honour. To revitalise the spark in a current affair, I have created for him *Aiguillettes de Canetons au l'Esprit de Femme*.

221

Aiguillettes de Canetons au Esprit de Femme

FOR TWO PEOPLE	
2 duckling breasts	
1 lb (450g) unsalted butter	
3 tbsp cognac	
3 tbsp port	
Juice of 1 freshly squeezed orange	
Grated nutmeg	
¾ pt duck or chicken stock	
1 lb stoned black cherries	
Salt and black pepper to season	

Buy a largish duckling and lift each breast off in two pieces with a filleting knife inserted on each side of the middle breast-bone. Or get your butcher to do it for you.

Enlist the assistance of a loving colleague. Have her strip naked and lay on her back on a comfortable bed, a soft pillow beneath her head. Spread her legs. Carefully insert the duck breasts into her vagina and let them marinate there for three or four hours. Your colleague may sleep if she wishes; I recommend that some soothing music be played, such as Satie's *Gymnopedies I, II, III*.

No-one should be surprised at this exotic method of marination; women in the Middle Ages frequently inserted fish into their vaginas before frying them for their husbands – this was both to ensure fidelity and to arouse desire. Penitentials of that period give a quite specific penance for this somewhat outré misdemeanour: seven days on bread and water. Indeed, it was browsing through Canon Pikestaff's *Penitential Practices of the Medieval Church* that inspired me to add my own particular touch to this well-known French classic, which specifies Monmorency sour cherries. In fact, any dark variety will do.

The breasts used to create my version of this dish were taken from a lady well-known in certain circles for her lavish distribution of sexual favours, and my dear Jeanne marinated it herself. I specify duck as an excellent substitute.

After marination is complete remove the duckling breasts, salt them lightly, and immediately sauté them in a deep pan over a moderate to high heat, turning them once. Ideally, the flesh should be half-cooked, pinkish in colour. Drain off the butter, pour in the cognac and set it alight. When the flames have died, season the breasts with the nutmeg and the salt and pepper. Remove and keep warm.

Now add the port to the pan, deglazing the juices. Put in the orange juice and reduce by half. In a clean saucepan heat the stock, then pour in the liquid from the sauté pan, stirring well. Add the cherries and poach them in the saucepan without bringing to the boil. Put the duckling breasts into the sauce and heat them through. Remove, drain and slice into fillets. Arrange them on a warm serving plate and pour over half the sauce, reserving the remainder for the sauceboat.

And that more or less concludes the extraordinary history of my life. I am content – there is no reason for me not to be, now. Inevitably, the task of judging whether this history is that of a man or a monster falls to *you,* but I offer no explanations, no mitigating circumstances, no considerations to assist you in your judgement other than those offered by these confessions themselves. The true genius, you must know, never resorts to self-defence.

If you are ever passing through Geneva, I invite you to try the gastronomic delights of my restaurant – ask anyone, and they will tell you how to find it. But be warned: if you intend to dine *chez* Orlando Crispe, you had better be a true *flesh-eater.*

Master Orlando Crispe
Le Piat d'Argent
Geneva, Switzerland